THE WHISPERING GORILLA

By
DON WILCOX

I0616779

ARMCHAIR FICTION
PO Box 4369, Medford, Oregon 97504

*For more information about Armchair Books and products, visit our
website at…*

www.armchairfiction.com

Or email us at…

armchairfiction@yahoo.com

A BEAST WITH THE BRAIN OF A MAN

Even reporter Steven Carpenter didn't suspect the incredible future that lay in store for him. It had all started because he'd found out too much about a corrupt businessman named Swangler. And Steven Carpenter—being the crusading type—was never afraid to splash what he knew all over the big city newsstands. Then one day someone took a shot at him. So before he knew it, Carpenter was whisked off to the wilds of Africa for his own safety. Hiding on the remote jungle estate of a reclusive scientist, he continued to pound out his finger-pointing news stories. Then one evening a stranger showed up and lit a match, and soon Steven Carpenter was written into the annals of medical history.

Here is another outrageous, yet highly entertaining tale from the master of wild science fiction, the "mad man," Don Wilcox.

FOR A SECOND COMPLETE NOVEL, TURN TO PAGE 79

CAST OF CHARACTERS

STEVEN CARPENTER
*He was a top reporter about to blow the lid off a huge scandal.
Then his enemies struck…and his life would never be the same.*

ROLAND FUZZIMAN
*He was something of a sideshow charlatan, but how often do
you get a chance to put a talking gorilla on stage?*

DR. DARTWORTH DEVOLI
*He was emersed in scientific research deep in the jungle. Then
one day he performed the medical operation of the century!*

ROSELLE CARPENTER
*When her husband was murdered it left a huge hole in her heart.
It seemed unthinkable that it could be filled by a 400-pound ape.*

PAUL SWANGLER
*On the surface he seemed like a respectable businessman, but
underneath was a soul-less man with a penchant for greed.*

"SURE" PEETSON
*He was a little on the thuggish side, yet very slick. He knew how
to pull the trigger at just the right moment.*

LAVERY
*When you're the managing editor of a big newspaper and your
best reporter's life is threatened, what the hell do you do…?*

CHAPTER ONE
To Light a Match

THE night was foggy, gray-black. It was well past midnight.

A car sped down the dimly lighted street, its motor quiet. There were three men walking along the sidewalk, and the sound of their voices was gay; one was laughing.

Tat-tat-tat-tat-tat... The sound of the submachine gun rose over their voices, cracking out the sound of death. The three pedestrians fell for cover. Only one of them, Steven Carpenter, knew what had happened after that. He had watched the other two fall, it was the way they fell that sickened him. That and the blood that ran down the pavement, sticking to his clothes...

*   *   *

The usual morning hustle in the city room of the *Daily Telegram* was quieter. On half a dozen desks lay the morning edition. There was a picture there of two men lying dead on the pavement. A third stood by, his face tear-stained. The newspapermen who walked by the desks spoke little. Some of them had been to the morgue. The City editor had all three of his telephones off the hooks.

At the far end of the long room, the elevator door opened. Steven Carpenter came walking down, waved to the City editor, walked through the door marked: Private—Managing Editor.

Lavery, the Managing Editor, turned his chair to face Carpenter.

"Where's my wife?" said Carpenter. "What did you do with her?"

"Hid her. Got her out of town."

"What the hell for?"

"I'll draw you a diagram," Lavery snapped, sarcastically. "Now *you're* getting out for awhile—while you can still walk out."

Carpenter faced him, his jaw rigid, a tall, thin man, his eyes bright. "I'm not going anywhere. And I want to know where my wife is."

Lavery nearly shouted, "Shut up! "I'm running this show. You're taking the next boat for Africa. Take a vacation."

"You can go straight to hell," said Carpenter. "I've got that munitions ring on the run, I know what they're after— war. And I'll keep at them, I'm no quitter."

There was silence. Presently, Lavery said, "Steve, I know that, I'm not asking you to quit. They got Hannigan and Forman last night, but they were after you. And last night they sprayed your apartment with bullets—trying to get your wife."

Carpenter started. "She isn't—"

"No, she's safe. You have my word on it. She's where no one will find her—not even you. Because you're going to Africa on a game hunting assignment. That'll take one day a month. The rest of the time you can keep on with that series of articles you started. Take your notes. Mail the stuff in, I want you to stay alive, you and your family. Your expose will explode things here. You'll come back in time for the explosion, just before election."

Steven Carpenter sank into a chair. He mopped his head. "Thanks, chief," he said. "Thanks for everything. But I'm not going to Africa."

"You'll be aboard the S.S. *Congo* in less than two hours."

Carpenter shook his head. "No," he said.

The motors of the S.S. *Congo* sent a dull roar upward into Stateroom 44. A solid, subdued roar, fitting accompaniment to the hammering of typewriter keys. The freighter was out of the harbor now. Steven Carpenter lit another cigarette as he began his column.

QUESTIONS AND ANSWERS:

Why was the S.S. Itaska *reported to dock officials as being laden with harmless chemicals, when any stevedore on the loading job knew that the mixture of these chemicals would result in deadly mustard gas?*

What was the real port-of-call of the American owned and Panama-registered freighter Celeste, *when she steamed out of the harbor with transport planes that require only two days to be converted to bombers?*

Was it farm machinery in the holds of the U.S.S. Brockton *when she sailed quietly at midnight last Saturday? Was it mousetraps? Or could it have been sixty thousand machine guns?*

The typewriter kept hammering. The floor became littered with paper. The room was filled with a blue haze that lay like a cloud, through which only fingers moved.

There was a knock on the door. "Come in," said Carpenter.

A sailor entered, carrying a tray. "Captain Forest's compliments, sir. He says maybe you'll want a sandwich and some coffee."

"Thanks," said Carpenter, rubbing his eyes. "Put the tray down on my bunk. And here—give these papers to the Captain. They're to go wireless immediately."

As the sailor closed the door behind him, Carpenter spoke aloud. "And let those dirty scoundrels directing the bloody mess see how they like it…"

*   *   *

"I DON'T like it," said the heavy man. "I don't like it at all. And I want it ended now." He had an iron-gray head, and his cheeks were puffy with good living. His little eyes roamed again over the bold type of the *Daily Telegram*, over the column, *QUESTIONS AND ANSWERS*. The cigar in his hand was unheeded as he faced the long table with the men around it. Now he spoke.

"We've got things running well now. Soon, when it gets too hot to continue running contraband, we'll make our big move. But before that—"

"Anything you say," said a man near him, a gray-moustached, carefully dressed man.

"Questions?" the heavy man spat out, still looking at the newspaper. "Well, we've got the answer. Spangler—you say you know where this Carpenter went?"

"Had him followed right to the boat."

The heavy hand crashed down on the paper and the cigar crushed.

"Get him!"

*   *   *

The deep, pungent odors of the jungle clung to the air, but there was something fresh in it. The faint breeze that cooled Steven Carpenter's face eased the heat a little. He rose from his bamboo chair and strolled across the low, wide verandah. The door to the house had opened and the light fell out to the dusty road in a long patch.

"It's so pleasant here, Dr. Devoli," said Carpenter, "that I'm really glad the lodging houses in town were filled. It's so peaceful here near the jungle's edge. Let me thank you again for your hospitality."

Dr. Dartworth Devoli stood in the doorway, donning a laboratory apron. Taller even than Carpenter, the top of the doorway was just high enough to brush his fine white hair. His unwrinkled face and strong bearing belied his age.

"The pleasure is all mine, Mr.—ah—Fenton," Devoli smiled. "I wouldn't live anywhere else, now that I've acquired this little corner of the jungle for my own. It's both a home and a laboratory, and that's all in the world I want; that, and my work. But it is a welcome novelty to have a guest here, especially a man of your intelligence. Does your writing allow you to travel as you wish?"

"Not always." Carpenter smiled slightly. "This is more of a trip for my health. But your work—that seems fascinating, from what you told me at lunch. I've thought of it since. An article on your experiments—"

Devoli raised a hand, the sensitive fingers spread. "Please, not a word. Perhaps in a few years, after this generation of gorillas has developed. Let Plumbutter have a chance. After that—but I hear Plumbutter's voice." A low growl had issued from the laboratory building where Devoli kept his specimens, a voice at once sensuous and cruel. "If you'll excuse me," said Devoli, bowing. "I'm being paged—jungle style."

Carpenter grinned. "The moon seems about to rise. I believe I'll go for a walk. See you later, Doctor."

Steven Carpenter strolled down a winding path bordered by deep-scented flowers and delicate, dark ferns. From everywhere the myriad noises of the jungle came to him, a uniform stridency that negated itself into a clean silence. He stopped at the edge of a clearing, silhouetted against the mammoth orange moon that edged over the tops of great trees. He was planning the next day's work...

"Hello."

The man had come up so quickly that Carpenter had not heard him. He looked uncomfortable in the loose white clothes he wore, and the moonlight caught a jagged scar that ran from a corner of his mouth.

"Hello," said Carpenter, after a moment.

"Nice night," said the man, fumbling for a cigarette.

"It's a honey," said Carpenter.

"Got a match?"

Carpenter produced a match. In the cupped flame in his hands, the stranger's eyes took on a peculiar glint as he looked up at Carpenter.

"Thanks," he said. "Just wanted to make sure who you were." He backed away. There was a gun in his hand, and as he spoke, the gun flashed three times.

Steven Carpenter fell heavily, with three bullets in his heart. The stranger listened a moment to the echoes of his gun, and when they had ended, he ran lightly down the road.

CHAPTER TWO
A Gorilla Speaks!

THE English Captain put on his cap. "Thank you very much, Doctor. The Department won't forget your cooperation. If we'd had to take the body with us now, half the damned town would be awake. We'll be here first thing in the morning. The necessary autopsy can be performed by you at your convenience." He nodded to the Lieutenant, who motioned to several men in uniform. All of them turned to leave.

Dr. Dartworth Devoli stared at the body lying covered on a bench. "You were a fine chap, Carpenter," he said aloud. The table beside him was covered with papers: notes, letters, news clippings, pictures. "Two hours ago you were alive," the Doctor mused. "A fine, healthy man, with a good mind and a conscience, and a job that ended it all. And this lovely girl who was your wife...what will I tell her? They followed you all the way here, from a country where they needed men like you."

The scientist sighed deeply and blew his nose. "That's life," he said, quietly. "Here lies youth and vigor dead—while an old man who scarcely knew him or his right name is the only one to mourn. An old man who has spent his years trying to approach making out of animals what nature gave you at birth. How wasteful...how tragic..."

Devoli rose and pulled back the cover from the dead man's face. A ray of moonlight came through the shutters and lighted the dead, agonized features. "What good did all the fighting do you? Your brain was no stronger than your heart. When they stopped that, they stopped everything."

But suddenly the aged scientist paused, and his hands trembled. "What am I saying?" he demanded of the empty room. "What am I thinking? Good Lord!"

His hands tore off the cover from the dead man. The blood from the bullet holes had clotted. For a moment the lithe, strong hands swept over the body. "Your brain, Carpenter... You were no more than your brain—but maybe..."

Devoli stood indecisive, his hands holding his head, his eyes burning. Then, swiftly, he rolled up his sleeves.

He placed the body upon a cot, rolled the cot over the threshold, through several rooms, into a half-lighted chamber. He touched a switch and a blaze of violet-white light flooded the room.

Now he scoured his hands in the deep white basin. The kettle that contained the surgical tools was boiling. The body waited upon the operating table...

Occasionally through the night the scientist would break away from his frantic work for a few seconds long enough to listen to the soft rhythmic sluss-sluss-sluss of the automatic blood pump. Now and then a slight adjustment of the control levers, then back to the operating table.

By the time he was ready to deposit a precious mass of tissue in the chamber of the automatic blood pump, the instrument was perfectly adjusted to the conditions of temperature and circulation necessary to keeping human tissue alive.

With a sigh of gratitude to his good luck, Devoli slumped into a chair. The sun was high. The caged animals were whining for their breakfasts. For minutes the white-haired man sat there, heard nothing, saw nothing—nothing except the rhythmic sluss-sluss-slussing of the automatic blood pump. He looked down at his scoured white hands, wondering at the miraculous surgery they had performed. The easier half was done.

One hand rested upon a small writing table. There was a pen, there was writing paper. He wrote:

My dear Mrs. Carpenter:

By this time you will have received my telegram informing you of the tragic death of your husband. I regret to inform you that it will be impossible, owing to conditions I cannot readily describe, to ship the body of Steven Carpenter back to you…

Now Dartworth Devoli paced back and forth before the cage of Plumbutter.

"This is the end for you, Plumbutter my boy," he muttered to the unconcerned animal. Plumbutter chewed contentedly at a straw. "I've invested a lot in you, Plumbutter," said the scientist, as he prepared a large chloroform pad. "Now I need you—need your body."

Plumbutter yawned—a little painfully, for his throat was still sore from recent operations, which the scientist had performed on his voice box.

Plumbutter was a four-hundred-pound youth of six years, a healthy, normal male gorilla. The scientist had hoped that Plumbutter would eventually shed light upon the intriguing age-old mystery of animal intelligence. In recent months the finest of Devoli's surgical skills had gone into equipping Plumbutter with every physical property necessary for speaking with a human voice.

Time and again during these past weeks the white-haired master had said to his dumb protégé, "It's a certainty that you and your tribe will never develop real intelligence unless you learn to speak. As soon as I get your throat in shape, you'll have a chance that no other ape has ever had." For Devoli was convinced that human intelligence and human speech were interdependent; and what a sensational victory for science it would be if an improved speech mechanism would result in a higher grade of brainpower in the gorilla!

But all of Devoli's fine aircastles for Plumbutter had suddenly shaken down to nothing in that strange moment of inspiration when the dead body of Steven Carpenter had been left at his door.

"I need you, Plumbutter," Devoli repeated. The husky gorilla grew drowsier with each inhalation of the chloroform. "I *think* the purpose is humanitarian," the scientist added, "though no scientist in the world can be sure of such things until he tries…"

FOR several weeks after the operation, Dartworth Devoli wondered whether his experiment had not been a dismal failure. But finally the springs of life within the animal began to take on enough vigor that the creature would creep about on his hands and feet and show an interest in food.

From all outward signs he was the same old Plumbutter with the same old jungle habits, old customary actions that he could have performed as well with no brain at all.

Then came the first indication of a change.

One morning the gorilla rubbed his great hands over his head, as if it were strange to him. His skull had been enlarged with borrowings from a foreign skull, and patched with silver plates, over which his own scalp had been tightly stretched. For almost an hour the creature seemed absorbed in stroking the furry dome above his ears, then he lost interest—if such simple behavior could be called an interest. It was simply a mechanical discovery on the animal's part, Devoli realized, and no proof that any consciousness had awakened in the new cortex.

There came a day when there seemed to be a symptom of growing curiosity in the gorilla—slight but perhaps significant. The animal showed a strong fascination for the mirror he held in his hand. Something more than the lively curiosity, which any monkey exhibits—rather an agitated concern—even an emotional disturbance!

"Carpenter!" the scientist called. "Steven Carpenter! Listen to me!"

The gorilla grew attentive.

"You are Steven Carpenter! Do you understand?" The scientist clutched at the bars of the pen fervently. The animal stood motionless before him as if entranced by his words.

"You were killed, Carpenter, but I saved your brain. Gradually your nerves will straighten out and once more you'll be a living, thinking man—"

The enthusiastic words suddenly broke off. Unintentionally the speaker had run into the snag he meant to avoid—that word *man*.

He might have passed over the slip lightly had he been sure that the big hairy creature before him did not understand his words. But he was not sure; as a matter of fact—*the gorilla behaved as if he had understood.* He slowly lifted his great, leathery black hands, palms upward, and stared at them. Then he returned his deep-set, burning eyes to Dr. Dartworth Devoli.

The scientist edged back from the steel bars unconsciously. He was uncertain what to make of the gorilla's strange manner.

Now the animal clutched the upright bars with his great hands and pressed his bulky head close against the steel fence. His lips pushed together thickly then opened to reveal his tongue between his chalk-white teeth. The tongue pressed at the roof of the mouth. At the same time the vocal cords gave forth a low hum. The scientist understood. The gorilla was speaking the word *man.*

"Your brain—it's working!" the scientist cried out. "You're Steven Carpenter...Steven Carpenter! Do you understand me? Your body was dead, but I've saved your brain—put it into a new body. *You can still live—and think—and be...you can be!*"

Again the gorilla studied his hands. His upright body drooped slightly, the huge head bowed, and the sluggish lips uttered a sound. It was a low, thickly whispered word, crudely pronounced but unmistakable.

"THAN-N-NKS." The deep subdued boom of that single word made chills race along Devoli's spine.

Then, as if the mental exertion had exhausted him, the gorilla lay down, a tired animal that wished to be left alone with his solemn thoughts.

The scientist capered about, pampering the beast with food and medicine, returning from his other duties every few minutes to study the mumbling lips.

Devoli tried to talk to him, to no avail. The beast simply stared off into space—or was he, by any chance, staring at that sprightly female ape two pens beyond?

Suppose, the scientist thought with sudden self-torture, that this prize achievement of surgical grafting should yearn for the jungle instead of civilization?

Suppose the animal instincts that dwelt within the viscera of this beast should prove more potent than the brain-stored memories of man. The gorilla equipped with the superior thinking machine of a man might decide to free himself from this prison and beat his way back to the deepest jungles to become the king of all beasts.

Dartworth Devoli's concern grew as the gorilla's distant manner continued…

Late one night as Devoli moved from gate to gate, stepping lightly so as not to disturb any sleepers, he came to the last gate, Plumbutter's own. He heard a soft tread from inside the fence. Suddenly a huge crusty hand came out of the darkness to clamp over Devoli's face and bind his head against the bars. A second husky hand slipped through the steel bars to snatch the keys. The lock sounded. The steel hinges sang a sharp note as the gate swung open, another as it closed. In the brief interval between those notes, the scientist and his prize specimen changed places. The lock clinked.

Devoli cried out, "Carpenter, in the name of decency—!"

Perhaps the chance words were well chosen. The shadowy form of the gorilla receding toward the black wall of the jungle stopped. An arm swung, and the ring of keys whizzed through the air to fall somewhere within the pen that held the scientist prisoner.

Before Dartworth Devoli, groping through the blackness, recovered the keys and extricated himself from the pen, the sounds of the gorilla's footsteps melted away into the silence of the jungle night.

CHAPTER THREE
Gorilla in a Stateroom

DEVOLI plodded back toward his house with faltering step. He reached the porch, slumped into the first chair, and there he sat for the rest of the night, his head in his hands, his fine white hair showering down over his slender fingers.

Sunlight and the call of hungry animals forced his stiff tired body into action. He stalked through the house, then suddenly stopped. An overturned chair arrested him.

His eyes flashed across the room to an open door, he flew to the storeroom where the suitcase of the late Steven Carpenter was stored. The suitcase was there—open! It had been rifled. The money was gone.

A knock sounded at the front door, Devoli looked into the grinning face of an American agent who lived in the nearby Congo village.

"Say, Professor, I just seen somethin's got your trained animals beat to a frazzle. Some guy made up like a gorilla—"

"You've seen my gorilla?" the scientist cried.

"*Your* gorilla? Hold on a minute. This wasn't no *real* gorilla, though this baby could pass in any zoo I ever seen. He came racin' down to the boat—"

"*Boat?*"

"Now let me finish, Professor? Whose story is this? I said *boat*. Almost knocked me over the pier gettin' up the gangplank, you never seen so much excitement in your life."

"You mean they let him get aboard a steamship?"

"Couldn't stop him. Or if they could, they didn't want to. He was wavin' a fistful of bills big enough to choke the Captain. An' the Captain looked like he was chokin' all right. Guess there ain't no law against these vaudeville actors gettin' made up if they want to get what they consider publicity. But I thought I'd come by an' tell you what you're up against."

Dr. Devoli sank to a chair. He was vaguely aware that his animals were screaming and chattering for food.

"Yessir," said the American, laughing, "with a fistful of bills like that actor was wavin', I wouldn't be surprised if they'd let one of them real animals outta your menagerie in the bridal suite! Coulda climbed aboard a chariot bound for Heaven, an' no questions asked. Them actors…"

THE steamship *Majestic* was two days out from the Congo coast, ploughing its course toward South America, en route to the United States. The weather had been rough, but it was clearing, and three stewards stood on the after deck, huddled by the rail. They seemed unmindful of the magnificent green swells of water through which the ship moved, or of the clouds that lifted from the horizon.

One of them reached into his pocket and brought forth half a dozen lengths of stiff, coarse hair.

"Now," he said, in a manner of one establishing a vital point in an argument, "what can you say to that? You'll have to admit he's some kind of animal, not a man. But he's trying to pass for a man, because he was clipping these hairs off his arms; I saw him through the keyhole. These hairs blew under the door."

"Haven't you gone in to see him, Joe?"

"No, thanks," said Joe. "Not since he growled at me that first time. I just knock and hand his tray through the door, and his big paw reaches out and takes it."

"Paw?"

"Well, *hand*—if you can call a claw as big as a platter a hand."

The three stewards sauntered down the stairs toward the stateroom in question.

"I'll bet he's a phoney, Joe—or else you are," one of the stewards jeered.

"All right," said Joe, half angered. "I challenge either of you to trade places with me and take him his dinner tonight. Go in and get chummy with the old boy if you feel like it. Which one of you wants to take me up?"

The challenge had a silencing effect. The subject turned.

"Does he eat like a man?"

"Eats three times as much as any human," said Joe. The words quieted to whispers. The stewards were before the stateroom door. Joe bent to the keyhole.

"There he is. You can see for yourself."

In turn the stewards bent for a keyhole view of the mysterious passenger. What they saw was a huge dark hairy head, the savage face turned toward them.

"Don't worry," Joe whispered, never guessing that his whisper carried clearly through the keyhole. "He never sticks his head outside the door."

The stewards bent for another look. It was an impressive face, with powerful protruding jaws, a wide rubber colored nose like a human nose pressed down flat and magnified, and a massive bony skull that gathered over the ebony eyes in a heavy ridge. The gorilla showed his teeth.

"Grinning at me!" one of the stewards gasped. "Nuts— that's no gorilla. That's an actor, and he's part of that theatrical company we got aboard. He's all dressed up to get the passengers excited about the troupe."

"Sss-s-sh!" Joe whispered. "He's listening to everything we say."

"You think he can understand—"

"Sure, I thought you said he's just an actor dressed up—"

"He's no actor," Joe hissed. "He's the real thing!"

"Don't give us that, Joe—"

The stateroom door opened. The big rubbery face grinned complacently and a huge hairy arm reached out in an easy dignified gesture. The white uniformed stewards made white streaks in three different directions.

"J-J-o-o-oe!" The soft booming voice reverberated through the corridors. The powerfully spoken word froze the three stewards in their tracks. Joe saw the huge crooked finger motion to him.

"Com-m-me her-r-re!"

Joe obeyed, retracing his steps gingerly. He stopped a few feet from the half-opened door.

"Don-n-n't be-e-e afra-a-aid," said the gorilla. "Go-o-oh geh-tt me-ee the man-n-ager-r-r of the the-e-eatrical-l-l com-m-mpan-n-e-e."

The deep soft husky whisper ceased and the door closed. Joe turned to the other stewards. "See?" he said. "Just like I said." But his voice had cracked, and he was as white as his uniform jacket. Then he went as fast as his wobbly legs would carry him, and the other stewards went their separate ways.

IN the salon Joe recognized the little, hot-eyed, black-mustached little man who was pacing around the table of card players: Roland Fuzziman, the troupe manager. Joe delivered the message with no explanations and left the dapper Mr. Fuzziman to do what he pleased about it.

Manager Fuzziman thought a moment. "One of my actors?" he repeated aloud to himself. "Room 44?" There were no members of his company there. But suddenly he brightened, corrected his tie. Undoubtedly a lady, he thought. An admirer too discreet to speak to him publicly. Undoubtedly a beautiful lady. A smile lay broadly on his face as he walked down to Room 44 and knocked on the door.

"Com-m-me in-n-n."

Fuzziman almost jumped back to the other wall. He gulped, and as his shock receded, his professional, theatrical ear functioned again, because it still was ringing with the deep, soft tones that had answered him. There was a rich resonance and a certain breathy, thick enunciation that he couldn't readily classify among the dialects he knew. He turned the knob and walked into the room.

This time Fuzziman's gulp was distinctly audible. He stared a moment, closed his eyes, then looked again. But slowly, as he gazed at the four hundred-pound gorilla, his manner changed, for Roland Fuzziman was a man who saw the world through eyes different from other people's. He blinked at the huge, hairy animal, strode up to it and slapped it on the chest.

"Say, buddy, you're good," the little man exclaimed. "Plenty good—in fact, damn good!"

He slapped the gorilla's chest again.

"Yessir, a very sturdy outfit, brother. Where'd you get it? Brehl and Brehl or Winklesteins? Any trademark on it? It feels like the real thing."

Fuzziman began to feel around at the wrists and neck, looking for a trademark. He couldn't even find a seam.

"Except for the head," Fuzziman cocked his own head critically, "that's the most convincing outfit I ever saw. The head's really too bulgy—but not bad."

The gorilla gave a low chuckle like an echo out of a cistern, and he bestowed upon the dapper little gentleman a wide grin full of even white teeth. His words came forth, slow, measured, deeply resonant.

"I wan-n-nt a job-b. Can-n you-u-u u-use me-e-e in-n a pla-a-ay?"

The cocky little manager was still too amazed at this theatrical creation to answer the gorilla's question. For a few minutes he could do nothing but walk around the huge creature, sizing him up from every angle and praising his appearance to the skies.

"That voice of yours," Fuzziman raved, "how do you manage that deep down in the cellar effect? It sounds like tom-toms from the depths of the jungle. You say you want a job? My boy, you're the answer to a manager's prayers. I've got a play I've never used because it needed a man monster. With a little rewriting we can change the monster to a gorilla—*hmmm!* By the way, what's your past experience? Are you at liberty now? Where are you bound for? Any previous contracts standing in the way?"

The gorilla hesitated momentarily, and his answer seemed to be a deeper, more disturbing rumble, as if he had thought of something.

"On-n-l-e-e a li-t-tle un-nfin-n-nished bus-s-siness in-n-n the Sta-a-ates," said the gorilla. "It can-n wa-a-ait."

Fuzziman fished two large cigars out of his pocket, placed one of them in the gorilla's teeth, and applied his lighter. The gorilla puffed heartily and blew smoke through the black nostrils of his flat nose.

FOR half an hour the manager smoked and talked; the more he questioned the gorilla, the more intrigued he became, and the more mystified. It was evident that the creature in the gorilla skin didn't care to lay all his cards on the table. Finally the manager put a pointed question.

"I'll check over that play tonight and see you tomorrow. How will I know you when you're out of that monkey suit? What is your name?"

"Jus-st cal-l-l m-e the gor-ril-l-la," came the slow reverberating answer. "I'l-l-l al-lwa-a-ays wear-r-r this-s cos-stu-um-m-me."

"Always? No, you can't do that. Whenever you'd try to go into a hotel or restaurant you'd have trouble. Women would jump out of their shoes. Men would call the police. No, you'd better—"

"I'l-l al-lwa-ays wear-r this-s cos-tu-um-me," the gorilla repeated.

Fuzziman studied the big hairy creature in awe. If this fellow preferred to be stubborn—

"It-t wil-l-l ad-ver-r-tis-s-se our-r pla-a-ay," the gorilla added.

"That's an angle! I'll let you wear it with a sign on your back. But still—you'll find it awkward traveling that way."

"That-t is-s why-y I wis-sh to-o pla-a-ace my-sel-lf in-n you-r-r car-r-re."

The little manager stood at the door, his mystified eyes still lingering upon his fascinating protege. This man, he thought, must be some sort of fugitive—perhaps a convict who had invented this clever means of hiding himself. Well, whatever he might be on the inside, Fuzziman liked his disguise well enough to take a chance.

"By the way, what is this unfinished business you mentioned? Revenge—or love—or—"

"Bo-oth," said the husky undertone.

The manager laughed. "You're all right, brother." He stepped back to give the gorilla a final slap on the furry chest and a pinch on the tough massive arm. "You'd be just one notch more realistic if you'd glue some longer hairs on your forearms."

The gorilla gave a rumbling answer and proceeded to crouch down on the floor. A sudden sickness had come upon him, owing to the effects of smoking the cigar.

Fuzziman, of course, never guessed such a thing. He went out with a head full of enthusiasm, tinctured with puzzlement. The gorilla's final gag, in answer to the suggestion of longer hairs on the forearms was a stunner that made Fuzziman chomp at his cigar all the way down the corridor.

The gorilla had replied, "Hair-r-rs? I'l-l-l gro-o-ow them-m-m."

ON the final night before the S.S. *Majestic* docked in New York the various and sundry talents of the passengers were collected and displayed in a stage show down on the second deck.

The feature of the night's entertainment was a preview of Manager Fuzziman's forthcoming stage play, *The Whispering Gorilla*. From the instant that the bulky silvery gray-brown gorilla's head and shoulders appeared at the window of the stage set, the audience was all eyes. And when the husky, soft whispered words began to roll forth in tones unlike any human voice ever heard, every listener was transfixed.

Three brief scenes from the play, then the curtain went down. The crowd went wild. The S.S. *Majestic* fairly rocked with the cheers and shouts of "Gorilla! More gorilla! Give us more!"

Fuzziman responded by staging one more short scene. Then followed curtain call after curtain call, Fuzziman brought the Whispering Gorilla back for a final bow, but still the audience wasn't satisfied.

"We want to see his face!" they shouted. "Take the mask off!"

Under the glare of footlights the dapper little manager turned to the dark hairy monster.

"How about it, fellow? Won't you give 'em a look at your face?"

The audience hushed to catch Fuzziman's words.

The place was suddenly deathly quiet—so quiet that the gorilla's whispered answer carried out to every listener.

"But-t I haven't-t an-ny mas-s-sk. This-s is m-y own-n fa-a-ace."

The audience greeted this with wilder applause than before. But after the curtain had fallen for the last time. Manager Fuzziman still stood beneath the floodlights like a man paralyzed. His eyes were wide, and upon his reddened face the beads of perspiration stood out sharply.

CHAPTER FOUR
Rumblings by W.G.

THE telephone buzzed.

Manager Fuzziman strode across the carpeted floor of Suite 909, the most exclusive suite in the very exclusive Radcliffe Hotel, and picked up the receiver.

"Metropolitan Press Bureau," said the voice. "We're downstairs with the press clippings on the first month's run of *The Whispering Gorilla.* '"

"Send them up!" snapped Fuzziman.

Fuzziman had been snapping at everyone that day, though he was by nature a gentleman. He walked back to the ivory table, sniffed at a box of cigars. Lighting one, he went toward the next room, from whence came the slow, painful clicking of a typewriter. Patient, crude strokes of heavy fingers.

Standing in the doorway, Fuzziman said, addressing the immaculately dressed and groomed creature at the typewriter. "You're working on that column of yours, I suppose?" There was no answer. "I don't like to keep talking about it," Fuzziman added, hesitantly. "I know you think it's really none of my business. Only you're meddling with dangerous stuff, I wouldn't have minded a column of harmless chit-chat, but—"

"Please," said the gorilla.

Fuzziman sighed. "You're a person of peculiar talents," he said. "I hope they won't lead you to tragedy." His words seemed to stop the gorilla, for the huge animal stopped typing and stared at the wall.

"Tragedy?" said the gorilla in a low whisper. "Maybe I've seen it. Maybe—" but he was silent.

"All right," said Fuzziman. "You know I don't want to pry. But I did want to tell you that I've read your column every day since it appeared two weeks ago and I'm rooting for you. You're doing a great thing. They say you'll swing the whole election. I only wish someone else was doing it."

"Thanks," said the gorilla. The typewriter again beat out its labored tattoo.

"Slow going, isn't it?" said Fuzziman. "You ought to get a stenographer."

"If my typing speeds up as rapidly as my speech did, I'll be all right." The animal's voice had the deep, melancholy resonance of a pipe organ, but the words were cleanly articulated, and the speech was fluent. "And I can't trust anyone to know who is really doing this column."

"Maybe I could get Lavery, the Managing Editor of the *Telegram,* to supply someone you could trust," Fuzziman began, when the doorbell sounded.

Fuzziman went to the door and three bellboys pushed in, loaded with volumes that contained stacks of papers. "Take them right in to the table in the inner office," said Fuzziman, with a wave of his cigar.

The bellboys obeyed, advancing to the room from which the clicking typewriter sounded. Two of them got as far as the table. The third one was knocked down in the rush—a rush inspired by the sight of a monstrous animal sitting at a typewriter and turning around to face them. The stacks of paper swished down in heaps over the floor, and the three bellboys hustled out of the suite in a near panic.

"What? No tips?" Fuzziman smiled wanly. He returned to the inner room and helped the gorilla gather the mass of clippings. "They're still afraid of you," Fuzziman said. "In spite of your nationwide publicity in advance of that radio program you've signed for, and in spite of a month's packed houses on Broadway, they can't decide whether you're human or not."

"Can you?" said the gorilla.

At that moment the door buzzer went off again. Fuzziman gratefully tore his eyes away from the gorilla's penetrating gaze and went to the door. As he opened it, he found himself face to face with a tall, slender, white-haired man. "I'd like to see the person called the Whispering Gorilla," he said.

"You and ten million others," Fuzziman snapped. "How'd you sneak past the house detectives downstairs? This is a strictly private—"

The tall man pushed a hand out and kept the door from closing. "I've come from the Congo," he said. "I am a personal acquaintance."

"THE Congo?" said Fuzziman. A queer chill went through him. The tall man's manner was strangely impressive. "What is your name, sir?"

The stranger did not answer; perhaps he did not hear, for his gaze was intent upon the door to the inner office. Fuzziman looked about to see the gorilla standing there in the doorway, statue-like, his knees bent but slightly, his huge head held high above his immaculate white collar.

The gorilla advanced a step. The stranger rose from his chair, passed his fingers through the locks of white hair that sprayed over his forehead, as if appraising the creature's appearance. He looked and waited. The gorilla came to him and extended a leathery hand.

The furniture quivered as the gorilla spoke. "How do you do, Dr. Devoli."

"How do you do," said Dartworth Devoli. "Mr. Ca—"

The syllable was only half uttered when a steel pressure from the gorilla's hand stopped it. "Mr. Gorilla," the speaker finished.

Then the newcomer and the gorilla stood silently, looking at each other. Fuzziman couldn't make out what was passing between these two. He didn't like it. It made him think of strange things. Things that made his throat dry, that forced him to clutch the ends of his coat. He took a deep breath through his mouth.

"I'll take a walk," said Fuzziman.

"You needn't," said the gorilla. "Dr. Devoli and I will visit in my private office. Dr. Devoli, this is Mr. Fuzziman, my personal manager."

The gorilla took the scientist's hat, ushered him into the next room and the door closed.

"Well, Dr. Devoli?" said the gorilla.

"I've come to take you with me, back to the Congo," said Dartworth Devoli. "You are one of my—patients, you know. I owe it to you to—"

"What of your other patients?" asked the gorilla. "How were you able to leave them?"

"Only by suspending several experiments. I left an assistant in charge. I felt that my first duty was to you."

"Then I welcome you to stay here and continue your duty."

Devoli smiled. "Your brain is working well, I see."

"Never better," said the gorilla. "Plumbutter's vigor was enough to enliven anyone's brain."

"Yes." The scientist's smile vanished. "Plumbutter's vigor is what I've been losing sleep about. You must come back with me. Live in my lodge. I'll give you every chance to get used to your new vigor—safely."

The gorilla's ebony eyes passed over the stacks of clippings, the typewriter, the yellow bulletin board where his first week's columns were posted. He got up and sauntered to the window and gazed out over the panorama of white skyscrapers. Devoli noted the lines of the well-tailored black suit, and was surprised to see how much it did to correct the gorilla's misproportions.

The gorilla turned about, his long arms unobtrusively folded behind him.

"I had to come back to America. Believe me, Doctor, I had to finish my job." The floor seemed to tremble at his words, and his voice fell to a low whisper, "No one else knows what I've found out. An old friend of mine named Bradford helped me collect it, but even he hasn't gone ahead. And it's vital that this work continue."

"No work is more vital than the salvaging of Steven Carpenter," said Devoli.

"But don't you see, Doctor?" whispered the gorilla. "That is exactly what I am doing. Steven Carpenter found the international ring of munitions makers; he unearthed their method of shipping contraband cargoes to belligerents, while at the same time retaining the government's protection. Sooner or later they will contrive to have a ship of theirs sunk—and then war! War because a nation at war sank a ship carrying munitions to the enemy! And they'll take the country to war when they're ready for it! They're almost ready. The election is almost here. If the ring elected its puppet Congressmen, then staged a torpedoing—"

The gorilla pulled a sheet from his typewriter. "Have you read the column I write as W.G.?" he said, laying the sheet down on the table before Devoli. The aged scientist looked at it.

"Are all these things true?" he said quietly.

The gorilla nodded. "Every word. I've had to begin anew. Had I merely continued, my old editor might have become suspicious, demanded to meet me. As it is, with so much of Carpenter's material duplicated, he considers it an independent source with the same material. But he must never find out who I am, for he might beat a trail for others to follow."

Devoli sat silently a moment.

"Do you know whom you are fighting?" he said.

The gorilla nodded his great head. "I think so. Every shipment has gone through the hands of the North American Shipping Alliance." He paused, then said, "Would you call your experiment a success if I quit my responsibility to my people and my country—to assume the life of an oyster?"

DEVOLI rose and his hands trembled visibly. "If you stay here to fall, as Steven Carpenter and others fell, my life work will fall with you."

The gorilla hesitated. "Why are you so sure I'll fall?"

"Your gorilla instincts will let you down. I can't let you make this sudden plunge into civilization. Remember, from the neck down you're—you're full of primitive instincts that will control you. You're dangerous. In a pinch—"

The gorilla lifted a finger and his guest silenced. Sounds of knocking at the door of the outer office. A mutter from Fuzziman.

"It's all right," said the gorilla. "My manager is there to answer. You were saying—"

Devoli tried a new tack. "What of Mrs. Steven Carpenter? Does she know what has happened?"

"No," said the gorilla quietly. "*No one* knows but you."

"Do you intend to ever let her know?"

"Never."

"But—aren't you curious to see her? You must be." The scientist searched the expressionless silvery black face. "Are you so strong—or so devoid of your old feelings—that you can resist the temptation to see her?"

"My manager often lets me drive about in his car." The gorilla closed his ebony eyes slowly and opened them to gaze out the window. "I have already seen her—many times—but she doesn't know it."

Suddenly the private conversation was terminated by echoes of harsh talk from the front office. Contrary to the usual procedure, Manager Fuzziman was not doing his share of the talking.

"Don't give me that stuff. Where's this W.G.?" said a loud, snarling voice. "I mean the guy that's been writing that column."

"But there is no—"

"Then what the hell did the *Daily Telegram* send a copy boy over here for yesterday?"

"None of your business!" Fuzziman snapped.

"But it *is* our business," said the second voice, with a deadly calm. "We're exterminators, see? We come after an insect."

The first voice rang out: "Get the hell away from that phone!"

The sound of a table falling, then Fuzziman's choked cry.

The gorilla had moved halfway to the door, his arms reaching.

"Stay back!" the scientist cried. A restraining hand reached out and held his neck. "Let me go." And as the gorilla opened the door, the scientist bolted through and closed it behind him.

The gorilla, standing against the door, his breath coming in labored gasps, his hands tightly knotted as he held them clenched, heard what happened.

"Get away from that man!" Devoli said.

There was an instant's surprised silence. Then, "You're W.G.?"

"Suppose I am?"

"We're goin' to give you a little lesson in newspaper reporting…" The gorilla had opened the door and he could see Devoli facing him, and the two thugs, with their backs toward him as he walked in, Fuzziman was rising from the floor. "Where you gettin' that stuff you run? Is Lavery puttin' you up to this? How do you know so much about Carpenter and Bradford—" His words were cut off as the gorilla took the neck of each man in one of his hands and suddenly whirled them around.

"My God!" gasped the thinner of the two. "W.G.—the Whispering Gorilla!"

"Sit down, both of you," the gorilla boomed. "You're going to answer some questions." The two men, released, began walking slowly toward the settee, which the gorilla had indicated.

But as they walked, the heavier man, his pockmarked face white, slid the hand away from the gorilla into the side pocket of his tan coat. Suddenly he whipped the hand out—and there was a gun in it…

Simultaneously the gorilla had flashed a mighty arm directly at his head. The heavy man flew off his feet and crashed into the wall. The ugly blue automatic in his hand spat flame.

Crack!

"Harry!" the thin gangster nearly screamed. "What did you…do…that…for?" He stood erect a moment, his hands fumbling slowly to his chest, where a dark stain was growing. Surprise alone lay on his face, and his eyes looked from one to the other. Then he crumpled up and fell limply to the floor.

The gorilla had meanwhile clamped his huge hands on the heavy thug. The gangster, bewildered, his eyes filled with terror, sat where he had fallen, still holding the gun.

The door burst open and two house detectives rushed in. "What's coming off—" The corpse stopped them. One of them went to the phone and dialed. When he finished, he said, "Homicide's on the way."

Both detectives were looking at the gorilla uncertainly. They knew he lived there, of course, but the sight of him...

"Will you excuse us until the police arrive?" said the gorilla. He ushered the Doctor and Fuzziman into the next room. There he faced his manager and asked, "Did you send for a copy boy to come here?"

"Ye-es," Fuzziman said, haltingly. "Your copy was going to be late—"

"All right," said the gorilla, quietly. "It's too late now. Now the real identity of W. G. will come out. All of the advantages of secrecy are over. We'll have to plan the fight differently, and God alone knows what they'll try next. There's hardly any time left with Election Day only two weeks away. *I have one ace in the hole that I've saved, but if I have to go to court...*"

Roland Fuzziman's eyes darted quickly to the gorilla's troubled face. Suddenly he remembered the gorilla saying to him, when he mentioned that no one could decide whether he was human. "Can you?" Somehow the question seemed important now.

Sometime later, when police, reporters, photographers had re-hashed the murder, re-enacted it a dozen times, Dartworth Devoli stood at the gorilla's side, placed a hand on the powerful shoulder, and whispered, "I'm staying with you till you see your fight through."

CHAPTER FIVE
W. G. for Congress

"YOU are listening to the Whis-s-pering Gorilla." To the radio world that voice was like an electric magnet translated into sound. It figuratively reached out of the amplifiers to touch each listener with a gentle but compelling hand.

"Here it comes," said "Sure" Peetson, fingering the jagged scar that ran from a corner of his mouth. He got up from his game of checkers and sauntered across the marble floor of the Carnation Club Lounge to the radio.

"And to think," his partner grumbled, "we been listenin' to that gorilla program every night, and *likin'* it up to now."

While the Whispering Gorilla theme song played. "Sure" Peetson reread the black headlines that had been folded in his coat pocket since afternoon.

ATTACK ON GORILLA FOILED, ONE THUG DEAD
"Plot Against Mystery Columnist 'W.G.' Leads to Door of Famed Whispering Gorilla."

"Sure" Peetson's eyes lingered on the paragraph that described the accidental killing of Fragathorp. "Bunglers," he muttered. "The boss should have given me this job. Haven't had a break since I came back from Africa."

"You may get your chance yet," said his partner. Other persons who gathered around the radio were discussing the same matter in other languages. The frequenters of the Carnation Club Lounge were as cosmopolitan as a Geneva conference. The circle quieted as the theme song came to a close.

"Where's the big boss?" Peetson whispered. "Isn't he listening tonight?"

"He's in a stew," someone answered, "cookin' up something for the gorilla. He's got a notion he's the only one who can handle this thing like it oughta be handled. Kid glove job."

"Kid glove! I could fix it with one bullet," said "Sure" Peetson.

The gorilla's voice returned to the radio. "Tonight, in place of our regular radio play, we bring you a short drama from real life, which occurred today in the offices of my associates and myself. This re-enactment has been prepared by Mr. Fuzziman, my personal manager, who witnessed the invasion of the two thugs and the killing that followed. The comments are those of yours truly, the Whispering Gor—"
Snap!

The gray mustached executive had marched across from an adjoining office to snap the switch. The Carnation Club Lounge fell silent. The big boss lighted a cigar.

Someone whispered to Peetson, "Get that paper out a sight, or he'll burn it up for you. He's been stamping out headline ashes all afternoon."

The gray mustached man paced in front of the silent group and puffed at his cigar. He began to bark.

"What the hell has this Whispering Gorilla got on us? Where does he get his information? Who is he, anyway?"

The dynamic speaker rested his glare on "Sure" Peetson. "You're all wrong, 'Sure.' This is no job for a gunman. If we'd known W. G. was the gorilla, today's fracas wouldn't have happened."

"I never said nothin'," said Peetson.

"Well, see that you don't get any funny ideas," said the big boss. "If that gorilla-actor got bumped off, the public might get stirred up enough to start investigating. Especially after the Carpenter business. So don't get any funny ideas."

"Let me remind you, Mr. Swangler," a well-dressed man with a foreign accent spoke up, "that a few tidy millions depend upon your—"

"I'll swing it—don't worry. In my own way."

"But these writings by W. G. are stirring up a very ugly temper among the people over here. What if our export syndicate should actually be investigated? Aren't you going to stop them?"

"Take it easy, Haeffner. You'll get everything you want a month after the new Congress meets. Election Day is on top of us. I'll give you America wrapped in a paper sack. Don't forget that I can step into any office in America as Paul Swangler, millionaire investor and director of enough corporations to make you dizzy. My connections with this ring were never discovered by anyone—"

Swangler's eyes caught upon the sharp look of Peetson, and he added, "Excepting one man, and he was promptly dispatched."

The circle of men became more comfortable. Drinks were passed, and the big boss clinched his impression of confidence by mentioning that he would release a few additional advance "dividends" that might be useful before election.

Before the group dispersed Paul Swangler gave a few orders. "Burgess, I want tickets to 'The Whispering Gorilla,' the stage play, for the rest of the week... Quaggy, you follow through on this Fragathorp manslaughter case and make sure Frag and Motini never heard of the Carnation Club. The verdict will be accidental death. The Whispering Gorilla will get a world of free advertising out of the hearings, but don't mind that. Just now we're giving him all the rope he'll take, see? Winterbotham, you keep up on Alan Bradford... And Peetson—"

"Yeah?"

"Check up on Steve Carpenter's widow."

"Sure," said "Sure" Peetson.

*   *   *

THE chauffeur throttled down. Fuzziman hailed the crowds with his unlighted cigar, and in the rear seat the gorilla kept nodding automatically and waving the tips of his fingers at the window. Beside him Dartworth Devoli sat in an attitude of tension, his eyes on the gorilla rather than the crowd.

"Keep moving," said Fuzziman to the chauffeur. "We're due at the theater in ten minutes." He chuckled. "The next time I engage a gorilla to make sure he doesn't write for the newspapers. We've had a traffic jam every night since the killing brought W. G. out of the dark... How's he feeling, Doc?"

The scientist turned the question to the gorilla. "How *are* you feeling?"

"Perfect," said the gorilla.

Devoli smiled and then grew sober. "If they demand a speech after the play, as they did last night—"

"I'll give it to them," said the gorilla.

"You can't keep up this pace for long. You've barely slept for two nights."

"I'll sleep after the election. As long as people want to stamp out the war cult I'll help them. Before I rest I'm going to get the exact dope on every man running for Congress."

Devoli gave a resigned sigh. "It's a good thing Plumbutter had a rugged constitution..."

*   *   *

The play ended with the usual uproar of enthusiasm. There were two quick curtain calls and then the house lights went up, signaling the end of the performance. But then came a general cry for a third curtain call. Applause broke out when the gorilla appeared again.

"Thank you," the gorilla bowed.

"Speech!" a voice called.

"This is not a political rally," said the gorilla. "I cannot tell you more than my column does. There are forces among you who would drive us to another war. These men control newspapers, they own Congressmen, they have unlimited power. They must be stopped. The people of this country do not want war. They must vote against the men who are intent on driving us into that war!"

Applause and cheers rang out. The darkness exploded with flashbulbs going off as photographers took pictures of the strange scene—an actor in a gorilla costume, holding a strange rally in a packed Broadway theatre. People were on their feet. The gorilla couldn't be heard anymore. He held up a hairy paw for quiet.

"Each day in my column, run by the free press of this country, I intend to discuss the candidates for Congress and on the day before election, three days from now, I promise to run the names of every controlled candidate—and their backers!"

But suddenly, in the stillness, a man sprang up in the balcony and shouted: "Maybe you should run for Congress!"

The crowd laughed and applauded. When at last the house quieted for the gorilla's response, the deep voice sent a tragic shiver through every listener.

"I thank you from my heart, but it is quite impossible for me to become a candidate."

A low murmur swept over the audience, then another man sprang to his feet and shouted:

"The Whispering Gorilla for Congress..."

Dartworth Devoli, shaking his head, led the Whispering Gorilla from the stage; the curtain fell. The audience buzz carried on out into the street. Fuzziman's chauffeur drove through throngs all the way from the theatre to the broadcasting studios.

"Who were the men who shouted out the nonsense about running for Congress?" Devoli asked.

"I didn't recognize either of them," said Fuzziman.

The gorilla said nothing.

CHAPTER SIX
The Man with the Scarred Mouth

THE next morning there were a lot of people in the lobby of the exclusive Radcliffe Hotel—mainly gorilla fans, some reporters, too. The management called up Fuzziman and advised that in order to keep the crowd under control that some of them should be allowed up to the gorilla's suite to speak with at least Fuzziman, or perhaps even the gorilla himself. Fuzziman spoke to the gorilla about it. He then called down and instructed management to allow a few up at a time.

Now he and three receptionists, quickly hired from an agency, were busy with the people as they filed through the sumptuous room.

"No, Madam, there is no intention to run for Congress. We are happy to have your kind words of support, though.

"No, Miss, we cannot give out any statements at this time."

A tall young man stepped forward "Please tell the Whispering Gorilla that I need to see him. I'm—"

"I don't care who you are," Fuzziman was saying. "You can't—"

The tall young man persisted. "If you'll only tell the gorilla that Alan Bradford of the *Telegram* wants to see him."

"Bradford?" said Fuzziman. He had heard the gorilla speak of a Bradford before. "Just a minute. I'll see."

The little manager pushed his way past the fringes of the crowd and let himself into the adjoining room. "Whew!" he said in a breathy manner. "You should see them, pal. They're four deep, and there's more coming in all the time downstairs. If some of them could have their way I think they'd actually draft you for Congress..." He smiled. "Kinda crazy, isn't it? Can you imagine someone in a gorilla suit in Congress?" He laughed under his breath. "By the way, do you know somebody named Bradford from the *Telegram?*"

The gorilla had been sitting quietly, a sheaf of papers spread out before him. Now he looked up. "Alan Bradford?" he said, nodding. "Yes. I've been waiting for him. Let him come in, please."

A moment later, the gorilla stood up to greet the young man who had entered the room. He offered his hand. "Don't be afraid to shake hands with me," he said. "I really want to shake your hand. I've heard about your work. You were associated with—"

"With Carpenter and Hannigan and Forman."

"Yes. And since their deaths, you've done nothing?"

"You seem to know quite a bit about our activities," said Bradford.

"My business is knowing about others," said the gorilla, quietly. "Naturally, since I became interested in this work, I found out a lot of things."

"About North American Shipping Alliance, for instance?"

"Yes." The gorilla stood quietly. "You have news?"

"Rather vital news."

"And you've come to me with it?"

"I'm not sure. I don't know anything about you. I mean after all, you're some actor-turned-activist in a gorilla suit." He chuckled slightly at his own words. "It's a bit nutty don't you think? Look, I know what you've been doing, and I know that Lavery trusts you. That should be enough, but yet I'm...just a bit leery."

"Of what?"

"What are you up to?" Bradford asked. "No one knows who you are. There are a million rumors about you. Why do you always wear this gorilla outfit? No man who was serious would continually—"

"I'm not telling you anything. Only this, I'm wearing this outfit for reasons that you'll never understand. Do you still doubt my sincerity?"

The young man was silent. "I've got to know what you'll do with what I tell you. It's too big."

The gorilla studied Bradford. "I see," he said. "You found out what ship they're going to have attacked and when."

Instantly Bradford was on his feet, facing the impassive gorilla. "*You know that too?*" he cried, incredulously. "It isn't possible—"

"I know a lot of things." The gorilla cut in. "I've known for some time what the Alliance was up to. I knew that when things got too hot for their racket to continue that they would play their ace—which is, to tell one of the belligerent's secret agents of a big contraband shipment, and then wait for the belligerent to torpedo it. There would be women and children aboard; we'd have another *Lusitania,* and war..."

The young man sat with a surprised yet perplexed look on his face. When he found his voice again he said, "They've chosen the night before election—two nights from now—for the sinking. The ship is the U.S.S. *Commodore.* When the papers scream the news on election morning, every pro-war candidate will be swept in."

The gorilla rose and took Bradford's shoulder. "Thank you," he said. "You've given me another ace. With this card to play, we can't lose."

"What are you going to do?" said Bradford. "There are people who would actually write your name in if you ran for Congress."

"No," said the gorilla. "That's what my enemies want. They engineered this whole Congress thing. They want me to run—it's a sly diversion of some sort. I can't quite figure it out, but it's impossible."

"But I don't see why," Bradford protested.

"Trust me. There aren't many days left for us and I need your help. Come back later today and bring a stenographer, someone you can trust."

WHEN Alan Bradford and the new stenographer returned later that afternoon, the gorilla was very much engrossed in his work. He stood at his desk reading a badly typed draft of his column. On one side of the gorilla stood the erect, white-haired scientist; at the other shoulder was Fuzziman, his cigar tilted high, his eyes following the words as the gorilla read them.

Bradford and the girl, having disposed of their wraps, entered. The reading stopped. The paper fell from the gorilla's hand and slid to the edge of the desk.

"Our new stenographer," said Bradford. "Mrs. Carpenter, may I present the Whispering Gorilla."

"How do you do," said the girl.

"How do you—" the deep voice faltered. The paper that clung on the edge of the desk trembled and slipped to the floor.

"And this," Bradford continued, "is Dr. Devoli, the Whispering Gorilla's private physician."

Devoli nodded as the girl warmly greeted him. "The name was—?" His hand was half-lifted toward the gorilla, his eyes were intent upon the girl.

"Mrs. Carpenter," Bradford repeated. "You've heard of Steven Carpenter?"

"Yes, indeed," said the scientist, his hand now trembling high upon the gorilla's back. The gorilla had bowed his head.

"And this is Mr. Fuzziman, the gorilla's business manager."

Fuzziman extended a cordial greeting, which helped to loosen mysterious tensions that had suddenly gripped the office.

Roselle Carpenter stood before the Whispering Gorilla's desk. "Mr. Bradford said that I am to take my first orders from you," she smiled politely, "so what would you have me do?"

The gorilla did not answer. He seemed to try to answer, then he turned away. For a minute or two his huge form was silhouetted against the window and he seemed to be absorbed in studying the skyscrapers and canyons of the city. When he turned back he picked up the paper that had dropped to the floor. His voice choked down, but the girl understood from his gesture toward the typewriter that he wanted the paper retyped.

Roselle Carpenter went to work. The gorilla returned to the window. And Devoli hastily left the offices for a cup of coffee.

Time passed slowly through the afternoon and evening wore on, and still the columns outside the door did not diminish.

It was past nine o'clock in the evening when Fuzziman rushed in breathlessly. "Where's W.G.?" he cried. Alan

Bradford and Roselle Carpenter were eating sandwiches from a tray.

"He's in his bedroom, eating alone. Said he wanted—"

Fuzziman rushed past them, threw open the bedroom door.

Bradford and the girl, following him and saw the gorilla sitting on his bed, a huge tray before him. There was something horrible about the way he was eating, something that made the girl tear her eyes away.

"Shut that door, you fool!" the gorilla roared. The tone of his voice was primitive, brutal, a great hoarse shout that was inhuman. Bradford shuddered as the door closed.

Some moments later, it opened again. The gorilla followed Fuzziman, a still trembling Fuzziman, out. He was calm now, his face almost pleasant, and when he spoke, it was in the deep whisper that enthralled those who listened.

"Bradford," he said. "The eminent and famous Mr. Paul Swangler is outside. He wants to see me."

"Swangler!" Bradford leaped to his feet. "Do you know—"

"Yes," said the gorilla. "I know. That was my first ace in the hole. I knew what Mr. Swangler was up to a long time ago."

"What do you suppose he wants here?"

"I'm going to find out."

"How?"

"By seeing him. Remember, we have one advantage. He doesn't think we know who he really is."

Roselle, who had been standing near the window, slowly rejoined the group. "Will you want me to make notes of the conversation?" she said.

"If you please," said the gorilla, not facing her. "Fuzziman, let Swangler in, please."

PAUL SWANGLER came walking into the room, a smile on his face. When his eyes fell on the gorilla, the smile faded a little, but he held it there. He took the gorilla's proffered hand unflinchingly. "I see the newspapers are correct in saying that you never take that costume off," he laughed.

"Cigar?" said Fuzziman.

Swangler silently took the cigar, lighted it. "I suppose you're wondering why I'm here?" he said. "I'll come to the point directly, and I would like you to do the same, I'm accustomed to quick action."

"Please proceed," said the gorilla, sitting down.

"In a nutshell, Mr.—uh—W.G., I've come to offer you my support for your campaign for Congress. I've been reading your column, and I've heard about your "speeches," and I agree with you one hundred percent. This country could use someone like you. I admit frankly that I have a selfish interest in this. Most of my money is tied up in peace time industries, and war would hurt me tremendously."

"I see," said the gorilla.

An awkward silence fell. All eyes were on Swangler. "Every wealthy man owes it to his country," he said, pompously, "to see to it that the best men are elected to govern." In spite of his pompous address, he had lingered significantly on three words: "Are you interested?"

"Yes, Mr. Swangler," said the gorilla. "Please continue."

"Thank you. Now, if I were to give you my support to the extent of, say, half a million dollars, which can be very useful in two days of campaigning, I would naturally expect to meet whoever is behind this movement."

"I'm sorry, I don't know what you mean."

"Come, come," said Swangler, jovially. "You know well enough. I mean, who writes your speeches? Who writes that column for you? Who supplied that list of 'controlled' Congressmen? I know well enough that you are—with all due respect—nothing more than the front for some organization, some man. Naturally, I must meet whoever is behind you."

"But the gorilla here writes it all himself—there isn't anyone else," Fuzziman blurted out, before the gorilla's swift warning glance could silence him.

"Indeed?" murmured Swangler. "You know, I'm inclined to believe you." He rose to his feet and advanced to the gorilla. "I'm fascinated by your costume," he said, reaching out a hand. "I could swear you were the real thing if I didn't know it was only a costume. Do you mind if I feel it?"

The gorilla stepped back from the outstretched hand swiftly. "Yes, Mr. Swangler, I mind very much."

The words brought a sudden silence to the room. Everyone tensed. Swangler hesitated, then forced a chuckle. "Professional secret?" he smiled. "I'm not offended, and I'm sorry if I've annoyed you." He turned around, both hands outstretched in a magnanimous gesture. "Shall we draw up formal papers for my backing?" he said. "You know, they always investigate these things. Let's keep our arrangement above board."

At a nod from Fuzziman, the girl left the room.

"It will be quite unnecessary for Mrs. Carpenter to bring back any papers," said the gorilla. "You see, Mr. Swangler, I have no intention of running for Congress."

"But my dear *fellow*—"

"I will continue to support those men whom I consider to be right. If you would care to lend your support to that, we can continue."

Swangler smiled. "Your modesty is refreshing to me, but I'm afraid that I must insist on your running personally. It isn't too late; your name can be written in."

"No." The gorilla said the word incisively, showing his teeth.

At that moment, Roselle Carpenter came back into the room, closing the door behind her swiftly. It opened a moment later and Dr. Devoli followed. "Mrs. Carpenter," he said, anxiously. "What's the matter? You've turned as pale as a ghost. Did something frighten you?"

The girl stood nearly still, trembling, visibly shaken. "It's…nothing," she managed to say. "It's just nothing."

Instantly Bradford was beside her. "What is it, Roselle?" he demanded.

The gorilla had come beside her. She faced Bradford. "It's foolish for me to be upset by such a trifle," she said, trying to smile. "I thought I was being followed."

"Followed?" said the gorilla. "By whom?"

"I don't know him. I saw him last night when I went home after shopping. This morning I saw him again. Now I thought I saw him outside."

"Here?" cried Fuzziman.

But the gorilla had thrown the door open.

AS ALL eyes turned to the adjoining room, the people in that room all turned to face those with the gorilla. There were dozens of people there, men and women of every description. As they looked at the cold, searching eyes of the gorilla, a hush came over them.

The gorilla was standing there, legs slightly apart, one arm on the door he had thrown open. There was something in his bearing akin to a beast about to leap.

Suddenly a nondescript man in a gray coat began to move. He had a long scar running from a corner of his mouth. "Let me out of here," the man mumbled, beginning to push his way.

The next moment a mighty roar echoed through the room and the gorilla leaped halfway across the packed room towards the fleeing man!

Instantly there was a panic. Screams rang out. The man in gray had gone mad. Clawing, shrieking, he was trying to get away.

"Stop! Stop!" Devoli was shouting, fighting his way after the gorilla. He plunged through the terrified crowd and seized the gorilla by the nape of the neck. "For God's sake, remember you're a man!" he whispered fiercely. The gorilla stopped suddenly. The next instant he was surging again, but the man in gray had fled.

The aged scientist bent close to the gorilla's ear. "Remember you're Steven Carpenter, for your wife's sake," he whispered.

The gorilla stood quietly. The scene in his mind—a moonlit night in the Congo, and a match light flaring up—faded from his mind with a great effort, Fuzziman was saying a few words to the frightened people still in the room as the gorilla silently followed Devoli back to the inner room.

Inside he stood once again in his impressively dignified manner.

"I'm sorry I—" the girl began. "I didn't think I would cause—"

Fuzziman came back inside. "What happened to you?" he said. "I've never seen you so angry before!"

"I don't understand," said Swangler. "That man came up in the elevator with me. He certainly looked harmless enough."

"If I ever see that man again, I'll kill him," the gorilla said. His voice was as calm and steady as a deep river. "With your permission, I bid you all good night."

He turned and walked into the adjoining bedroom. Those outside could hear the click of the lock inside.

"Well," said Swangler. "He certainly sounds as if he means it."

"I'm sorry you had to witness this," Fuzziman said to Swangler. "W. G. isn't an excitable sort, usually. I hope you won't think anything of it."

"If that man follows Mrs. Carpenter again," said Devoli, "his life may not be worth a plugged nickel. He better stay out of sight."

"You really think," said Swangler, in a low voice, "that he would kill that fellow?"

Devoli shrugged. "Don't know for sure. Maybe not. Then again he might choke him in an instant."

Swangler laughed. "One would really think W. G. was a gorilla, to hear you speak. Well, I guess that's as much as I can accomplish tonight. If W. G. shows any sign of changing his mind, Mr. Fuzziman, please let me know."

Several minutes later, Swangler had gone.

THE others stood about for some moments until the gorilla's voice came from behind the door, muffled yet clear, "Fuzziman, you and Bradford take Mrs. Carpenter home. She's had a harrowing night. Bradford, did you get a good look at that man outside?"

"Yes," said Bradford, shouting.

"Don't shout. My hearing is quite acute. Remember that face. He was Swangler's bodyguard. Never mind how I know. Just keep him away. Good night."

Quietly, the two men and the girl put on their hats and coats and left.

When they had gone, the gorilla's lock clicked and he came out.

"How do you feel?" said Dr. Devoli.

"I almost lost myself," said the gorilla. "That man was the one who shot me that night in the Congo."

"Good Lord..." Devoli muttered. "No wonder you went off like that."

The gorilla sank into a chair, his hands over his eyes. "Did you see how frightened she was?" he whispered. His voice was shaky. "I'm dead, Doctor, and I've left a wife to be hunted by the lowest scum on earth. I can't lift a finger to protect her." He rose suddenly, and his bloodshot eyes gazed at Devoli. "You weren't here to see how repulsed she was when she caught a glimpse of me eating. You should have seen her face."

"Hold on," said Devoli, anxiously. He took hold of the gorilla's arm.

The gorilla buried his head in his hands. "I can't," he whispered. "I just can't bear it. I love her so much. It's too much for a man to bear."

Suddenly the gorilla lifted his great head and laughed and the tears rolled down his silvery-black face. "*Man*—I called myself a *man!*" He faced the Doctor with his legs apart. "Look at me, Devoli! You made me this! You made me live again—a monster. Why didn't you let me lie there? Why—"

"*Carpenter!*" the aged Doctor snapped. "Stop this! You knew what you were doing! You've work to do these next two days. *Carpenter,* listen to me!"

The gorilla stood there looking at the old man before him. "You call me *Carpenter,*" he said quietly. "Thank you, Doctor Devoli."

He crossed the room and sat down. The Doctor brought him a glass of water and several pills, which the gorilla took unquestioningly.

"These will keep me from waking up during the night," said the gorilla. "But in the morning it will be here again. Do you know why Swangler and his crew want me to run for Congress? No? Because then they'll expose me—*as a real gorilla!* They're sure of it after tonight."

"But you're not running," said Devoli.

"No. Swangler came here tonight to find out if there was anyone behind me. Instead he found out I'm a real gorilla. His next move is clear."

"What do you mean?"

"I mean," said the gorilla slowly, "that the indicting of Swangler's thug for that accidental killing that took place here comes up tomorrow—and they undoubtedly have a subpoena waiting for me."

The Doctor's face turned white. "That's impossible! They'll challenge your identity—force you to prove who you are!"

The gorilla nodded. "Either that—or another way." Then he rose and went slowly back to his own room. "Good night," he said.

CHAPTER SEVEN
Plot for a Victory

A DOOR closed gently and "Sure" Peetson stood before Paul Swangler.

"You sent for me?"

"Yes," said Swangler. "You know what today is?"

"Sure. Two days before Election Day. Today's the second."

"Fine. Now get out of town. Go up to Mattson's place in the mountains, and don't show up until after election."

Peetson's face clouded up. "But, boss, I want to be around—"

"You heard me. Get going."

Paul Swangler watched "Sure" Peetson close the door behind him. He stepped to a phone and dialed a number. "Hello, Stetley? Swangler. Yes, the subpoena was served on him at the crack of dawn this morning. No, I can't be there, though I'd like to be around to watch the fun. Right.

Tomorrow's the day he was going to publish that list of Congressmen we own. He'll be up in the Bronx Zoo by then. Do I really think he's a gorilla? I'll be damned if I don't! Sounds insane to me too, but wait till you see what happens in court today. Certainly. There'll be no list tomorrow, and there'll be a fine Election Day the day after that. Call you after it's over."

Then, smiling to himself, Paul Swangler put the phone back and sat down to the breakfast that waited for him on a silver tray.

The corridors of the Court of Special Sessions were packed. Somehow the word had gotten around that the gorilla was going to appear. Early in the morning, the streets around the court had been roped off. The area was dense with newspapermen, though it was a routine appearance against a criminal that was going to bring the famed gorilla to the court.

Or was it? Hints had circulated...big doings...startling developments... The crowds waited impatiently, wondering.

Cheers rolled down the street when the gorilla's car came into sight. One could see him sitting there with his manager on one side, and a distinguished old man on the other. The car drove up to the great stone stairway that led to the court and stopped. The police cordons battled the wild mob for gangway, and a loud shout was heard the din.

"Look...he's still in his outfit!"

The photographers clustered around, impeding progress with their pleas for the gorilla to pose. The gorilla posed patiently, silently. His face was grave, as were the faces of the men with him. Presently they began walking up the long stone steps.

"Say something to us, W.G.!" a shout rang out.

The gorilla turned. "The newspapers will say everything I have to tell you tomorrow," he said, his voice deep and booming, and amidst a smatter of cheers he resumed walking.

Police ushered them through the corridor into a small room to one side of the courtroom, to wait until the gorilla would be called. Inside, Fuzziman sank to a bench, while the gorilla stood, his eyes on the floor.

"What are you going to do?" Fuzziman panted.

Devoli held up a hand. "You've asked the same question a thousand times this morning. Let him alone."

"I'm quite all right," said the gorilla, slowly. "Did you get the money, Fuzziman?"

"Ten thousand dollars in cold cash," said Fuzziman, plaintively. "Had to get the bank president up to get it. What's it all about?"

"Soon," said the gorilla. "Soon enough. Thank God Election Day is only two days away." He said nothing more until the policeman came to call him. Then he rose and walked into the courtroom with the two men behind him.

A sound like water rushing up on a beach greeted his appearance in court. Half the spectators stood, the better to see him, and the gavel rapped imperiously. "Order in the court! Sheriff, see that order is restored…"

The judge's eye swung back to the gorilla. He turned to the District Attorney. "Mr. Attorney," he said, "is this the witness for the State?"

"It—he is, your honor," said the District Attorney. "But he has requested that he be left out of the case. Mr. Roland Fuzziman is here on my subpoena, and he is quite capable of presenting the State's case."

"If it please the Court," said a man, rising from one of the tables in the enclosure, where the gangster sat, shifty-eyed, "that gorilla has been subpoenaed by the defense."

"Do you intend to have this—uh—person testify on the stand?"

"I most certainly do, your honor."

"In that case, the Court requests this person to remove his ridiculous and abhorrent costume at once."

Now the wave of talking and comment that rose up drowned out the gavel. The gorilla advanced to the bar and waited for the noise to die down. At length, when the sheriff had ejected a spectator, and order was restored, the gorilla spoke.

"Your honor, what if I do not choose to remove my costume?"

The judge leaned over. "Do I hear you correctly, sir? This Court has ordered that you remove that costume at once. Please give your name to the clerk."

"I must refuse," said the gorilla quietly.

The judge rapped down on his bench. "This Court is quite aware of your theatrical and political activities, but it cannot countenance an effort to reduce this Court to a laughing stock. Unless you obey my order immediately, I will be forced to hold you in contempt."

"I have no alternative," said the gorilla.

"Are you quite aware of what you are saying?" said the judge. He adjusted his spectacles, and his voice was softer. "I know the fight you are waging is a good one, but I cannot approve of your methods. Please consider your answer carefully."

"Your honor," said the gorilla in his magnificent voice. "The furthest thing from my mind is the desire to cause any undue sensation here, or to obstruct justice in any way. But there are other kinds of justice, and I have fought for my own kind more than I can tell you. I cannot explain why it must remain impossible for me to comply with the order of this Court, but I can tell you only that it would ruin everything I have worked for. I must therefore accept your decision to hold me in contempt."

The judge nodded his head in a mystified manner. "You are a very courageous man," he said, quietly, "in your own peculiar way. I hold you in contempt because I have no other alternative."

The attorney for the defense sprang to his feet. "I must protest! I demand that the witness the defense has summoned here be forced to testify!"

"*You* demand?" said the judge quietly. "The Court has already demanded. If the witness chooses to be cited for contempt, there is nothing more."

"But I protest against this outrageous—"

"Sit down!" the judge snapped. "It is quite within the ability of this Court to hold even a defense attorney of your fame ni contempt." He faced the District Attorney. "Call the sheriff to hold this witness."

The gorilla spoke up, "If it pleases your honor, may I press upon the understanding of the Court to grant me immediate bail?"

"I protest! I most emphatically—"

"*Sit down!*" The judge glared at the defense attorney. He turned to the gorilla, his voice altered. "Bail granted. Five dollars, and I remand you to your own custody until further notice from this Court. Please pay the clerk. And now, please get on with this hearing..."

"Thank you, your honor," the gorilla murmured. He turned to Fuzziman. "When you're through here, you'll find me at the hotel." Then he was gone.

PAUL SWANGLER had barely finished his leisurely breakfast when the phone rang. He walked over to it and lifted the receiver, then listened.

"What? You blundering idiot! You let him get away—you damned fool! You—" Viciously, he slammed the phone down, his brow furrowed. Immediately the phone went off again.

Gingerly, Swangler lifted it. "Yes, I heard," he said, after a moment. "No, it isn't over yet. Stop crying, Stetley. I promise you that column will never appear. Of course I can still stop him. It's my last trick, but it can't fail. Now sit down and relax, I'll get to work right away."

Swangler pressed the receiver button down, holding the phone in his hand meditatively for some moments. Then he lifted his hand and dialed. He spoke, "Is Joris there? Swangler...Joris? Listen, get up to Mattson's place in the mountains right away, Peetson's on his way there now. Get him and bring him back to town. Got that? Bring Peetson back to town without fail..."

Swangler held the button down and dialed again.

"Hello, Rollins? Swangler. There's a change in plans. The Victory Dinner is coming off tonight instead of tomorrow night. Did you hear what I said? I don't care what you have to do. Hire two dozen private planes if you have to, but have them all there tonight. I want every one of our candidates there, understand? Senators, Representatives, too. No...I can't tell you what it's all about... Can't you guess? What do people hold Victory Dinners for? Victory...*Tonight!*"

Now Paul Swangler replaced the receiver and sat down again. A slow yet careful smile spread on his face and he murmured to himself, "Peetson, you're going to give your all for the cause tonight." The smile didn't fade.

CHAPTER EIGHT
Discovery and Loss

WHEN the gorilla returned to the Radcliffe Hotel, he found a small crowd already forming. He pressed his way into the private elevator that went to his suite, then past the people in the outer room. In the inner room, he found Alan Bradford and Roselle waiting.

"Then it's true!" Roselle exclaimed. "Dr. Devoli called—said you hadn't testified after all!"

"Yes," said the gorilla slowly. She hadn't looked at him when she spoke, he had observed. The gladness was in her voice, but not in her eyes.

Bradford came forward. "What do we do now?" he said.

"I'll call you in a few moments," said the gorilla. "I want to be alone while I collect my notes. I'm going to dictate my pre-Election Day column in a few minutes, and I want you to be around to add what you can. No, don't leave. Stay here; I'm quite content to stay in my bedroom."

He tried to smile, then realizing how horrible a grimace it must appear, he quickly stepped into the bedroom. He then sat down before the mirror and looked at himself for several moments. "Lord," he half-whispered, spreading a hand over the eyes he was forced to close. He shook his head and stood erect. "In a few days it will all be over," he said to himself. "And then?"

But he erased the thought from his mind. He opened the drawer of his desk with a key, fumbling as his huge fingers strove to move the little key. Then he arranged a sheaf of papers before him.

For several minutes he wrote with a great pen that stood nearby, each sentence a painful effort. His huge head was a study in concentration as he worked. Then he laid the pen down and seemed to be listening. His immeasurably sharpened sense of hearing had caught fragments of conversation from the next room. Now he went to the door and stood close to it.

"It's a beautiful day outside," Bradford was saying. "Real fall weather. In a few days we'll be able to enjoy it like normal people. As soon as W. G. blows this business up."

"Alan," said the girl. "What is he going to do after that?"

Silence. "I don't know. I've never thought of it."

"Alan, who is he?"

"I don't know. No one knows. He's just…"

"Just what?"

"Don't ask me, Roselle. You know as much as I do. You saw him that day when he was eating like some—"

"Like some animal."

"Yes."

"Alan, do you really think he *is?*"

"*I don't know,* I tell you. Not even Fuzziman really knows. Did you see what happened to him when he tore after that man who was following you? Fuzziman trembled all the way to your home; couldn't talk either. I wish I knew…no, I don't… I don't want to know. It frightens me. It isn't possible."

"But Dr. Devoli—he must know."

"Maybe he does. He whispered something to the gorilla that night, but I couldn't hear. It was the only thing that quieted him."

"I noticed," said the girl. "There was only one man who ever fought for me that way—the man I loved."

"Steven," said Bradford. "One of the finest men I ever knew. But, Roselle, he wasn't the only man who loved you. Roselle, I've thought about saying this to you for weeks, but I know it must take a long time for a woman like you to get over losing a man like Steven."

"Much more time, Alan, please," said the girl, her voice barely audible.

"So—I see," said Bradford. "I thought— Well—maybe a man can't feel these things like a woman. But I love you, Roselle."

The door leading from that room to the front one closed as Bradford left. After that there was silence, and only the girl's weeping could be heard.

THE gorilla sat down again. There were great tears in his small eyes, and a sob choked in his throat. His great black fingernails bit into the rough flesh of his palms, and he lay his head on the desk and wept. He lay that way until Dr. Devoli silently entered the room.

"Carpenter," the Doctor whispered, "you need all your strength now. You outwitted them this morning. Now we're almost finished. I know how you're suffering, man, but you've got to hold on a little while longer."

The gorilla turned away. "I'm all right," he said. "Go out and talk to her. She's feeling miserable. I've got to end it. Send Bradford in to me."

When Bradford came into the bedroom, the gorilla kept his back to him for some time while he spoke. "Bradford, get this down: The North American Shipping Alliance is owned by Mattson, Stetley and Swangler, through proxies. In three months, exactly 853,000 tons of contraband has been shipped on illegal permits. Among the contraband has been poison gas, machine guns, bombers, grenades, automatic rifles, trench mortars, tanks, scrap iron. On my desk you'll find complete lists. Beside it is a sheaf of affidavits from the proxies with sworn testimony that they have been paid to hold title to shares really owned by three men; also, testimony from the foreman of the Newark warehouse, testimony from—" and there the gorilla stopped.

Bradford waited expectantly. He had left the door slightly ajar, and through it came the sounds of Devoli and the girl speaking. Bradford looked closely at the gorilla's ear. A shiver swept him as he realized that the ear was twitching as it listened to the conversation.

"Dr. Devoli, I've been wanting to ask you something. Are you the same Dr. Devoli that wrote me a letter once…from the Congo?"

A thoughtful look came over Devoli's face; it was a good twenty seconds before he finally answered. "Yes…Mrs. Carpenter, I wrote you a brief letter at the time of your husband's death."

"Why have you never mentioned it?"

"I—I thought perhaps the hurt was still too keen…"

"You must know that I loved my husband deeply."

"Yes, of course."

"Then surely you realize how much I've hungered for word of him—even though he is gone. Why haven't you told me?"

"There wasn't much to tell. I'm sorry to say that I was so busy with my animals during your husband's short stay that I had little time to talk with him. Had I realized what fate lay in store for him… But there's no need to say that now. I remember distinctly how often he spoke of you."

"What sort of things did he say?"

"He wished he had brought you with him."

"Yes, he wrote me that… I wish I had gone." She was crying again.

"Close the door!" the gorilla whispered. He had turned to face Bradford as he spoke, and he was shaking. His eyes were more red-rimmed than usual, and his hands were closed fists.

Bradford closed the door, eyeing the gorilla. "What's the matter?" he said softly.

"Nothing. I'm not myself today. Maybe you'd better go for the day."

"Today?" said Bradford, his eyebrows lifting. "Two days before Election Day? With all that vitally important material to be—"

"I can handle it myself. Take my car. And take Ros— Mrs. Carpenter with you. It's a beautiful fall day outside. Take her for a ride. You can both use the rest... *What are you staring at?*"

"NOTHING," said Bradford. "Nothing but that paper clip."

"What about it?"

The gorilla's eyes went to the paper clip, then back to Bradford.

"What about it?" he whispered.

"Nothing," said Bradford. "Yesterday I watched you sharpen pencils. You held one between each pair of fingers and sharpened them that way."

The gorilla had come very close to Bradford now.

"I'm thinking," said Bradford, his face ashen, the words coming from him as if by torture, "that of all the men I ever knew, only one ever fastened papers with the clips on the *side,* instead of on the top—and that same man held pencils in his hand in that peculiar way—*and that man was Steven Carpenter.*"

The gorilla's hand shot out stiffly, gripping Bradford by the throat. The huge arm pushed him against the wall, and a thumb and forefinger pressed against his windpipe. Bradford's body shot backward. His legs whipped over a chair that clattered to the floor. He stood pinned against the wall, unable to struggle, helpless in the grasp of the great animal that held him there.

The gorilla held him like that for ten seconds. Then he let his hand relax and breath rushed back to Bradford's lungs.

"Steven Carpenter is dead," said the gorilla, his eyes boring into Bradford's. "Never forget that you know that. I saw him die."

Still unable to speak, Bradford nodded his head. He brushed a hand up to his eyes. "I understand, W.G.," he managed to whisper.

The gorilla helped him to his feet. "I'm sorry," he said. "Do as I said. Take her for a ride. Help her to forget. I know your friend couldn't have prayed for a better man than you. Now go—I've got work to do."

Later, when Devoli came in, the Doctor said, "What happened in here? Bradford looked ill when he went out. And you don't look well either."

"Nothing," said the gorilla.

"You didn't lose your head again?" said Devoli anxiously. "You're getting to a point where you go off easily. Remember what I told you at the beginning. No matter how much it dismays you, you're essentially a brute from the neck down."

"*Only* from the neck down, Doctor?" said the gorilla, gently. "Have you ever taken a good look at my face?"

The Doctor looked away. "You're a long way from the Plumbutter whose face I knew. I'm worried. Deeply worried."

Then he went out and left the gorilla to his work.

IT was late in the afternoon when Alan Bradford came rushing into the gorilla's room. His clothes were torn, his face was cut in several places. "Roselle!" he cried. "They've kidnapped her!"

Instantly the gorilla leaped to his feet. "Who?" he roared.

"I don't know. They rammed into our car out on Long Island, forced us out with guns and took her with them. I fought, but they knocked me out with a gun butt. When I came to, I was lying on the side of the road with a crowd around me. I didn't wait for the police and came here. There was a note lying on me when I got up. Here it is."

The gorilla's heavy fingers fumbled with the paper until he threw it down on the desk with a loud cry of frustration. "Open it! Read it!"

Bradford read: *"Don't worry. Nothing will happen. Just wait for our call later in the day."*

The gorilla stood as if transfixed. "This is Swangler's work," he said intensely, the veins on his great neck standing out. "I'm going to kill him…"

The rage stood out on the animal's face, and his mighty arms swung up as if to come with force enough to shatter everything in sight.

But just as he moved toward the door, the telephone rang.

Swiftly, Devoli stepped over and took it. His eyes were fixed on the gorilla, one hand upraised in warning. "Hello," he said. "This is Dr. Devoli. Yes, Swangler, we have your note. Just a moment, please."

Devoli spoke to the gorilla, "Are you man enough to talk in a civilized fashion over this phone? It's Swangler, and you'll have to be calm."

The gorilla snatched the phone from the Doctor. Then he held it away at arm's length, while his breath came less rapidly, and the hair on his neck, which had seemed to rise, settled down.

Then the gorilla spoke, "I'm listening…" He said nothing else until the end, when he said, "We'll be there. If anything's happened to her, I'll tear you to bits with my hands." And he hung up.

"She's safe?" Bradford cried.

"Swangler says so," said the gorilla. "He says he only took her to persuade us to come to his Victory Dinner tonight. He says that Roselle will meet us there."

"I don't understand it," said Devoli, watching the gorilla as he began to pace the floor. "But whatever it is, I think we can be sure that she's safe if Swangler says so. Until tonight, there's nothing we can do."

But Bradford had caught the Doctor's glance.

"There's a lot we can do," Devoli said. "And we'd better do it. That list, for instance, and those names. Come on. After all, I'm sort of fond of the girl too," he added wanly.

The gorilla looked up at him and shook his head. "All right," he said, and walked into his bedroom.

Only Devoli stayed behind, his white forehead furrowed in thought.

CHAPTER NINE
Death Comes to a Party

"THEY must be nearly all here now," said one of the bellboys close to the door of the Carlton House. "What a bunch. I bet this is the biggest party this hotel ever saw. All these Congressmen and millionaires."

"There's one I know," said another bellboy. "That's Senator Green. And down there, that smooth-lookin' bird, that's Paul Swangler. Ain't that Swangler, copper?"

"Hell, yes," grinned the cop. "That's him. 'Scuse me, lads. Here comes the main treat of the evening."

The policeman joined several others going toward the doer of the hotel. Outside the scream of many sirens was growing as it approached. The sounds echoed down the canyon-like streets.

Around the corner sped four motorcycles, the policemen on them riding like centaurs. Up to the Carlton they swept and then the sirens died. Behind them a long, black limousine drew up. The door opened and three men stepped out. Last of all was the gorilla. The four began to go through into the hotel.

"Holy smoke!" ejaculated one of the bellboys. "It's the whispering gorilla himself!"

"The main treat—I'll say," said another. "He's about the only guy that was missing 'til now. Who are those other guys?"

"Damned if I know."

The gorilla walked through the lobby and a hush followed him as people caught sight of him. His huge face was composed and his eyes looked straight ahead. Like the three men with him, Bradford, Devoli, and Fuzziman, he was immaculately clad in full evening dress, and he was an arresting, majestic figure.

At the entrance to the Grand Ballroom, Paul Swangler came up to the group. The men bowed politely and went past Swangler inside.

There, standing not far away, with several men around her, stood Roselle Carpenter! She was radiant in her gown, a deep old rose velvet. She hastily excused herself and came up to meet the men.

Every eye seemed to rest on the little group as they stood there.

"Did they hurt you?" the gorilla said, his voice low.

"No." She was actually smiling. "They were very nice to me. They sent someone over to my place for my clothes and took me out to dinner." Her gaze rested on each of the men, lingered momentarily on the gorilla, but he was looking out over the assemblage.

"All right," said Dr. Devoli. "Now that you're safe, let's get out of here. I don't like this one bit."

"Not so fast, Doctor," said the gorilla. "Let's look about here. We've got the columns all set up and ready to go, but we may pick up a detail or two here."

"I agree," said Bradford. "This is a Victory Dinner, but it's our victory. Let's stay."

"I don't like it," Fuzziman spoke up. "It's cockeyed. Why should they invite us here tonight? And wasn't this scheduled for tomorrow night? There's something going on here that I can't put my finger on."

"We'll stay," said the gorilla. "I'm going to find out why Swangler wanted us here so badly that he kidnapped Ros— Mrs. Carpenter to get us here."

The orchestra began to play at that moment. Bradford murmured something to the girl, but she laughed and shook her head. "No, Alan," she said. "I'm going to have the first dance with—W.G."

The gorilla turned slowly to the girl, his eyes full upon her. "Thank you," he said quietly. "I don't dance."

"But you must," she insisted, coming closer. "I'm asking you to."

The gorilla caught Devoli's glance from the corner of his eye. He could almost feel the Doctor wincing. His heart was beating furiously, his breath caught. "Of course," he said.

He advanced and took the girl's hand in his own. She put an arm around him, and they danced out on the floor. If everyone had been watching the group before, now they stared openly. As if by some magic, photographers appeared everywhere, and flash bulbs began popping. People stopped dancing to watch the strange couple, and everywhere the conversation followed them.

BUT the gorilla danced. He was awkward, his feet wouldn't do what he wanted them to, but he danced. And as he danced, the vision in his arms spoke to him, and laughed, telling him little things that had happened that day.

And slowly, a great anguish grew in the monster's breast, and a rage tormented him. This woman was his wife. Had he lived, his life would have been spent thus, always in her arms, always beside her. The love he had always had for her burned a thousand times more fiercely now.

By the time he had finished the dance, his brain and heart were in a quandary. How hazy everything was. He wandered out of the hall and into one of the lounges, and there Devoli found him. "Are you all right?" the Doctor asked.

"Devoli," said the gorilla. "Look at me. Am I really so hideous?"

"Not to me," said the Doctor. "I've grown so accustomed to you that I scarcely see you. I see only the being underneath."

"Thank you, thank you!" the gorilla cried. His voice was uneven, husky.

"What's the matter?" Devoli said, anxiously.

"I've been thinking," said the gorilla. There was pain, unbearable pain, in his eyes. "What if I actually told Roselle who I—"

The Doctor suddenly held a warning hand up to his lips. His eyes sent the gorilla's gaze past a wall of potted flowers that separated the lounge from the one adjoining. Bradford and the girl stood there, close together, their conversation very low.

"It's impossible for you not to eavesdrop, with your hearing," said Devoli. "Let's go before you hear something you'll be sorry for hearing."

The gorilla started walking. "We're too late," he said, choking. "I heard it." He was aflame inside. But he had to conceal it. He had to.

When they joined Fuzziman, Devoli took the little manager aside.

"Roland," he said. "At the first sign of anything funny, get hold of W. G. and don't let go. I'm afraid. I've never seen him like this. He's *very* worked up tonight."

"He's not the only one," retorted Fuzziman. "Look over there." He moved his chin to indicate a small group of men who were facing them. "You know what's looking at us now?" he said. "About a hundred million dollars. That's Stetley, the fat one, and next to him, the small man, that's Mattson. And those other babies are no paupers either. They got a lot to laugh about, but I wish they wouldn't do it right in our faces."

"Tomorrow night at this time," the gorilla broke in, "we'll be doing the laughing."

"Don't underestimate them," cautioned Devoli. "Look, the dinner's going to begin."

Liveried servants were standing at the entrance to an adjoining dining hall, and as four deep-toned chimes sounded, the guests were beginning to pour through the doors. In a moment Bradford and the girl appeared and the little party began to move forward.

Paul Swangler himself waited for them. "We've allowed you complete freedom up till now," he smiled. "But from here on, you're our prisoners. You may not know it, but W. G. shares the guest of honor seat tonight."

"You're too kind," murmured Devoli.

The guests of the evening were too well bred to stare too openly as the partygoers took their seats. Famous names and famous faces were beginning to feel a little put out at their total lack of appeal beside the sensational W. G.

The dinner began quietly enough. Halfway through the first course, Paul Swangler, seated as Toastmaster, near the gorilla, rose to his feet. Five hundred banqueters turned to him.

"We are gathered tonight," he began, "to celebrate the victory of our Party—a victory, which will be ours within forty-eight hours. There have been those of us who have felt doubts about our ultimate success, but tonight those doubts will vanish. For, as one of the guests of honor, we have here tonight a nationally famous figure. I refer to the Whispering Gorilla, for lack of a better name—and where indeed might I find one?"

General applause and polite laughter broke out.

"You will be surprised and pleased, I am sure," Swangler continued, "to learn that our victory has been assured by the presence of our guest of honor—rather, by the presence of both our guests of honor."

Many of the guests exchanged wondering glances. Swangler was speaking in riddles. Devoli was frightened. The gorilla was restive, his hands trembling.

"Do I make myself clear?" said Swangler. "But I am afraid I do not. The Whispering Gorilla promised us a rather gory bit of news in his tomorrow's column. Many of us were perturbed at his threats. Does not his presence here signify otherwise? Perhaps not. But let me introduce our other guest of honor, to clarify matters—"

The gorilla was rising, a low growl in his throat.

Swangler waved a hand to the guards at the entrance. The door opened and "Sure" Peetson walked in.

He was dressed in ordinary street clothes. He stood confused a moment, looking about the vast room, as if he had wandered in accidentally. He started to turn around and walk out, when he heard the pounding footsteps.

"Stop him!" Devoli cried. Fuzziman had leaped up and tried to halt the gorilla, but he was cast aside like a toy. The gorilla was running straight toward Peetson!

Now Peetson saw him, took in the whole scene at a glance, saw Swangler—and understood in one paralyzing instant. "Swangler!" he screamed. "That's why you brought me here—*for him!*

FIVE HUNDRED people recoiled as the scene unfolded… The Whispering Gorilla shedding his veneer of civilization and turning animal…the jungle beast stalking, running toward his kill…bounding…and suddenly the screams rang out…

Over the wing of a table the gorilla vaulted, barely touching his knuckles. His flying black tails made him look like a monstrous bird, a monster from hell. Now Peetson began to run—but too late! The gorilla had seized him about the throat… Police were rushing up, guns drawn, bewildered, afraid to shoot… People fainted…chairs turned over…men went pale

And over it all came a blood-freezing cry from the gorilla, a cry from deep in his chest, higher each instant, insane with blood lust.

The gorilla stood for an instant with the body of the screaming gunman in his huge arms, then he whirled, leaped over a table and out of a balcony window.

As he had run past his friends at the table he heard them cry out to him. "Don't—this is what Swangler planned for you!" but it had had no effect on him. Now as he stood on the balcony, seeing the street below, he wanted to dash the body he held down. But he didn't. Swangler had wanted him to. He wanted to kill. The moonlit night in the Congo, the match light—all of it came back now to the gorilla…the door opening and Roselle seeing the way he was eating…dancing with her an hour before…all of it lost.

Lost—he was lost! He was an animal. Now he knew it. There was no control now. Only the desire to kill—to kill the man who had taken away more than life from him. His voice was a cry of desperation, of madness and sorrow.

Behind him now were the sounds of pursuit. Police were scrambling out to the balcony. The gorilla leaped up to the balustrade and ran along the wide window ledge of the building.

Now he had been seen in the street below. The wild yelling of people rose up. And then he remembered again that he was doing what Swangler had planned—but there was no help for it now. He was an animal, acting like an animal... What was it Devoli had said about the brute within him?

The window several feet ahead on the ledge swung open. Police were crowding there. He looked behind. They were following. He wondered why? If he wanted to, he could drop the body once and for all. Why didn't he drop it? Swangler had wanted that. Swangler had planned it. Why was he holding the body? They were closing in on him now.

With a snarl, he bent over, seized the ledge and began climbing down the alleys cut in the stone building. There was a theatre marquee below.

Huge masses of people had formed below. The roar of the mob beat on his ears. The great electric signs were blinding him. Down he climbed, slowly, slowly to the marquee below. All the windows above were filled with people—people everywhere, and their voices all shouting at him.

But Devoli's voice he remembered. It came to him even over the crowds, over the memory of Roselle's voice as she had laughed when they danced.

He remembered he had to save the body he was carrying on his shoulders. The body was still now; it had stopped struggling and crying.

All his life came back again: his home—*and the golden moon of the Congo*—the music of Roselle's voice *and the gun roaring in the Congo*—a face more lovely than a dream—*and his own, a monster's!*

Now he stood on the marquee, swaying, and the body seemed to come alive again. He listened to it scream, holding its mouth close to him.

"Don't kill me! Don't kill me! I'll tell you everything! I'll tell the world!"

"You'll tell the world?" said the gorilla. His voice suddenly died away. He was so tired. He stood there gently, while down below and from every side, cameras were going. Slowly he lowered the man Peetson, and the man collapsed at the beast's feet. This was what Devoli had meant—and Roselle. All he had fought for. They had tried to stop him, but they hadn't. He had won, even for Steven Carpenter. It was over now. It was victory.

The gorilla stood there in the midst of chaos, alone on the marquee, staring down at the body at his feet. His whole life was like a dream, fading faster...faster. "Tell the world," he was whispering when the police climbed up to him.

Then, when the clubs crashed down on his head, all the gorilla could remember was Devoli telling him that he was still a brute inside. "Your primitive instincts—guard them!" They were hurting him, killing him, but he didn't raise a finger. He fell heavily, quietly, and a single groan came from him, and then he was still...

BUT after that, it seemed as if it had been only the beginning. That was when "Sure" Peetson began to talk, late that eventful night, and didn't stop until he had run through six editions and two extras. The headlines followed each other down the pages, now of Peetson, now of the gorilla. The column that had become famous as *"Rumblings of W.G."* ran in bold letters on the front pages. The printer's ink ran like the blood that had been spilled that night on the marquee...

U.S.S. COMMODORE TURNED BACK BY NAVY ORDER.

CONDITION OF GORILLA UNCHANGED.

RAID ON JERSEY SHIPYARDS: ALLIANCE OFFICERS JAILED.

GORILLA'S INJURY BAFFLES DOCTORS.

SWANGLER CONFESSES, IMPLICATES CONFEDERATES.

GORILLA IN BARRED ROOM—NO VISITORS.

The spotlight had fallen and in its scope half a dozen cities blazed. The answer came in a flood of votes, like rain to soothe. The answer came with a mighty roar.

At the end of the week, the news came through.

Special IP Dispatch: The Whispering Gorilla has been pronounced an animal, and unfit for everyday association with humans. It is believed that the present physical condition of the gorilla influenced the decision...

American Newscast: The Whispering Gorilla and his devoted personal physician, Dr. Dartworth Devoli, will leave today for the Doctor's home in Africa. The Doctor said today that his world-famous pupil will henceforth live in a jungle habitat to which his basic instincts are more suited. The permanent injury to his brain, committed by terrified police the night of the gorilla's sensational seizure, has deprived him of all the faculties, which convinced millions of people that he was a human masquerading as an animal, instead of the opposite, which was true…

THE thousands who swarmed at the freight docks could see little. The ship's gigantic cranes were hoisting cargo, and all that could be seen was the pointed top of a steel cage and the striped shadows that played over the forms of four persons who stood beside it.

"Sorry," said Dartworth Devoli to the other three, "that I couldn't have allowed you to see him during the past week, but you see how it is."

The great gorilla sat in a corner of the cage. Part of the bandage around his head had become unwound, and the end hung over part of the gorilla's face. He kept shaking it away and it kept coming back. Then he began chewing on the flowers that filled part of the cage.

He still wore clothes, and now he fumbled in a pocket and found some odds and ends. His head kept turning here and there, attracted by movement or by a flash of light.

"His conscious mind is gone for good," said Dr. Devoli. "He is rapidly losing his civilized habits and soon only gorilla instincts will govern his life."

The giant crane swung down, fastened to the cage. It began lifting, and the gorilla peered about him, noiselessly.

"Goodbye, W.G.!" Fuzziman called. He had to turn his eyes away.

Alan Bradford looked after the cage until it disappeared, unable to speak or move.

The men were shaking hands.

"Goodbye," said Dr. Devoli. "I'm an old man now, and my plans are uncertain. We may never meet again, but I've loved you all." His aged, aristocratic face was firm in defeat, and proud.

The whistle of the boat drowned out their farewells.

The last the two men and the girl saw was the aged scientist standing on deck, waving to them as the ship began to move.

In Bradford's arms, Roselle was weeping softly. "He was so alive, so kind," she sobbed.

"I had come to feel that I'd known him for years. I felt almost close to him at the end..."

THE END

If you've enjoyed this book, you will not want to miss these terrific titles…

ARMCHAIR SCI-FI & HORROR DOUBLE NOVELS, $12.95 each

D-101 **THE CONQUEST OF THE PLANETS** by John W. Campbell
THE MAN WHO ANNEXED THE MOON by Bob Olsen

D-102 **WEAPON FROM THE STARS** by Rog Phillips
THE EARTH WAR by Mack Reynolds

D-103 **THE ALIEN INTELLIGENCE** by Jack Williamson
INTO THE FOURTH DIMENSION by Ray Cummings

D-104 **THE CRYSTAL PLANETOIDS** by Stanton A. Coblentz
SURVIVORS FROM 9,000 B. C. by Robert Moore Williams

D-105 **THE TIME PROJECTOR** by David H. Keller, M.D. and David Lasser
STRANGE COMPULSION by Philip Jose Farmer

D-106 **WHOM THE GODS WOULD SLAY** by Paul W. Fairman
MEN IN THE WALLS by William Tenn

D-107 **LOCKED WORLDS** by Edmond Hamilton
THE LAND THAT TIME FORGOT by Edgar Rice Burroughs

D-108 **STAY OUT OF SPACE** by Dwight V. Swain
REBELS OF THE RED PLANET by Charles L. Fontenay

D-109 **THE METAMORPHS** by S. J. Byrne
MICROCOSMIC BUCCANEERS by Harl Vincent

D-110 **YOU CAN'T ESCAPE FROM MARS** by E. K. Jarvis
THE MAN WITH FIVE LIVES by David V. Reed

ARMCHAIR SCIENCE FICTION CLASSICS, $12.95 each

C-34 **30 DAY WONDER**
by Richard Wilson

C-35 **G.O.G. 666**
by John Taine

C-36 **RALPH 124C 41+**
by Hugo Gernsback

ARMCHAIR SCI-FI & HORROR GEMS SERIES, $12.95 each

G-11 **SCIENCE FICTION GEMS, Vol. Six**
Edmond Hamilton and others

G-12 **HORROR GEMS, Vol. Six**
H. P. Lovecraft and others

If you've enjoyed this book, you will not want to miss these terrific titles...

ARMCHAIR SCI-FI & HORROR DOUBLE NOVELS, $12.95 each

D-111 **THE MOON ERA** by Jack Williamson
REVENGE OF THE ROBOTS by Howard Browne

D-112 **SON OF THE BLACK CHALICE** by Milton Lesser
SENTRY OF THE SKY by Evelyn E. Smith

D-113 **OUTPOST ON THE MOON** by Joslyn Maxwell
POTENTIAL ZERO by S. J. Byrne

D-114 **OUTPOST INFINITY** by Raymond F. Jones
THE WHITE INVADERS by Ray Cummings

D-115 **TIME TRAP** by Rog Phillips
THE COSMIC DESTROYER by Alexander Blade

D-116 **THE OTHER SIDE OF THE MOON** by Edmond Hamilton
SECRET INVASION by Walter Kubilius

D-117 **DANGER MOON** by Frederik Pohl
THE HIDDEN UNIVERSE by Ralph Milne Farley

D-118 **THE WAILING ASTEROID** by Murray Leinster
THE WORLD THAT COULDN'T BE by Clifford D. Simak

D-119 **THE WHISPERING GORILLA** by Don Wilcox
RETURN OF THE WHISPERING GORILLA by David V. Reed

D-120 **SPECIAL EFFECT** by J. F. Bone
WARLORD OF KOR by Terry Carr

ARMCHAIR SCIENCE FICTION CLASSICS, $12.95 each

C-37 **THE GREEN MAN RETURNS**
by Harold M. Sherman

C-38 **THE SHAVER MYSTERY, Book Five**
by Richard S, Shaver

C-39 **MARS CHILD**
by Cyril Judd

ARMCHAIR MASTERS OF SCIENCE FICTION SERIES, $16.95 each

MS-9 **MASTERS OF SCIENCE FICTION AND FANTASY, Vol. Nine**
Poul Anderson, "The Star Beast" and other tales

MS-10 **MASTERS OF SCIENCE FICTION, Vol. Ten**
Robert Moore Williams, "Time Tolls for Toro" and other tales

THE FACE OF A BEAST, BUT THE SOUL OF A MAN

Steven Carpenter had a reputation as one of the best reporters in the business. Tough assignments were his forte, and he was known to be cool, calm, and fearless in the face of danger. Then a paid assassin brought his life to an abrupt end late one sultry African night… Yet he still lived! A strange, fantastic experiment had seen to that. His brain was now inside the skull of a gorilla—and the gorilla could speak and reason. But the life he had once known was gone, and slowly but surely the blood that flowed through his veins began to take over, dulling his humanity and increasing the latent jungle instinct inside of him. And when a regiment of German soldiers turned up, they decided he was the perfect specimen for a new kind of Nazi soldier! Soon the fate of those he cared for depended on Steven Carpenter holding onto his humanity for just a little while longer.

CAST OF CHARACTERS

STEVEN CARPENTER aka OLOWGA
Who was he really? Steven Carpenter knew that blood in his veins would eventually overpower the last of his humanity.

JOE ABBOTT
He was pretty shot up when Devoli had taken him in; but he soon felt better and was on the mend—until the Nazis showed up.

MAJOR VON BRUCKNER
This slick Nazi officer was as cold and cunning as they came, driven by a shameless ego and an insatiable thirst for power.

DR. DARTWORTH DEVOLI
He was the scientist who had created the Whispering Gorilla—an accomplishment the Third Reich was most interested in.

JEANNE CHAUMONT
This beautiful dame had German Army officers eating out of her hand, but what was her real motive?

DR. FREIDRICH
He was faced with an ultimatum—keep Devoli alive at all costs. Failure to do so would…well…this is the German Army after all.

GENERAL GLEICHENHAUS
He required much from his officers, but even he had a hard time believing that a gorilla could be trained to operate a submarine!

RETURN OF THE WHISPERING GORILLA

By
DAVID V. REED

ARMCHAIR FICTION
PO Box 4369, Medford, Oregon 97504

CHAPTER ONE

"CARPENTER, I'm coming in. Is it all right?"

He had heard the knocking on the heavy oak door but he made no response. Again Dr. Devoli called to him. Carpenter had been standing at the barred slit in the wall that was his window, and now, afraid that the Doctor would look in, Carpenter moved away from it, flattening himself against the wall.

"Carpenter! Speak to me!"

He would come in anyway, Carpenter thought. He would come and after that there would be no peace, and he would bring back the pain and the memories...

"Go away," Carpenter said, wearily, and the sound of his own voice, as always, frightened him. "Leave me alone. I'm all right." He had had difficulty forming the words, he thought. Soon, if all went well, he would be unable to speak. In a few hours he would drift away to that quiet world where there was no thought and no pain.

The Doctor had gone away and now Carpenter stood at the window again, looking across the bright sunlit plains that stretched far away to a horizon marked by towering trees. That was the jungle, the dark, uneasy, savage jungle, but here life seemed quiet. He heard the sound of cattle as half-breed Arab boys drove them home, and he heard the subdued stridency of insects...

"No," he said aloud, but it was no use. He was thinking again, and the ache that was constantly with him was there again. He remembered another life, a life that once was his, but it was a fleeting thing. A face rose up from the mist of his memory, a woman's face, but the image was blurred. Everything was blurred now but he couldn't stop the thinking, the trying to remember.

A breath of wind blew through the window, bringing the smell of the jungle and his nostrils quivered and he straightened involuntarily. And now stronger thoughts came to him, and memories that crowded out the others, and he thought of the great trees and the vines, and the birds of brilliant color, and of life that was green and fresh and a world that was still and quiet.

And now, though he tried to think of the face and the other life, it would not return, but he could not forget it. "One or the other," he said aloud, listening to the sound of his voice, and he trembled.

He went away from the window and sat down on the bed, staring into the darkness of his little room. He was a captive here, but freedom was his for the taking. Why did he sit here, letting the wind bring him the smells of the life he knew and wanted? The life he knew and wanted... Which was it? Which life?

"One or the other."

His voice was half a sob, half a cry of rage. He could take the bars in his hands and tear them away. He held his hands out before him and couldn't look at them. He sprang up, feeling the enormous strength of his body, the might and the terrible power that was his and with a single leap he was at the window, his hands curling around the bars. In a moment it would be over, the decision made. But was the decision his to make? Did he dare trust his own thoughts by now?

"Tonight," he said aloud, to himself. "Tonight, quietly again, without Devoli knowing. I'll go again tonight."

As he turned away from the window, something glittered on the floor. A shaft of sunlight had slanted through and caught the bit of mirror lying there. The bit of mirror he had stolen so long ago. He had hidden it; how had it gotten to the floor?

He stared at it fearfully, but already its fascination had won the struggle. Slowly he bent down and picked up the mirror. He held it up before him so that the light poured on it and on his face.

The face that looked at Steven Carpenter from the mirror was the face of a gorilla. Its eyes were small and dark and bloodshot, its mouth like a red scar, its teeth huge and powerful. The mirror fell from view and the gorilla disappeared as Carpenter hid the mirror under his bedclothes, but when he looked down at his body, he saw the great, naked expanse of his chest and his massive, hairy arms and his squat, strong legs.

"One or the other," the gorilla sobbed.

CHAPTER TWO

DR. DEVOLI paused before he began unlocking the door. For a moment he considered looking in through the window to see what Carpenter was doing. He decided against it; it made Carpenter nervous. Not that he had ever said so—he said little these days, but the Doctor had once or twice caught him ducking into corners when he spied a face at the window. The Doctor wondered whether, in spite of his strict orders against it, any of the houseboys or the other help around the place ever looked in at Carpenter. Did they suspect that this gorilla was in reality...?

It struck him now, as it sometimes did, that he always thought of the—the *thing* inside this hut (for actually it was neither man nor beast) as Steven Carpenter.

He unlocked the door, listening for sounds from within, holding ready the strange rifle-like tube in his left hand. Because of the way Carpenter had sounded when he had knocked before, the Doctor had decided to administer the injection at long range. Already it was two days overdue, but the danger involved hardly occurred to Devoli; he had lived with it long enough. He knew too well the price of error in his calculations—the possibility that he might one day enter this hut and be confronted not by Carpenter, but by the gorilla in whose body Steven Carpenter had lived for two years.

Swiftly he opened the door, let himself in, closed it behind him. He saw the gorilla sitting on its bed. As he swung the tube up, the gorilla started to spring forward.

"No! Devoli, for the love of God—don't!"

The tube spat out a green phosphorescence, a stream of innumerable tiny objects like bullets. The stream plunged into the gorilla's chest. For an instant it was as if green lightning had danced on that huge, agonized body. The gorilla stopped, clutched at its chest, then fell heavily to one knee. It looked oddly man-like in that position. Only a single groan had escaped its tightly drawn lips.

The Doctor stood at the door, waiting. He glanced at the sweep-second hand on his watch. The gorilla dragged itself to its bed. It had too little strength to lift itself and it remained there, its great head lying on a pillow, its eyes closed. Devoli waited, his face drawn with compassion. He brushed a hand across his eyes. It was bad for Carpenter to see him reacting that way; the thought of pity had a profound, horrible effect on him...

When the gorilla opened its eyes again, they were clear. It raised its head and looked at Devoli. "I'm all right now," it said, and its voice was like an incredibly deep whisper, a tired, low voice.

Devoli said, quietly, "It took almost five minutes today."

"You were late again," the gorilla whispered. "You remember what I told you...someday you'll be a little too late... I'll be waiting for you behind the door..."

A slight, involuntary shudder ran through Devoli. He had seldom seen him like this. He was really bad today. How much dared he tell him now? His eyes wandered about the room, as if from among the familiar objects, from the gloomy corners, he might find an answer.

"Listen to me, Carpenter, listen carefully. I won't be able to give you these injections as often as you need them. The drugs are becoming scarce. The war has made shipment very uncertain. I'm trying to develop a substitute, but there may be times when I won't be able to give you anything for weeks. Do you think you can find the strength to hold on?"

THE gorilla had listened carefully, and as Devoli finished, it stared at him. "The strength to hold on?" it cried in a horrible, guttural sound, "Do you think there's any strength left in me?"

"You're a man, Carpenter. You must be strong."

"A man..." The gorilla rose up and went to the barred window, its gait a halting, dragging thing. "For two years you've called me a man. Sometimes, when the drugs are still functioning in me, I almost believe you. I forget the bars in my little house... I almost forget the body whose prisoner I am... But do you think I don't know what's been happening to me, Devoli?"

"There's nothin g happening that can't be cured in time."

"You don't believe that yourself," the gorilla whispered. "You don't know what it is." It held its head in its two huge hands. "The brain in here is Steven Carpenter's now, but when the drugs are eaten by this body, even the brain begins turning. Do you think I don't know what's happening?" it cried brokenly. "Do you think I don't know that this monstrous, beast's body is devouring my brain—that little by little the blood that runs through these veins erodes the mind that lives on the blood of this animal? I do know, Devoli, and I've known for a long time—without your drugs even the awareness of my identity ceases! Without your drugs I am no longer even this ghastly parody of a man but a gorilla, a beast of the jungles!"

"You mustn't let yourself think along such—"

"No?" the gorilla snarled. "But perhaps my thoughts aren't my own any more! Perhaps these millions of little cells of my body do my thinking. But the prospect doesn't frighten me, Devoli," it said, its voice softer now and a throaty rumble. "Not anymore. It won't be worse than living here this way. You'll either have to let me free…or kill me…as you should never have let me live…"

And now, Devoli thought, seeing Carpenter break down again and seeing the tears run down that distorted, black face, it would be all right for awhile. As long as Carpenter had the capacity for self-pity, he was safe. As long as the sight of himself in the fragment of mirror he kept carefully hidden from Devoli, but which Devoli knew—as long as that sight filled him with loathing, just so long was Steven Carpenter removed from the fate he had recognized.

"I'll see you tonight," said Devoli, going to the door. "Tambo went into Tiola for the mail and I'm expecting some magazines. Maybe we'll get new chapters of that serial you're reading."

As he went back to the main house, the Doctor remembered the words Carpenter had used…you should never have let me live. How many times had Devoli himself asked that question? His mind returned again to that night two years before…

All he had known then was that Steven Carpenter was an American newspaperman, writing articles for a New York newspaper. Devoli hadn't known that Carpenter had been ordered into hiding by his paper because there had been attempts on his life, that he was writing a series exposing a powerful criminal syndicate. He had known Carpenter only a few weeks then, and he had come to respect and admire this intelligent young man who lived nearby. Carpenter had even become interested in the Doctor's experiments with gorillas, in those long ago days when Devoli believed that the intelligence of a gorilla might be enormously advanced if only it could be taught to speak.

AND then one night the Doctor's servants had carried Steven Carpenter into the Doctor's house. He was dying. An assassin had followed him thousands of miles to Sao Paulo to empty a gun into him. How well Devoli recalled every detail of that memorable night. No one but a scientist, immersed in his work, perhaps blind to every consequence but the success of an experiment, would have dared what he did.

What had impelled him? He had not even believed he had one chance in a thousand, but he had looked at the corpse and he had felt...he could almost remember the words: *"...two hours ago you were alive. Here lies youth and vigor, dead, while an old man who scarcely knew him or his name is the only one to mourn. An old man who has spent his years trying to approach making out of animals what nature gave you at birth. How wasteful...how tragic..." What good did all the fighting do you? Your brain was no stronger than your heart. When they stopped that, they stopped everything."*

And then he had thought of it. He had shouted it aloud. *"Your brain, Carpenter! You were no more than your brain!"*

That had been the beginning. With his magnificent skill as a surgeon, Devoli had performed a miracle, though it was weeks before he knew. And after that...

Devoli shook his head and muttered to himself. So much had happened since then. He thought back to the wife Steven Carpenter had had, the work he had left unfinished, but to which he returned. And the aftermath. But that was before either of them had had any inkling of what was to follow. He could have left Carpenter a half-crazed beast long before. What had stopped him?

What was there for Carpenter to live for? But the Doctor shrank from the question. Once he had given life to Steven Carpenter—to the brain that was the man. What had given him the right to so awful a decision? And what perverted sense of power made him assume he now had any right to decide on Carpenter's death? Just because he told himself that this was slowly becoming a *thing* that was not Carpenter? Was it for him to say?

But the end was approaching swiftly. Devoli had told only part of the truth. The drugs were no longer uncertain—they were impossible to get! A substitute? Perhaps. It might take years to find it.

Meanwhile there were enough of the drugs left for five or six more injections. Already it was a matter of perhaps two or three weeks. After that there would be nothing left to combat, however feebly, the virus that was destroying Steven Carpenter. The brain the Doctor had put into a gorilla's body was being claimed by that body. The monster lay in wait, sucking, eating, devouring...

Now Devoli stood on the verandah of his house, looking out over the peaceful fields. The weight of his age lay heavy upon him, but the weight of his responsibilities was overpowering.

*   *   *

BY now there was a considerable number of men around the great table. The face of the table was highly polished, and where it was not covered with papers and maps and charts, some of which had fallen to the floor, it reflected the decorations on the uniforms of many of these men. Tobacco smoke lay like a weightless veil in midair, and the Colonel waved a hand to clear the air around him. From where he sat at the head of the table, his eyes traveled down the row of intent faces on his left, until they rested on a man who sat apart from the others.

The Colonel said, "Then your research is finished, Major?"

Without answering the question directly, the Major said, "In 1940, this wonderful animal that became known as the Whispering Gorilla first appeared in New York. It came originally from Africa, presumably from the Gold Coast, where Dr. Dartworth Devoli was then living. As far as we know, the gorilla ran away from Devoli. Somewhere it had gotten enough money to buy passage to New York on the S. S. Majestic. The story begins there."

"This man Devoli?" the Colonel inquired.

"An Englishman," the Major nodded. "Perhaps not too aware of the war, but thoroughly loyal. At any rate," he resumed, "the gorilla sailed alone, locked in its stateroom, its true identity hidden by the amazing boldness of its action. Presumably it was an actor who had undertaken a wild, provoking role as a publicity trick. This theory was aided by the interest of a man named Roland Fuzziman, a theatrical producer, who was aboard with his troupe of actors, returning from a tour of South Africa.

"We do not know what Fuzziman really thought. In spite of many evidences that he alone could gather, Fuzziman seems to have avoided concluding that the gorilla was, in reality, a true gorilla—possibly to preserve his own peace of mind. He was able to persuade it to join with him, and together they made a fortune in New York in a play written around the gorilla.

"For some reason still not clear to us, the gorilla later took to broadcasting as W. G., which obviously stood for Whispering Gorilla. Possibly the idea was Fuzziman's, or someone who paid Fuzziman, but what happened was that the gorilla became a radio crusader, investigating crime and corruption, and attacking especially a certain Paul Swangler, the head of a large criminal syndicate..."

The Major paused to light a cigarette, enjoying the effect of his words, and he smiled, saying, "Fantastic, is it not? To think that for months this jungle beast, trained by an obscure experimenter to speak like a man, could live among humans with none suspecting the truth. Its steadfastness in clinging to what was thought to be an excellently contrived costume only aided the deception. Actually, gentlemen—would any of you remotely imagine such a thing?

"It was Swangler who first thought of it. Enough, at any rate, to attempt proving it. The gorilla had brought one of Swangler's hirelings to trial. Here Swangler played a trump: He subpoenaed the gorilla as a witness for the defense. When the gorilla came to court—it must have been an amazing spectacle—it naturally could not obey the judge's order to remove its disguise."

THE Major paused again, savoring the dramatic triumph of the story. When he judged the pause to have been just long enough, he said, "The trial, however, failed, and the criminal went free. The gorilla, held for contempt of court, was freed on bail. And here Paul Swangler played a master card. He arranged a scene that so infuriated the poor beast that it went berserk in full sight of thousands of people. Only then, after police had captured and subdued the gorilla, did the astonishing truth become known..."

"Come," said the Colonel, irritably, "what happened? End it."

The Major shrugged and held up a mass of newspaper clippings. "The gorilla had been beaten within an inch of its life. Dr. Devoli, who had followed the animal shortly after its escape, was able to save it, but he saved only the wreck of that magnificent beast. The animal's brain had been irreparably ruined. It became an animal again, sickly, dull-witted. It returned…" He held up a large picture of a gorilla in a strong wooden cage. "…in this cage to Africa, with Dr. Devoli."

"And Dr. Devoli…?"

"Has, as we know," supplied the Major, "never stopped his work with these beasts. Our agents have given us ample evidence of this. The jungle surrounding Devoli's home is filled with gorillas, surely a strange animal to be found in any numbers in French West Africa. We have heard incredible stories of what these gorillas do in the jungle. The Doctor's laboratories have always held at least one specimen. And there, gentlemen, is where we must seek the assistance of Dr. Devoli. For the intelligence which he seems able to breed in these beasts is a weapon we must have."

The Colonel asked, "Your plans are concluded?"

"Yes. Our agents and partisans are stationed."

"Your credentials are ready?"

The Major nodded.

"What route will you take?"

The Major looked at a map before him. "The area," he said, "is untrustworthy. One cannot be certain of the strength of the Vichy French there, or of the numbers of the Free French. Therefore…" He traced a line from Libya down into French West Africa. "…once we are in Kutiala, we go to Kuora, along the Banifing River to the Bagoe, and at the triple junction of the Bagoe with the Baniegue and Bafing rivers, we go to Tiola. From there it is a short way."

"Yes," the Colonel agreed. He added, as an afterthought, "See that our people in Dakar are wide awake until then."

BECAUSE the moon had started rising, every shadow became treacherous. The tall man who stood alone against the flat brick building listened, then answered the low whistle. The tropical moon hung fat and golden, and the air was moist with the salty breath of Gore Gulf. Across the clear area of the railroad yard, a long line of boxcars moved slowly into sight, crawling behind two donkey engines that sent up huge yellow smoke plumes. They were coming into Dakar, and they could have come from only one place—from St. Louis, 160 miles north, in the Senegal country.

A second man suddenly appeared. He had slid around the exposed corner of the building and come up beside the first man. Within a few seconds, a third man duplicated this appearance. He said, without looking at the other two, "It's coming in now."

"From St. Louis, Hans?"

"Yes. Over a hundred cars, and more coming."

They waited until the cars were closer, but at the last moment the engines swung away, traveling over a series of switches. When the engines stopped, fifty yards of open, moonlit track lay between the men and the cars.

"Hans, why are they stopping there?"

"I don't know. Perhaps they've changed plans."

"They seem to be very careful. What do you think?"

The tall man said, "We'll take the chance. Ready?"

Together, the three men leaped from the shadow and began running across the tracks. Halfway across the open space, the tall man stumbled and went down. He fell with his head on the corner of a tie and the blow stunned him momentarily. Unsteadily, he rose in time to see his companions reaching the cars. Then, though he didn't understand it at the moment, he saw the boxcar doors slide open, and saw the little orange flames spurting from inside the cars, keeping quick time with the flat crack of guns. Simultaneously, a huge searchlight swung its white beam on the scene.

One of the two men had been shot down almost at once. The other had ducked under the wheels of the boxcar. Half a dozen shots snarled together, at least one of them from the man under the car. He came out from the other side. The searchlight lanced across, picking him up as he tried to duck into shadows again.

That was when the man who had fallen found his revolver. He raised the barrel and took deliberate aim. Once…twice…five times his gun spoke, and after the fifth shot the searchlight was dark, and the hunters had only the moon to guide them.

He began running back, heard the guns spit behind him, heard the chase divide to include him, saw the gravel before him leaping. He reached the brick house and crouched there while he reloaded.

By then he had decided he couldn't get out of the yards alive, but he had six bullets in his revolver, and he meant to use them well.

THE Prefect of the *Gendarmerie Centrale* at Dakar was burning with a quiet, bitter fury. He listened to the District Captain end his recital, then he said, "The final result of this affair, then, is that only one of the three men was killed?"

"The other two were most certainly wounded," said the Captain, energetically. "The one who ran under the cars left a trail of blood. The other, the destroyer of the searchlight, was hit twice. Yes, he was *seen* to have been hit twice."

"And twice wounded he was still able to shoot down four of his pursuers—finally to escape?"

The Captain murmured, "A most remarkable shot, was he not?"

"And the explanation of this bloody affair?"

"The military authorities gave none. As usual."

The Prefect hammered a fist down on his desk, but his voice, when he spoke, was restrained and thoughtful. "I am not a political man," he said. "I leave politics to the army. But these Germans cannot so overrun our city. Dakar is not a *Boche* shooting gallery. Armistice or not, they must be taught where authority in this city resides; they must be taught that we French can still administer justice. This is a lesson I propose to teach them."

He met the Captain's eye and added, "Let us speak again with Dr. Bonat. Perhaps we know a few things the Germans do not suspect, eh...?"

It was perhaps an hour later that a young woman came into the Prefect's office. She was tall and slender, and her eyes were a clear blue, a blue that seemed to enhance the perfection of her long blonde hair, though this was but one feature of her loveliness. She sat down alone with the Prefect.

"Jeanne," said the Prefect, "we are hunting the two survivors of that business in the railroad yard tonight. A doctor told us that he treated a man for gunshot wounds a few hours ago. Two wounds, the thigh and upper chest. A foreigner, said the Doctor, and he thought he could not guess at the man's nationality. Still, he spoke once or twice in delirium, and he mentioned a place. I am sending you there to look for such a man. I am sending you because a strange man might be watched in the interior these days. We no longer know whom to trust."

"And if I find him?" asked the girl.

"Telegraph immediately from Goundam."

"Where is the place I am to go?"

"Tiola," said the Prefect. "Near the triple junction of the Bagoe, Baniegue and Bafing rivers."

NIGHT was slowly enveloping the jungle. Far to the east, the peak of Mount Mina was still touched with sunlight, and the plateau seemed dark indeed in the electric blue of twilight. One of Dr. Devoli's houseboys pattered across the floor to light an oil lamp that hung from the high bamboo ceiling.

"Your interest both flatters and confuses me, Major Brooks," said Devoli. "However, my work, as you call it, ended two years ago."

The Major allowed a smile to flit across his granitic features. "Much as I admire your reticence, my dear Doctor," he said, "I know otherwise. That knowledge comes from an excellent source."

Dr. Devoli said nothing, waiting.

"From Military Intelligence," said the Major quietly, nodding. "From headquarters of the British Expeditionary Force in Cairo." He took a large, bulky envelope from his breast pocket. Moving aside the drinks that stood on the rattan table, the Major laid down several passports, a newspaper clipping from the London Daily Sketch, containing his picture in an army Major's uniform (though he now wore clean white linens), two letters signed by Ministry officials in London, a letter of introduction from General Sir Hugh Gaystone in Cairo.

Dr. Devoli handed back the papers. "Naturally, Major, I am at your service, though I cannot understand—"

"All in good time, Doctor. Forgive me if I seem to lean toward mystery." He smiled. "You might call it an occupational disease in my work. But to clarify matters—you are still experimenting?"

"It seems past denying, Major, does it not?"

"Then perhaps I might have a look at your…ah…subjects?"

Devoli looked out across the settling gloom that hemmed in the open verandah. "It's rather late," he said, but he led the way down the stairs, pausing at the door long enough to light a lantern.

A pathway, worn through thick grass, led to a group of other buildings nearby. One of the barns was lighted, and a tall, half-naked Senegalese was squatting on the floor, mending harness. An Arab boy came out of a hen house, carrying water. Twenty feet farther on was a small building, a hut, separated from the group. It was low and windowless, save for one barred aperture in its walls.

The Doctor stopped before a door with a double padlock. He knocked softly on the door and waited. Presently a voice, either abnormally deep or somehow muffled, said the single word, "Doctor."

A scarcely audible sigh escaped Devoli. He leaned against the door and said, "I'm coming in."

A full minute went by before the voice answered. "All right."

Devoli said, "There's a man with me."

"All right."

Devoli thought: *He doesn't know what I'm saying...he must be far gone tonight,* and he said, "Stay close to me, Major," and slowly, very slowly, he opened the heavy door. Then he thrust the lantern so that its light shone behind the door and he nodded to the Major.

AS the two men entered, the outer perimeter of light moved across the floor, past a heavy table on which were piled newspapers and magazines and phonograph records. The light moved past a chair, on which stood a phonograph, past a bed, carefully made and covered with fresh linen. There was a shoe under the bed, a large, square shoe, and not far away was the shoe's mate, but this second shoe had been torn apart, mangled and ripped to shreds. Now the light searched a corner...and caught the green and orange slits of glazed, reflected light from two eyes that could see in that darkness.

The light moved up—swung crazily a moment, then righted itself as Dr. Devoli freed his arm from the Major's sudden grip. The lantern shone full in the corner now.

Sitting on its haunches, its back against the juncture of the two walls, sat a huge gorilla. Its leathery features glistened and its powerful, hairy arms rested on folded knees, and though it was otherwise entirely unclothed, one of its feet was encased in a white cotton sock.

Dr. Devoli said, "Why are you sitting there?"

The greatest beast moved its arms slightly and kept looking at the Major. Presently its mouth opened, showing pink gums and wicked teeth, and moving its lips silently for a moment before it spoke, the gorilla said, "You know I like to sit here."

"But I gave you one of my best chairs."

After a long pause, the gorilla said, "He is afraid of me."

"The Major is a friend. He has no reason to fear you."

The gorilla shook its huge head and said, in a throbbing whisper, "You looked behind the door...when you came in...so you must fear me...all of you..."

The Doctor turned away from the gorilla's inscrutable gaze and led the Major out. Preoccupied with his own thoughts, Devoli walked in silence toward the house, when he noticed Ali, the eldest houseboy, had come out on the verandah with a lantern. Now, suddenly, the wind changed and brought the sound of approaching horses.

The Major's brow was covered with a thin film of sweat, and noticing how shaken he appeared, Devoli had waited for the Major to regain his poise before he spoke. But now Brooks said, in a voice that fought to remain even, "Are you expecting anyone?"

"A friend of mine, an American."

"Visiting?"

Devoli nodded. "How'd you know?"

"Intelligence didn't mention him."

"Naturally. He's only been here a week or so."

THEY were on the verandah steps now, waiting with Ali. In a moment a wagon and team of horses came riding into the light. A tall young man climbed off the wagon, calling, "Got a dozen cans of tuna fish, Doctor!" He limped slightly as he came up on the verandah, carrying a small sack, one of many piled in the wagon. He was silent now that he had seen the Major. He wore denim trousers and an open shirt, and hanging from a loose cartridge belt at his hips was an open-holstered revolver. His sandy hair was close cropped and his skin deep copper.

"Major Brooks, Joe Abbott," said Devoli. "Let's go in and have a drink. Ali, hurry and get some of that battery ice, quick."

"I'm afraid I haven't time, Doctor," said the Major. "My friends are expecting me back."

"But I assumed you would be my guest, tonight at least. Surely you don't intend traveling back to Tiola alone? The nights here aren't as quiet as they appear."

"I'm sure of that," Major Brooks laughed. "No, Doctor, I'm not traveling alone, and I'm not going to Tiola. I've several friends waiting for me a short way down the road and we've our own plans, but—"

"Are you sure?" Abbott interrupted. "I mean, I just came down the road and I didn't see anyone."

"They saw you," the Major smiled. "You may be sure of that."

"This isn't particularly healthy country for an Englishman," said Devoli, winking at Brooks. "The Vichy French might not believe he came here merely because he was interested in my experiments."

Abbott spoke before he caught the Doctor's slight signal. It was too late to stop then. He asked, "Your experiments?"

"With the gorilla," Devoli nodded.

"There are more than one, aren't there, Doctor?" said Brooks.

"Why, yes," said Devoli. "I was referring to the species." He called toward the kitchen, "Benno! Saddle our guest's horse."

Abbott had seated himself on the verandah rail, and as Ali came out with the drinks, he took one and lighted a cigarette.

"May I have one, Mr. Abbott?" Crossing over, the Major held his hand out for the package. He took a cigarette and observed, "I see you haven't been away from home very long."

Abbott said, carelessly, "You can get American cigarettes in Cairo, Major. And I answer direct questions very nicely," he grinned. "Just in case you want to ask any."

"Not at all. I just can't help feeling a bit curious about an American in French West Africa, these days, especially."

Abbott took a light from Brooks. "It's no secret. I work for the New York *Telegram*. I've been reporting the African front."

"British or American?"

Abbott shrugged. "Can't tell 'em apart, can you? We've had our tanks and planes there since Rommel's last push. Maybe more are coming; it figures. Anyway, I ducked in here between assignments and I'm due out soon. You might call this a quick vacation."

"You know," Major Brooks smiled, "I once met an American in the Victoria desert in Australia—the only other white man, except for my party, for hundreds of miles. I'm becoming accustomed to meeting you Americans everywhere. We've the war to thank, I suppose." He smiled, drained his glass, and said to Devoli, "I hope to be back soon, Doctor. Perhaps tomorrow. See you again, I hope, Mr. Abbott. Goodnight."

Joe Abbott waited until the Major's horse had disappeared into the darkness before he said, "Sorry I almost missed your signal."

Dr. Devoli smiled, looking at Abbott. "Surely," he said, "you didn't miss the signal I directed at Major Brooks?"

"No," said Abbott. "I didn't miss it."

"Then what do you think?"

"Suppose you tell me, Doctor."

"All right," said Devoli, quietly. "It's simply this: My house, my servants and I have been under surveillance for some time."

"By whom?"

"By people connected with Major Randolph Brooks."

Abbott said, "Just who is this Major Brooks?"

"He's from British Intelligence," said Devoli. "At least he says so. My guess is that our friend the Major is a Nazi spy."

Joe Abbott let his breath out softly and crushed his cigarette.

CHAPTER THREE

"HE HAD a lot of identification with him," said Devoli, looking out across the dark plain. "He even had a letter from a friend of mine who I know is in a hospital in Coventry. But he also had a newspaper clipping from the *London Sketch* with his own picture in it. The top of that page was dated this past February, and it was page 32. Do you see what I am saying, Joe?"

"Frankly, no."

"It's a small matter, a detail," said the Doctor. "The Germans are usually good at details, but no London newspaper, no newspaper in Britain, for that matter, has published a 32-page edition since shortly after the war began. They haven't enough paper." He regarded Abbott wanly and said, "Why do you think they're here, Joe?"

Abbott hesitated. "What about your experiments?"

Dr. Devoli sat down. "There are no experiments. The things the Major spoke of have been dead for two years. He used it as an entrance here. He's looking for something, Joe."

"If you mean me, you're wrong."

There was a silent interval before Devoli spoke. "Joe, I've asked no questions and I'm asking none now—but for your own sake you must realize these men are hunting you. There's nothing else for them here. And now that they've found you—"

"You're wrong, Doctor," said Abbott, tight-lipped. He fumbled with his cigarettes again, finally lighting one. "I'll tell you the way it was. You've been more decent than I could have hoped. All you know about me is that I crawled in here two weeks ago with two bullet holes in me, saying that Alan Bradford had sent me..." He paused, drawing on his cigarette thoughtfully. "The *Telegram* had sent Alan to Cairo to cover the African front. I'd known him in New York. I had a plane and sometimes I flew his paper's men on stories. I met him through one of the finest newspapermen that ever lived—fellow called Carpenter..."

It was the strange way that Devoli had suddenly reacted that made Abbott pause. "What's the matter, Doctor?" he asked.

"Nothing. Nothing at all. Please continue."

There was an elusive little thought chasing around in the back of Abbot's mind; it had been there before. He said, "I'd been ferrying bombers for the British for a year. When we got in, I applied for our own service, and they got me to ferry ships for the Chinese, I kept applying for combat service and my orders finally caught up with me in India, I got to South Africa and came up to Dakar, hoping I'd cross to Rio. Then I met Alan at the American consulate in Dakar.

"He told me he'd run across something hot—Nazi work in Dakar, but he needed help and there was no one he could trust." Abbott blew out smoke, grinning. "Just my dish. I dug up an Austrian refugee I knew, an underground worker named Hans Kronenfeld, and we worked together. Alan knew the Spanish were loading barges of sealed trains from Morocco to St. Louis, and from St. Louis they came to Dakar by rail. One night we got into the railroad yards, but something went wrong. One of us—Hans or Alan, I don't know which—was shot down, killed…" Abbott drew a long breath before he went on. "But maybe the other got away. The last I saw, he was ducking under cars. Alan had told us to meet here if we became separated. He said you were an old friend, that you'd shelter us until we got together again."

"And now?"

"I'm waiting. If you let me, I'll wait here another week. One of them may be alive, you see, and he'll come." The Doctor stood against the rail, saying nothing. Abbott asked, "Do you believe me?"

"Is it important?"

"No," said Abbott. "If you don't believe me, I'll go to Tiola. I'll manage to hang on there. But somehow, I'd like you to believe me."

"Tell me," said Devoli, "in the shooting—what happened?"

"I'm a good shot, Doctor," Abbott said, briefly.

"Then you could be prosecuted for murder. France isn't at war, you understand. Why are you so certain the Major isn't hunting you?"

JOE ABBOTT shook his head. A soft, bitter smile lit his face. "They wouldn't know where to come for me. Only two men knew—and one of them is dead. If they caught the other, I'm waiting for nothing." He shrugged. "But neither of them would talk."

The Doctor brushed a hand across his face. He said, "I believe you, Joe. That's why I'm so confused. Because it doesn't make sense, don't you see? I believe you and I've trusted you from the start—but if these men aren't after you, what are they doing here?"

"I don't know. Didn't you get any idea?"

Devoli sighed. "He spoke only of my experiments, and because I knew almost from the start that he was an imposter, I let him go on, hoping he might say something in an unguarded moment. But he didn't, and when you came and I saw how interested he was in you—in that pack of cigarettes, I decided he had been wasting time, waiting for you…"

Abbott said, "Alan gave me the cigarettes." Almost absently, he mused, "Certainly a Nazi would be interested in finding an American here, especially if he wanted something here. He would hardly need his elaborate credentials if he was only after me…" He looked up at the Doctor curiously. "I knew there was something I meant to ask. What was that conversation you and he had about gorillas?"

Devoli motioned toward the flat-topped building in the darkness. "I'd shown him a tame gorilla I keep there."

"A *what?*"

"A gorilla. Entirely harmless. I've never mentioned it to you because it isn't important."

"But the Major knew about it?"

"Yes," the Doctor sighed. "There's a long story connected with that gorilla. Anybody might know about it. The Major asked to see it, probably to waste time until you…but we've eliminated that…"

"We have indeed!" Abbott snapped. "And maybe we've begun to uncover something. What is the story connected with the gorilla?"

Devoli shook his head. "I'd rather not." His gray eyes seemed clouded. "It's dead now, forgotten. Let it stay that way."

"But Doctor—don't you see that if it really is—"

Devoli interrupted with a wave of his hand. "I suppose you're right. We ought to eliminate every guess." The muscles of his jaw had hardened perceptibly. Quietly, he said, "Do you remember the Whispering Gorilla?"

"Yes, yes, of course I do," Abbott replied. "I knew Alan then and he was mixed up in it." His eyes shone as he asked, "Then you mean you've got the original W. G. here in that—but of course! Then you must be that Dr. Devoli who took the gorilla back to Africa later…"

"I am that Dr. Devoli."

Abbott sucked his breath in sharply. "I remember it now. You're the Dr. Devoli who buried Steve Carpenter when he was killed in Africa…and this is the place where Carpenter lived those months he was hiding from Swangler—"

"No," said Devoli, interrupting. "I was living in Sao Paulo then, in Portuguese Angola, far from here."

"But you did know Carpenter. How oddly tangled—"

"Please!" Devoli cried. He regained his composure quickly, and looking into the darkness, he said, "I'm sorry. It's just that the memory is very painful to me. I'd rather not speak about it…"

Presently Abbott said, "But the Whispering Gorilla is alive?"

Devoli nodded.

"Then the Major obviously knew all about it. But what made him think you were experimenting with it? And what made him think there was more than one gorilla?"

"I don't know."

"What happened when you took him to see it? Anything?"

"Nothing."

"Still," said Abbott, "it seems that the Major is interested in the gorilla, and that somewhere he has gathered peculiar ideas about what you're doing here." He added, "Will you show me the gorilla?"

"He—it must be asleep now, and the way it's been acting…" Devoli hesitated, then said suddenly, "Joe! Sometimes I inject the gorilla with a special drug I've been developing. Do you think perhaps…"

"Sure. Maybe one of the houseboys watched you one day. It might look like experimenting. What does the drug do?"

"A strange thing," said Devoli, softly. "Stranger than I care to say…" He stared hard at Abbot, then said, "Wait here."

RETURNING in a few moments, the Doctor carried a small black bag. He gave Abbott one of the verandah lanterns and led the way along the path to the building that stood by itself. He knocked on the door. There was no answer. In the silence Devoli opened both locks and went in. He took the lantern from Abbott and advanced to the center of the room where the lantern's light lit every corner, and then he knew that the room was empty!

Suddenly the Doctor bent down in one of the corners. The floorboards had been carefully lifted up, nails still showing, and stacked together. Under the place where the boards had been was a large hole, dug in the soft earth under the building. It was a shallow hole, curved to come up in the field behind the house.

"Joe, go to the barn," said Devoli, crisply. "Wake up Tomba. Tell him to get my rifle. Quickly, for the love of Heaven!"

Abbott ran to the barn. Tomba, the tall Senegalese, had wakened instantly. He fastened a stout belt to his middle, from which hung a broad, sheathed knife like a large machete. Then, from a hidden leather case, the native took out a high-powered express rifle and a box of shells. He had responded automatically, without a word.

Dr. Devoli was leaning over the bed when they ran in. Tomba had hesitated a fraction of a moment when Abbott waited for him to cross the threshold. Now his large, liquid eyes searched the room swiftly, and finding it empty, they grew composed.

The Doctor spoke briefly to Tomba in a native dialect. Tomba shook his head. Devoli said to Abbott, "He can't get a scent from the bedclothes—too fresh. And the gorilla seems to have escaped with all his clothes. No, wait..."

He stooped under the bed and brought out a large shoe that had been ripped to shreds. "Is this enough, Tomba?" The native nodded. "Good!" He tossed the shoe to the Senegalese. Abbott watched the native as he held the shoe close to his quivering nostrils, then closed his eyes and kept moving the shoe from one hand to the other, in satisfaction.

Abbott said, "I've got a hunch. Ask Tomba what he knows about the gorilla disappearing."

"What do you mean?"

"I'm not sure—it's just an idea. The way he looked when he came in, as if he half expected to find it gone."

The Doctor addressed Tomba in his native tongue. Tomba nodded vigorously, his eyes still closed. "Tomba!" Devoli cried. "You mean you knew he ran away tonight?"

"Not tonight, boss master. Other night."

"You mean it's happened before?"

Tomba's eyes opened in surprise. "Happen many time. Maybe ten, twenty. Happen many time."

"Why didn't you tell me?"

"Me think boss master know. Boss master business not Tomba's business."

Dr. Devoli seemed to shake the spell that held him with difficulty. Finally he said, quietly, "Ready?"

"Tomba ready."

"Come on."

ABBOTT took the rifle, waited a moment as the Doctor slipped a hand through the long loop of his bag, then followed Tomba to the outside of the house. He started to go back for the lantern when Devoli, reading his mind, said, "We couldn't take it even if we needed it, and we don't with Tomba along." By the time Abbott's eyes had become accustomed to the darkness, they had left the house far behind.

The eager Senegalese went ahead now and then, running about in a crouching position, returning to lead Devoli and Abbott. Presently Abbott realized, from the instinctive bearing he had taken on the stars, that they had made a wide circle around the whole group of houses and were now heading south...south, toward the towering fringe of jungle that bordered the quiet plains.

The sky was a field of soot, glittering with stardust. A wind ran through the patches of tall grass, and calls came from lonely animals that wandered over the plain. They had been moving swiftly for perhaps a quarter of an hour when Abbott asked, "Do you know where we're going, Dr. Devoli?"

"To the jungle, as far as I can tell."

The next time Tomba went ahead, Abbott asked, "Can he be trusted?"

"I keep my rifle in his care."

Tomba returned and said, "Animal go in jungle."

"Have you ever followed him before, Tomba?" Devoli asked.

"No, boss master! Tomba be afraid!"

"We want to follow. Are you afraid?"

"Not with boss master and big gun. Tomba not afraid for jungle, only animal."

They went on again, and the terrain grew more difficult. The brush was thicker now, tearing at them with barbs and spines. At first there were trees that stood like solitary sentinels, then these too began to group themselves, bound together with long, twisting vines, covered with hideous moss, with lovely night flowers. The jungle had closed in on them, obscuring the sky, black and evil. Life breathed all about them, malodorous, simple, whispering, piercing the night with cries of surging, fear-plagued things that crawled and crept and flew. They stumbled through grasping marshes, the air moist and fever-laden and fetid, and the parasitic vines reached for them like living tentacles.

Abbott, hard-pressed to keep pace with Tomba, his scarcely-healed thigh wound throbbing, held Devoli, but the aged Doctor kept brushing his hand away, refusing assistance though his breathing was labored and harsh. Abbott knew only the comfort of the gun he held, his fingers caressing the cold barrel as if for reassurance. Once he asked, "How far are we going to follow it?"

"Until we find him. He can't...have gone far if he's done this before...he's always been back by morning."

"But it could easily travel miles through these trees. Why don't we wait for it to return?"

"I've got to find out what he does here, now that I know he comes..." Devoli's breathing was fierce. "Don't ask me any questions...please...please..."

TOMBA saw it first. It was no more than the merest patch of light, quivering in the distance. The giant black cocked his ears and listened to the new sound. It was like a massed whisper, soft, guttural. Tomba led them forward cautiously now, changing the direction of his approach to keep the wind coming toward them, until the leaping tendrils of the fire were distinct, and the vast shadows that surrounded it had begun to take form...

They were forty yards away when they first realized what they were looking at. Tomba stopped, and when Devoli and then Abbott crept past him, he followed Abbott. Closer and closer they inched, until the dark, squatting forms ahead were no more than a few yards away. Abbott stared at the scene before him.

There was a clearing there in the jungle, a triangular wedge, lighted by a wood fire. Beginning a few feet from the edge of the fire were rows of gorillas, great, mute, shaggy beasts that sat in silence now, forming crowded, concentric rings. In the center of the clearing, close beside the fire, sat a single gorilla. It was dressed like a man, wearing a shirt, a crudely knotted tie, a coat and trousers and one shoe—for the other foot was bare.

Dr. Devoli gasped something, and instantly Abbott closed a hand over the Doctor's mouth, until, feeling the old man grow quiet, he released him and lay quietly beside him.

The gorilla in the center seemed to be paying no attention to the others, though they watched him with steady, unmoving eyes. The central gorilla was holding a long, sharpened stick over the fire, turning it as one might a spit. Now, as he pulled out the stick to inspect it, Abbott saw that a medium-sized bird had been run through with the stick. The gorilla was cooking it over the fire! The bird's head and feet had been torn off, the feathers carefully plucked, and the skin had been broiled to an even brown.

The gorilla examined the bird, removed it from the stick, and began to tear it apart, devouring it and spitting the bones into the fire. Now the other gorillas—there must have been several score—moved restlessly, and from some came low, disturbed sounds.

ABBOTT lay in the tangled grass, unable to move, feeling something of the nameless fear inherent in nightmares. From blurred eyes, fighting the weakness that swept through him, he watched the gorilla that was dressed like a man, staring, horribly fascinated, into the pinpoints of its eyes where the reflected fire danced...

When the gorilla had finished eating, it continued to sit there, looking into the fire, feeding it occasionally from a pile of wood that lay nearby. Now the great whisper that Tomba had first heard came again, the sound of these gorillas, harsh and querulous.

The gorilla dressed like a man turned its head from side to side, listening.

Then, slowly, it stood up. It uttered several dry, rasping sounds and the other gorillas answered it. The conversation, if such it was, went back and forth for a minute—the single voice and the chorused answer, though sometimes one or two alone answered. Then the central gorilla sat down. It put its head in its arms and began rocking to and fro. Once it looked up and stared about it strangely. Slowly, the rigidity of its great neck relaxed. Its face was buried again in its huge hands...and then, in the deep silence, there came muffled sounds filled with great anguish. The gorilla was crying...

SUDDENLY, hell broke loose. Later Abbott remembered how Devoli had sprung up from the ground, he remembered seeing the Doctor's fire-lit figure trying to reach the gorilla, and the black sea that had swallowed him. The bag he had carried had been flung high into air. It was an odd thing to remember, that bag, hanging in the blood-red glow of light over the fire. Abbott hadn't seen it come down...

Powerful hands seized him. Fangs came alive in the darkness, and surging, shaggy forms, ever closer, until he could no longer breathe. Through the chaos and terror that had engulfed him, one thought alone remained—the open-holstered gun at his hip. He fought like a madman, writhing, smashing, until he tore one of his arms free, finding the gun—

He still held it, after he had been dropped to the ground. In the sudden silence, he heard the deep, whispering voice speak, "Put down the gun!"

Abbott's hand trembled, then loosened, and finally dropped the gun.

The Whispering Gorilla was standing only a few feet away. One of its great arms sheltered Dr. Devoli. The Doctor had fallen to his knees. His clothes had been virtually torn from him, and his face was crusted with stains of blood. The gorilla lifted the Doctor into its arms. Around the three men the other gorillas stood motionless.

Devoli's eyes opened. "Carpenter...take...us...home..." he gasped.

The Whispering Gorilla gazed immutably at the aged, still man in its arms for several seconds. "Yes, Devoli," it said. "I'll take you home."

Its voice, low, throbbing, had frightened Abbott more than anything else. It spoke to the other gorillas and two of them came from the edge of the clearing. One of them bent and turned Tomba over. The native's eyes were wide open, staring without emotion into the leathery face. The gorilla lifted Tomba; the other took Abbott...

ABBOTT looked up into Major Brook's face and he thought: *This doesn't make sense.* No continuity, he thought. He remembered so little. The flow and gradual ebbing of consciousness, the numbing pain that had swept everything before it, the feeling of movement, the thought—it could not have been long before—that they were almost home. And now the Major. It must have taken no more than a few seconds for Abbott to come to full awareness, to restore meaning and order to what he had seen and heard during the very moments he was recovering, but time had become a pain-filled eternity.

Just instants before, he had heard men talking about Tomba as they had carried him away. Devoli was gone. There seemed to be lanterns everywhere now, moving briskly about in the surrounding fields like so many gigantic fireflies. Abbott was lying motionless on the ground; Major Brooks was standing over him, and beside the Major stood several of his men, two of whom held lanterns. All this came slowly into focus as Abbott took a deep breath, propped himself up, and tried to rise. And then, turning ever so slightly, into his field of vision came the forms of three gorillas. They had been standing on the other side of him, as silent and unmoving as automatons.

A thousand pinpoints of stars came swirling out of the night to blind him. He felt his arms buckle under his weight, felt himself falling back to the soft, wet earth. Pain stabbed through his chest, nausea welled up in his throat, and slowly, so slowly, the world receded again, and sounds grew faint and pleasant, and darkness came rushing...

The last thing he heard was Major Brooks' voice as he said, "Pick him up and carry him to the house," The last thing he felt were the great, hairy arms that lifted him up. It was meaningless to him.

CHAPTER FOUR

THE gorilla stood at the barred window of his home, and running through his mind were dim shadows that he knew were thoughts. Outside sunlight glinted on an airplane's wings. He watched the plane circle and swoop down with infinite grace. Like a bird, a great bird that carried men in its belly. He knew birds, the birds of the jungle…

"*I am Carpenter,*" he thought. "I *must remember…*"

For long moments he would forget that, forget why he had to know who he was. He saw another plane dip gently and begin the long glide to the field that bordered the road. Where did the road lead? Had he ever known? All morning the planes had been coming in. They were silent, and that must have been because the men in them had shut off their motors. He knew what motors were. There was a reason for what these men did. They were hiding. They were evil men.

"Evil," he said aloud, and a great bitterness grew within him. "*Evil,*" he thought. "*How simple all judgments are to me. I no longer am concerned with the complexities that make human beings. For me all things require no more than a rudimentary reaction. Pleasant or not pleasant, good or bad, good to eat, bad to eat, friend, enemy…evil…*"

The world had shrunken. It had become a simple world. Sometimes he felt it was the only world he was happy in, but that was when he was not thinking. He was thinking now, because his heart was bitter, because there was an ache in his mind. It was easier to think when emotion seized him. Perhaps that was because emotion was the attribute of human beings. The capacity for emotion was the last link between him and the world he had once known. Was that what Devoli's drugs did?

The drugs. They had come less often. Maybe soon they would be gone. Did he fear what would happen after that? Devoli feared it, but Devoli could not understand. Freedom was waiting for him.

"Free to be an animal," he said aloud. "A gorilla."

As he spoke, the two gorillas who sat on the floor in his house looked up and regarded him. They had been half-asleep. They were his friends, Moga and Yawwa. He uttered a soft, reassuring sound to them.

"Which is stranger?" he thought. *"The fact that I am still able to think, however imperfectly, like a man—or the fact that I can speak to these animals? Why do I know that the sound I just made will satisfy them? If I were to translate the sound to human speech, what would it mean? What do they think of the other sounds I make, the sounds that are words?"*

They feared him. That much he knew. He had seen it the first time he had gone to the jungle. The way they watched him as he walked on the ground when they went through the trees...though the first time he had tried, he had been as skillful as they, his arms instinctive in their power, his sense of balance perfect. These were the things he had never had to learn, the things he owed to the blood that coursed in his veins.

They were scarcely thoughts as they raced through his mind; they were ideas, misty, half-formed, fragmentary and fleeting...

He had been alone in the beginning. The first time he had gone to the jungle he had met...*one of his kind*...it had been a female, and she had fled, only to return later, when he offered no pursuit. Little by little, others had come out of the deep recesses of the jungle, to live here at its edge. The word of this strange one of them had spread. *Olowga,* they called him. The strange one.

They had seen the things he did, the things of which his mind was capable. The house he had built of boughs. The pit he had dug to trap a water buffalo. The time he had directed them and caught half a herd of deer. The great forked stick he had used to kill a python. The water he carried from the river, in skins he had sewn with unwound bits of vine. The fire he had made one night, and how they had scattered in fear and panic. They had learned that he could control it, and they had come to expect it of him.

Would these things persist? He knew without thinking. They were still the attributes of the man within him, the man who was dying away, the expression of skills he was losing. Or was it that he no longer wanted them? He had long since begun to feel that the difference between cooked and raw meat was immaterial. He had given up his house. He often went through the trees now. He found pleasure in being with the others. He knew he wanted the jungle, that something deep and fundamental within him wanted it, though he sometimes returned to it in the clothes that Devoli had given him, though he spoke to them sometimes in human words.

One day he would go to the jungle and he would not come back. He had thought of it the night before. What had made him come back? And that too, he knew without thinking. It was the deep love, the devotion he felt for Devoli…

HIS mind was growing cloudy again, but he fought it. He had to remember. The night before, when he had brought Devoli back from the jungle, he had found these strange men everywhere. They had been looking for Devoli. Was this man who led them Devoli's friend? What should he have done, finding these men? He had wanted to ask Devoli, but Devoli had been sleepy and tired.

No, that was not it. Devoli had been hurt. He had been…the word would not come to him. Unconscious. That was it. He could not ask Devoli.

The man had been greatly afraid of him at first. He was their leader. The others called him Major Von Bruckner. He must have been a German. The Major had come across him and Moga and Yawwa, carrying Devoli and Tomba and the friend, and the Major had called for others in a loud, fear-stricken voice, and men had come running with their guns and lanterns, surrounding them. But they had not tried to hurt him. He had seen that at once. It had confused him, knowing the man was evil, for he had known it the first time he had seen him.

And then the Major had shouted to him. Put Devoli down on the ground, he had shouted. He, confused, unable to ask Devoli, not knowing if the man was a friend of Devoli's, had put Devoli down. The other men had cried out in surprise. They had been amazed. And when the Major shouted again, telling Moga and Yawwa to put down Tomba and the friend, he, Olowga, had told them, speaking his own language, the language he knew instinctively, to put down the bodies.

Later he was glad he had spoken softly to Moga and Yawwa, for the man seemed to think that all three of them would understand him. When the Major asked them to do other things, he conveyed the orders to Moga and Yawwa, speaking less often than he signaled them, for their language was not only of sounds, and it had seemed as if they understood everything.

He had been able to think, the night before. He had thought it would be good to let the man think what he did, but he could not remember why. Was it because be thought that if the Major was Devoli's friend, that he should have known that only he, Olowga, could understand. But he did not know what Devoli had told the man. He knew only that there was one thing Devoli had not told him…who *he* was.

Then the Major had told them to stand away, and he had been very careful with Devoli, seeing he was hurt, and he had told the others to call a doctor immediately. It made him wonder seeing that, and also because the man was concerned with Tomba and the friend of Devoli. And when he and Moga and Yawwa had obeyed the man, the others had put away their guns.

The man had spoken to the others, exultantly, that the gorillas would take orders from anybody. He thought that Devoli's training had instilled unquestioning obedience in them. It had made him wonder, knowing the man was wrong, but he obeyed, and Moga and Yawwa with him. Even later, when the man had ordered them to go to his house, this little house that had been Olowga's home for so long, they had gone.

The hole he had made under the floor had been filled in, and the boards nailed down again. Who had done it? Moga had wanted to run away during the night. He had said that his great strength could destroy the house and the men who stood outside guarding it. He did not know why Olowga wanted to stay there. But he, Olowga, knew, Devoli had been hurt. He had to stay to see what would happen to him. He had to find out what these strange men were doing here.

Another plane dropped silently out of the sky.

"OF course, I sent whatever you required—your naval officers, technicians, material—all this at a time when we can hardly spare a thing. I had expected matters to develop more slowly, so, naturally, I was curious, Von Bruckner, though the affairs of the Intelligence Division are best left alone."

Major Von Bruckner was about to speak when he saw the transport plane coming in. He watched it as it fishtailed across the adjoining field, looking unreal because its outlines were blurred by the heat. He was glad of the momentary diversion; he had almost agreed.

It would have been an error. Colonel-General Gleichenhaus had not flown in from Tripoli to be told that this was none of his business. The General had made that clear by the fact that he chose to speak to Von Bruckner in English, though he spoke it with a horrible accent. It was as if to say that what transpired between them was not intended for the ears of the Major's staff officers, ignoring the fact that three of them, Mayer, Beidermann, and Prinzler, sat a few feet across the screened verandah, and all spoke English. It was a sign, nothing more, but one did not ignore signs from Generals of the Afrika Korps.

"Of course," said the Major, politely.

"Captain Mayer, how many planes have come in so far?"

The Captain rose to his feet. "The last for today arrived a moment ago, Major."

Von Bruckner had kept up the pretence by addressing Mayer in German, and now, in English, he said to the General, "I believe everything is in order, General. If you care to join me?"

As they waited for the staff car to drive up, the Major went on. "As you say, General, we had expected to proceed more slowly. My original intention was to win this Dr. Devoli as a friend, posing, as you know, as a Major Brooks of British Intelligence. However, by a stroke of luck, I discovered at the last moment that Devoli was harboring an American agent. An accomplice was at that very moment in Tiola, and both these men had taken part in a daring raid on the Dakar railroad yards recently. Perhaps you heard of it? No? Well, under the circumstances I had to move more quickly. I am sure you will agree we could waste no time in taking this place over."

General Gleichenhaus stepped into the car and the Major followed. The three staff officers sat in the front seats. "But how could you hope to win this Dr. Devoli after such a move?" the General asked, with a frown. "I understood you to say that his confidence was essential."

"By a stroke of luck, I discovered that too much emphasis had been placed upon that aspect. It developed that the gorillas were so well trained in obedience that they immediately took our orders."

"You are positive?"

"Of course."

"I can only say, Von Bruckner, that you have been very lucky, to use your expression. But I believe the English have also an expression of pushing one's luck too far. One must plan. One must think. One must organize. Luck is for anyone, with no favorites."

"Of course."

Von Bruckner's impassive face gave no sign of his feelings. He detested this little, self-important General with his decorations and disapproving air. What did he know of thinking or planning, seated at a desk in Tripoli, signing papers? Here he, Von Bruckner, by swift movements and quick deductions, had accomplished a task that might have taken months, and this pale General frowned and lectured.

At least he would find nothing to criticize in what had been accomplished in a scant twenty-one hours. There was organization.

THE adjoining field, a plain that stretched flat and smooth for miles beside this road, had been made into an airport. During the night power mowers had cut five lanes across the field. The cut grass had been left in place, so that from the air or the road, the field looked the same, but small signal flags marked the lanes as runways.

A long shed had been erected next to Devoli's barn, housing six large trucks that had come in before dawn. Another structure sheltered gasoline tanks; a third, ordnance supply; a fourth, quartermaster, and amply stocked. A wing had been added to Devoli's house, to serve as barracks for the hundred-odd men who had arrived from Dakar and Tiola. All had been landscaped, even with large trees, and including the new kitchen, all had been painted the same faded colors of the original buildings. Sixteen planes had come in that day, and they had been unloaded, serviced and refueled with dispatch, hidden from view during the operations. It was no mean accomplishment.

The car had driven half a mile down the road before it swerved off and headed toward a grove of trees. They were almost upon the grove before they saw the men there. The General took the salute and inspected the scene.

Eight or ten men were there, grimy and covered with sweat. They were busy with what appeared to be three machines. The machines were a mass of gears and wheels, and three naval Lieutenants Faber, Diemler, and Braun, paused in their work long enough to be introduced to the General. In another corner of the grove, other men were hammering a huge affair of canvas and wood. Even as they watched, the canvas began to form the outline of a dummy destroyer, mounted on concealed wheels, complete even to wooden guns and painted turrets and rafts.

"Faber," said the Major, "how near completion are you?"

Lieutenant Faber patted his machine.

"This one is done, Major. Only the shell remains to be put on, a matter of a few minutes."

"Excellent, Faber. Do you think you could demonstrate for General Gleichenhaus?"

Faber clicked his heels and saluted. "An honor, General."

Waiting in the car, then, Von Bruckner, feeling the General's continued silence an invitation to speak, said, "You remember the great importance which our naval office in Tokyo attached to the small submarines of the Japanese?" Absently, he had spoken in German, but the General, stony-faced, answered in English.

"It amounted to nonsense in the end."

Inwardly furious, Von Bruckner persisted in German. "*Gewiss,* but for good reasons. First, their limited range; they had to be transported to within a hundred miles of their objective. Second, only two small torpedoes were carried, and while the submarine itself was meant to form a third, large torpedo, there is no record of any submarines having done so, although—"

"Are you questioning the willingness of the Japanese to die in action?"

"I did not say that." Von Bruckner forced a smile. "There are always men who will commit suicide to achieve a necessary success, even though the supply of such men is limited and uncertain. But you must remember that warships are equipped with detectors which can hear the submarines long before they are close enough to attempt ramming."

"It seems to me," said Gleichenhaus, "that we are discussing matters far afield from those which usually concern the army." He kept his eyes on his boots, deliberating his words, before he added, "I am to assume, however, that you have found a way to aid the navy?"

Von Bruckner saw Faber approaching them, and realizing that the conversation was about to end, he decided to end it by sticking a verbal dagger into the General. "Not the navy, sir, but the Third Reich." He turned abruptly to Faber and said, "I see you're ready, Lieutenant."

THEY followed Faber back to the machines. The completed one had been covered with a shell, and it now completely resembled a tiny submarine, though it rested on three wheels. Lieutenant Faber waved and climbed through a small hatch into the submarine. When he closed the hatch, his only means of vision was through the periscope.

The dummy destroyer had been hooked up to two motorcycles, and at a signal from Captain Beidermann, the motorcycles started off across the field, towing the huge dummy ship behind them. When it was some two hundred yards away, Faber's tiny U-boat started forward, following the destroyer at a much slower speed.

The destroyer kept pulling away and the U-boat followed for a few minutes, the periscope fixed on its stern. Then, slowly, the U-boat maneuvered in a smart turn and paralleled the course of the destroyer, though much slower. A few minutes more and the U-boat nosed around so that its bow pointed an imaginary line that the destroyer would soon cross. And now the destroyer began to zigzag, altering its speed from moment to moment, while the U-boat adjusted and stayed close.

On came the destroyer. Suddenly the U-boat hissed once—twice, a third time! From its bow sprang three tubular projectiles, each on two wheels. They hit the ground and kept going, each in a slightly different direction, fanning out to form a triangle, of which the U-boat was the apex. Instantly the destroyer swerved. It swung its starboard sharply and the first projectile missed it by a wide margin—but the second hit the port side amidships squarely and went through it. And now, as the destroyer slackened speed, the U-boat, which had kept going in, came up to the destroyer and stopped.

IT was over. The motorcycles began towing the destroyer back, and Faber came out of the U-boat hatch, driving it back. Laughter and cries of approval had followed the demonstration, but General Gleichenhaus only nodded his head sharply. "That is all, Major?" he asked.

"Yes, sir."

"Very well. Please see that my compliments are presented to the Lieutenant." So saying, he went back to the car, the Major and the other officers following. As the car rode back to the house, the General said, "Perhaps, Major, I did not understand completely what your plans were when I heard them at the Berlin conference."

Naturally, Von Bruckner thought, because the plans weren't really discussed there—only the mechanics of the plans. But he said, "No?"

"For instance, Major, I perceive that your clever duplicates of the destroyer and the U-boat are for the purposes of training, and I think they are admirably conceived. Likewise, the three naval officers who were sent here are U-boat specialists. But tell me, Major, do you hope to teach your gorillas to operate such U-boats?"

"Not only these, sir, but the real ones, which are run exactly the same way, with several important changes that are—"

"In fewer words, Major, you believe that you can teach gorillas the very complex business of operating a U-boat, and not only that, but learning to navigate and stalk other ships? Gorillas?"

"Yes, sir," Von Bruckner said, doggedly. "These gorillas have an incredible intelligence. They have been taught to speak, to operate other machinery, to do many tasks. I do not expect that it will be an easy matter to teach them, and we may find that certain things will have to be changed. Also, I do not expect that it will be done quickly. I am prepared to spend a long time here."

"It *is* very peaceful here," the General said, pointedly, adding quickly, "Tell me, Major, why must you have gorillas to man your boats?"

"As I mentioned before, sir, the Japanese experiments failed for good reason. It our gorillas work out, we will overcome the difficulties inherent in such small ships. Our range of operation will be twice theirs, because there will be no necessity for our craft to return. All will be expected—taught, in fact—to destroy themselves by ramming the enemy warships. The torpedoes are incidental, a hope, one might say, but the other, predicated on the gorilla's complete fearlessness, and its inability to forsee its own death or fear it—"

"And what is to prevent your gorilla's U-boats from being heard?"

Major Von Bruckner had avoided the point in the hopes of just this question. That it was sarcastically put suited him even more.

"A most interesting idea, General," he said, quietly. "The model U-boat you saw operated was powered by an engine. It is the noise of the engine and of the generators that warships detect. But that engine can be shut off, and the method of propulsion changed to an incredibly powerful gear *which uses nothing but muscle power.*"

Von Bruckner paused then, waiting for the question. The General, aware by now of what Von Bruckner was doing; hesitated a full minute before he said, irritably, "And the muscle power for this powerful gear of yours—"

"Will come from the incredibly powerful muscles of the gorilla," the Major finished, smiling. "When the enemy is sighted, the engine is shut off. The generator is silenced, and the gorilla wears an oxygen mask. He propels his craft silently. Perhaps he lies in wait for the enemy outside a harbor; perhaps he enters the harbor itself. His intelligence guides him to the largest ship, or a pre-determined ship. He releases his torpedoes and follows them himself…"

The General regarded Von Bruckner in astonishment. "Utterly fantastic!" he spluttered. "I cannot believe that you seriously—"

"If I may interrupt the General," Von Bruckner pursued, "the Soviets are using trained dogs to hurl themselves at tanks, carrying large explosive charges."

"But the intelligence required for a dog to blow up a tank—"

"Assuredly, but the intelligence of these gorillas is beyond all belief. They approach humans."

"Do you mean to sit here and tell me, Major, that you ordered this vast quantity of material, these technicians and officers, in the furtherance of this…this fantastic scheme?"

"I expect to be here for some time, General, and I thought it wiser to have whatever I needed at once. Besides, I had full authority from Marshall Von Zweig to ask for what I wanted."

THE car was driving up to the house now, and the General said, "I can't believe it. No, I can't." He seemed to be mumbling to himself, then he said, "I really must see these gorillas of yours."

The Major opened the door for the General, and a genuine look of disappointment seemed to cross his hard features. "I regret, sir," he murmured, "that I am under strict orders to allow no one not expressly of this command to see the gorillas. No one, my dear General, by order of Marshall Von Zweig." And he added, mentally, *See what you can do with that, my pompous little goat.*

At that moment, as the General came out of the car, the screened door of Devoli's house opened and a man and a girl came out on the verandah. General Gleichenhaus glanced at them, then looked inquiringly at the Major. The girl was a beautiful thing. Von Bruckner, startled by the appearance of the girl, whom he had kept out of sight from the time the General arrived, said quickly, "She is Jeanne Chaumont, a Colonial French police agent from Dakar. She has been very useful to me."

"I don't doubt it," said Gleichenhaus, with a crooked smile. "I see you did order everything you'll need here for a long stay."

Von Bruckner, furious with himself for his unfortunate expression, persisted. "She is Dr. Friedrich's assistant too. The Doctor is taking care of Devoli. How is Dr. Devoli?" he called to Friedrich, raising his voice.

Dr. Friedrich, a tall, moustached man, shook his head. "Herr Abbott is doing nicely," he ventured, "but Dr. Devoli is another matter.   A man of his age cannot be expected to survive experiences that—"

He didn't finish what he was saying, for, suddenly, forgetting for the moment where he was, chagrin still burning in him like a live coal, Von Bruckner leaped up the stairs and seized the Doctor by the coat lapels. "What do you mean—survive?" he ground out, his face as gray as stone.   "You incompetent fool!   I told you Devoli must not be allowed to die!   He is vital to our plans!"

Dr. Friedrich bit his lip until it was white.   "I did not say he was dying, Herr Major.   He has suffered a concussion and shock.   His wounds are infected.   But he will not die, Herr Major.   I will see to it, Herr Major."

Von Bruckner's hands dropped to his sides.   Now that his rage had burned itself out, he became aware of the sudden stillness.   He turned back to the General, fighting to compose himself.   His officers, Mayer, Prinzler, Beidermann, had masked themselves with blank looks.   Several soldiers, passing by, had stopped and now rapidly walked on.   The girl had moved into the background.   In this dead silence, Gleichenhaus let a sigh escape him as he said, "Perhaps, Major, you will have another stroke of luck, and the essential Dr. Devoli will not die, after all."

The Major said, "Let us hope so.   In the meantime, General, will you do me the honor of lunching with my staff?"

Gleichenhaus turned and sat down in the car.   "Thank you, Major, but it is quite impossible.   I stole a few hours from most urgent duties to see for myself what you were doing.   I will have to account for the materiel you requisitioned, you understand."   He smiled his sour little smile.   "I have seen quite enough.   My plane is ready, of course?"

The Major glanced at Prinzler, who nodded.   "Of course."

"Goodbye, gentlemen.   Good strokes of luck."

THE car lurched away as they saluted.   Von Bruckner looked after the car bitterly.   The little General had heard a story that would have stupefied a man with brains.   The idea behind the use of the gorillas was unqualifiedly brilliant, but all that smug, blind little man had said was, "Fantastic!"   What would he say in the report he had so transparently hinted he would write?

To the devil with him! What did he matter? If—no, when the project had been successfully completed, and he had no doubt—very little, at any rate—that it would be successful, he would remember to deal with Gleichenhaus. But that was a long way off, and meanwhile he might create trouble. Von Bruckner remembered with a sudden qualm the cases of champagne he had ordered, the smoked hams, the fish... A lot of capital could be made of that...

Nevertheless he smiled as he turned to Jeanne Chaumont, offering her his arm and saying to his officers, "Miss Chaumont will substitute for the General, gentlemen. I believe the gain is ours."

Possibly because the remark was more successful than the Major had anticipated, judging by the pleased grins of his officers, or perhaps because the mere sight of this lovely woman raised Von Bruckner's spirits—she was at once a reminder of past luck and a promise for the future—he showed no irritation when Dr. Friedrich stopped him at the threshold, saying, "Herr Major, have I your permission to see the native Tomba? His condition is critical."

"*Ach,* how wrong you are," Von Bruckner laughed, good-naturedly. "I had him hanged an hour ago." He bowed gallantly as he opened the door for the girl, and he added, "I am afraid, Doctor, that unless Herr Abbott shows more cooperation, you will shortly lose another patient."

CHAPTER FIVE

IT WAS all like a dream to him. He had lain in the little house all morning, sleeping fitfully in the stifling heat, standing occasionally before the barred window to watch the men busy with their trucks and motorcycles, unable to understand their activity, hoping for the sight of Devoli. The sun had passed its zenith when the wind changed, and the smell of the jungle had come, sweet and tormenting. More than once, Moga had tested the bars, but he, Olowga, had been unyielding, and finally Moga had slept again, stirring at each slight sound.

And then the Major had come, opening the door, telling Yawwa to go outside. But Olowga's eyes had told Yawwa not to move, and when Olowga himself had gone out, the Major seemed satisfied. He had seen the men gathered outside, unerringly felt the tenseness in them, but they had been unarmed. He hardly cared what they wanted, but it was so good to be outside again. The Major had kept talking to him, asking him to speak, finally ordering him. Olowga had not spoken. He spoke to no one but Devoli.

And then he had heard these men talking among themselves, and dimly, he had thought it was odd, the way they sounded. He had heard them the night before, and sometimes during that day, and he had understood what they were saying, though the sounds they made were strange. And then, suddenly, knifing through his brain had come the thought, the realization: *They speak German— and I, Olowga, understand them because Carpenter spoke German! I am Carpenter! I must remember!*

It had awakened him. He had felt the blood pounding through his brain. He had been able to think. When they told him to get into a truck and rode him down the road, he had remembered the road, and his magnificent eyes had taken in everything these men had done, the houses they had built, the grass they had cut, the things they had so carefully hidden. He had seen the men in the grove long before the truck turned off the road.

And his ears, keen, attuned to the least rustle of a leaf, had picked up much of the things the men in the car behind had said— how they had wondered whether he could really talk, how necessary Devoli might prove to be, how important it was for them to understand what had transpired in the jungle the night before. He had understood, then, that it was for him to understand what these men wanted…

The machine had fascinated him. He had stroked its dark, gleaming shell, understanding instantly that it was a small replica of a German U-boat. Behind a row of trees a few hundred feet away, he had mentally reconstructed the form of the huge object there, and known it to be a model of a destroyer. He had listened to the patient explanations of the young man in blue, the Lieutenant Faber, as he pressed the buttons that lay under the shell, moving the levers.

Once the Lieutenant Faber had said to the Major, in a quiet voice, "His eyes, Herr Major, his eyes...such fire, such intensity. I cannot bear to look into them. But how much of this does he understand?"

"We will know soon enough. Explain everything to him, and then we will see how much he retains each time. Be careful with your pronunciation; Devoli's English is quite precise."

AS he had stood there, listening to everything, he had seen the other men come in. They had stayed close to the trees at first, and the air had been heavy with their fear, with their difficult breathing. He had felt that fear dissipate. Once the Lieutenant had taken his hand and pressed it down on a slender lever, and the machine had quivered with life. Of course he had known that it would, for the Lieutenant had long before explained that this was the motor control.

Carpenter had been a skillful man with machines all his life. His father had owned one of the earliest garages in the days when the automobile was being born, and Carpenter had worked in that garage in his youth. He understood every little mechanism in this machine. He understood it because it was instinctive in Carpenter...

There was little to understand here, he knew. Everything had been simplified. He watched the Lieutenant climb down into the shell and maneuver the machine about, and he thought: *Shall I show them I know everything? Is it wiser to seem to learn more slowly?"*

But then, like a wave of fever, he had felt his mind grow cloudy. It was like a physical sensation when he was thinking; the other times it had come upon him slowly. Olowga, Olowga, he thought, remembering how he had torn the clothes off himself the night before, bringing Devoli home, his mind decided, the jungle waiting for him, and the hateful clothes torn to rags.

He had no time. *No time.* This mind was not his to control. It played tricks on him. He had to find out quickly what these men wanted. He had to help Devoli quickly, if help was needed.

He had waited until the Lieutenant had come out of the machine, and then, without waiting for a command, he had gently brushed the frightened Lieutenant aside and climbed into the machine. The Major had cried out to him to stop, but he had closed the hatch over himself, and the next moment he was maneuvering the machine. He had let it run about over the field, turning it this way and that. The periscope had shown him how far he had gone from the grove, and he had started back.

And then, going back, it had come again, the numbness, the ache in his brain. He had cried out, fighting it, beating on his head with his hands—and the violent movement in that cramped space had made him swing over a row of levers. Something under his feet had hissed, and the machine had jolted him, and when he looked through the periscope, he saw three projectiles darting through the grass, heading straight for the grove!

He had seen the men leap aside, and the projectiles disappear harmlessly, but even after that the men were jumping about and pounding each other, embracing each other. He heard their shouting, their wild outcries, but faintly, far off, as in a dream. As...in...a...dream...

He remembered only that he had to stop the machine, and he had stopped it in the grove He had climbed out and stood there, and heard these men laughing and crying and shouting, and the Major standing before him and saying things to him and the Lieutenant Faber, and in the confused disorder of his brain, he had wondered what he had done that had made these men so hysterically jubilant. It had been like a dream...

And now he stood there still, moments after he had come out of the machine, watching them. "The torpedoes!" one man shouted. "Show him how to operate the torpedoes!" "Teach him to stalk the destroyer!" another cried. "Navigation in one lesson!" "Make him work the gear! The gear, I say!" *"Sieg heil!"* "Bring out the destroyer! Put a British flag on it!" *"Sieg heil! Sieg heil!"*

IT MEANT nothing to him. He was tired. He stood there until the men grew calm, and the Major quieted them. It was strange, he thought, the way the Major could quiet them all by speaking a word. But he had not quieted the happiness that lay in their eyes. Nor had the Major quieted the joy in his voice when he said, "First, Faber, we must show him how to operate the gear! The gear is first in importance, because we must see if his strength is equal to it."

"And the idea of an objective!" Faber cried, trembling with excitement. "We will have him head towards the truck—no, the motorcycle! We will station a motorcycle on the field..."

Lieutenant Faber explained the mechanism of the gear. The motor was to be switched off, and he was to put his arms into two cylinders, which, moved back and forth, would propel the machine, while leaving his hands free for other necessary tasks. It was very simple.

When the Lieutenant had finished, Olowga made no sign that he had understood. "Begin!" cried the Lieutenant. "Enter the machine!"

Olowga stared at him. He had comprehended, vaguely, what he was expected to do. He thought: *I will kill them all. I can kill them all if I want to.* Killing was easy for him. Fragments of fresh memories ran through his mind. He often killed in the jungle. It was good to kill. But he had never killed a man. Moga had wanted to kill men that day, and Olowga had forbidden him. Devoli was a man. Yes, that was it. He could not kill these men because they had Devoli with them. There were many of them. What was the Major shouting at him? All their joy was fading. There were too many. If he killed these, by the time he had reached Devoli, they would have killed him...

"I don't understand it," said Von Bruckner, worried. "What could have happened to him? Why doesn't he at least show he understands?"

"Get into the machine!" said Faber. "Do as I say!"

Olowga heard the motor coming. It was an automobile, with two people in it, coming to the grove. A man and a girl. A girl. He had not seen a girl since...since... A little fire began to burn inside his brain. Memories, always memories, rising from a past that had never belonged to him, and people, ghostly, and words and names, and the fire consuming him...

THE car stopped a short distance away and the girl came towards them. The Major quickly headed her off. None heard their voices, but Olowga heard. He heard Prinzler mutter softly to Beidermann, "She has no business here. He is making a fool of himself. He must order her away," And he heard the Major say, "This is no place for you, *fraulein*. Perhaps you had better go back."

"The gorilla," she whispered. "I heard the men talking about it. I heard the strangest stories." He could see her looking past the Major toward him, fascination in her eyes. "For just a moment," she begged, and her hand touched the Major's, pressing it. "Just one little look." And the Major, undecided, yielding as the girl took his arm and led him.

How beautiful she was. He had forgotten how beautiful women were. Once there had been a woman... Her hair was long and blonde and it shone like white water, and her skin was like the petals of the blossoms that grew in the jungle. It was so long since he had seen...he wanted to feel the touch of—

Her scream paralyzed him, froze him after he had taken the first step toward her. He realized, confusion swirling in his brain, that he had started walking toward the girl, his hands outstretched. Instantly the men had jumped away, the Major swiftly dragging the girl. She had screamed, her voice piercing him like a dagger, drowning out the hoarse shouts of the men. And then he had seen the fear in her eyes, and the horror, and more...the loathing...and it had brought the fire that was in him to a blaze that blinded him.

But now he stood there, afraid to move lest he frighten her, but he could not take his eyes away from her. The image of a woman's face kept rising from the ashes of his memory, superimposing itself over the vision of this girl. She was bringing back things that he had long forgotten, that had been buried. He kept looking at her, remembering.

"How he looks at me," the girl whispered. Calmness was returning to her. "He seems to be looking right through me..."

"Strange, the way he started towards you," Von Bruckner mused. "I could have sworn his whole body trembled when you screamed." An odd smile flitted across his face. "As if the sight of you..." Whatever he had been about to say was left unfinished. "Faber!" he called. "Try once more, please."

And now, Faber had hardly spoken to him when he climbed swiftly back into the machine. A great, unquenchable fury had welled up within him, and because he could think more easily now, he knew the danger of what he felt. He tried to force the image of the girl, and of what he had seen in her eyes, from his mind. Moments before he had been sinking into the welcome abyss of forgetfulness...

The motorcycle started across the field. He followed it, then turned off the motor and began moving the gear. He felt the power of his great arms surge through the cylinders that held them, he felt the machine shake with the rage and anguish that beat in his breast. There was forgetfulness again in this, in the knowledge of his strength, in its use. He had to overcome his emotions, for in them lay the secret of pain...

THE motorcycle had become a living antagonist for him. The enormous power of his arms was moving the machine faster than it had moved before. The motorcycle twisted and turned, unable to shake him off. He saw the driver's face once. Fear had slowly begun to grip the man as the machine followed. Not that he could catch it, but that he always spun about in such a way as to head it off. It was good to feel himself working, to be living again, feeling his mind grow numb again.

Later, when the motorcycle had gone back to the grove, and the Lieutenant Faber's form had come into view of the periscope, waving him to stop, he obeyed. He had no eyes then for anyone but the girl. He heard the overjoyed laughter of the men, witnessing their demonstrations once more, aware that their jubilance was greater than before.

He was very tired when he crawled out of the machine. He stood there, stretching his huge, hairy arms, licking his chops, letting his eyes roam over these men as they danced and hugged each other. He had done more—far, far more, than any of them had dreamt he might. He saw Von Bruckner, in his exuberance, sweep the girl up in his arms and kiss her, and a moment later, apologizing, the girl had laughed at him.

He thought about that all the way back to his house. His mind had divided itself into two separate entities. One mind was clear and understanding, the other dark and brooding and numb. But it was the clear mind that directed him when they came back to his house.

Lieutenant Faber, brashly riding in the back of the truck with him, had put a metal brassard on his arm. "I order you not to remove this!" he had told Olowga. How bold and confident these men had become. But he knew what they wanted to do, and when the Lieutenant brought him to his door, he, Olowga, went in swiftly and closed the door on the Lieutenant.

He kept his weight against it and called Moga to him, and then he took off the brassard and put it on Moga's arm. The Lieutenant, startled, was pounding on the door, demanding that it be opened. When Olowga let the door open, the Lieutenant hesitantly walked in, and Olowga saw him recoil from the heavy odor that lay there. The Lieutenant said to Moga, "You must stay here." Then, he pointed to Olowga, who was closest to him, and he ordered him to come out.

So in the end, it was Olowga who went through the tests on the field again—and later, maneuvering it so that Yawwa took the second brassard. Olowga came a third time.

As for why he did it, he himself was uncertain. He had wanted to see the girl again. Her face haunted him. But when he came back to the field the second time, she was gone. Nevertheless he had done what they wanted of him, and he had seen their growing acceptance of his intelligence, and their undiminished joy. He had gone the third time, toward dusk, because he knew he had to, but the reason for it was lost. He wandered through the maze of voices and directions without really understanding anything, carried by instinct…

With one difference. It had never happened before.

Somehow, as his mind had grown weary, he knew it was for the last time. *"I am Carpenter,"* he had been able to tell himself, but nothing within him had stirred. Yet, strangely, he had known that something should have happened.

It was as if he had found, somewhere, the strength of purpose to carry him here…but no further. In that amazing moment, in that last bewildering spasm of clarity, he had been like a drowning man who knew he was going down for the last time, but who welcomed the surcease from struggle.

He looked out of his little window into the gathering twilight, and he remembered Devoli, and one thought spun slowly in the murkiness of his brain...

CHAPTER SIX

SHE came into Devoli's room quietly, holding the door open. Dr. Friedrich glanced up at her and nodded. "Thank you for returning so soon, *fraulein,*" he said, wearily. "I don't know what I would have done without you." He got up and went to the door. "I will be here in this next room. Perhaps I can sleep for an hour."

"How is he?"

"The same. A short while ago he regained consciousness for a little while, poor man. He babbled incoherently. Meaningless things."

"Do you remember anything he said, Doctor?"

Dr. Friedrich held his hands over his eyes. They were bloodshot, half closed. "No. My English is not very good, besides. If he should wake up again, please call me immediately." He swallowed, and his eyes looked away. "Immediately," he repeated. "This case is very important to me. You understand, *fraulein.*" Then he went out.

She sat in a chair beside Devoli's bed. How old and worn he looked. His white hair was still matted, and scarcely closed cuts and wounds covered his face and arms, though the larger ones had been bandaged. A large blue vein in the center of his high forehead dilated as he breathed, and the sound of his breathing was shallow and irregular. Now and then he moved as he slept, and his long, burnt fingers opened and closed on invisible objects...

How long she sat there before she heard him speak, she didn't know. She had turned away, leaning on the window sill, looking out into the field where a solitary airplane had warmed up and left—the last of those to go that day. When she heard Devoli's voice, she turned back quickly. His wrinkled eyelids had opened, and the hot, feverish eyes were looking at her. He looked at her for a long time.

"Who are you?" he breathed.

"Jeanne," she said, softly, "I am a friend of Alan Bradford's."

"Where...where is he?"

"Safe, in Tiola."

"Where is...Abbott?"

"He has gone somewhere He will be back later."

The old man was silent, then, presently, he said, "Who was...the man that was sitting here...before?"

"A doctor. You are very ill."

"He...is a German," Devoli breathed. "Where did he...come from? And the noises...I hear noises...all day..." His eyes were rolling back into his head and his hands were clutching. "Tell...Abbott...to be careful of Major Brooks..." he gasped.

He lay very still for a few moments and then he began to speak again, and the girl listened intently. "Carpenter..." he moaned. "He must be careful of him...the drug...not much left...give it to him... I owe him his...life... Be careful."

"Doctor," she said, softly, taking his hand in hers. "You must make an effort to tell me what you mean. What drug?"

DEVOLI seemed to stiffen as she spoke. He opened his fever-laden eyes again and looked at her. "I...must trust you, Jeanne," he said, his chest laboring with the effort of speaking. "Go to the...cabinet. Take the large...can of tobacco. In it...at the bottom...you will find three capsules...they are all that is...left. I lost the rest...last night. Give it to...Bradford...for Carpenter... He will understand..."

"No," she said quickly insistently. "You must tell me. What is the drug for?"

"For the gorilla. If...he becomes...unmanageable...give it to him. It...it will clear his...mind..."

She got up swiftly and went to the cabinet. She opened the can of pipe tobacco there and took out three capsules. They were some two inches long, filled with a pale green powder. Carefully, she wrapped them in a bit of handkerchief and pocketed them. When she returned to Devoli's bedside, she asked, "Who is Carpenter?"

Though the old man's eyes were open, he did not seem to see her. "Carpenter," he gasped. "Forgive me..."

He spoke after that, but she didn't understand what he was saying. Once he repeated his instructions to her, but brokenly, meaninglessly, and if she had not heard him before, she would not have understood. She listened to the throaty whisper of his voice as he went on endlessly, then she got up and went into the next room.

She shook Dr. Friedrich gently, and he sat up at once.

"Yes, *fraulein?* He is awake?" He put his shoes on and followed her back to Devoli. There Friedrich sat down, listening to the old man. After a few minutes he forced a little glass of liquid down Devoli's throat. It spilled on his chin and wet his pillow, and the doctor gave up. "What is he saying, *fraulein?*" he asked. "The Major must know."

She shook her head. "I'll tell him."

After awhile, Dr. Friedrich said, "You can go now, *fraulein.* I will sit here with him. He is much better now."

She went out as quietly as she had come in. Downstairs she heard Von Bruckner's voice, raucous and joyful, loudest of all in the chorus that was singing the Horst Wessel song to the accompaniment of an accordion. Smiling, she entered the room and went to the Major.

*　*　*

JOE ABBOTT sat down at the table without answering the taunting greeting of Major Von Bruckner. Time enough later to heave a bowl of soup in his sneering face, Abbott thought. Meanwhile it would be better to see what was going on, and the way champagne was flowing, he guessed he had a good chance to find out.

Why had they brought him here, invited him to this dinner? It was one of the myriad mysteries that confronted him. Their Dr. Friedrich had bandaged his wounds and cared for him, and though he had asked questions about the cuts and bruises that covered him from head to foot, he had not pressed for answers. That had come later, when Von Bruckner and Lieutenant Kohler had come to the room they had locked him in.

It hadn't been so bad, all in all, he decided. Dr. Friedrich had told him that afternoon what had happened to Tomba. Poor Tomba. Abbott had heard him screaming all morning. And when Kohler had given Abbott a duplicate of the beating he had given Tomba, it had been fruitless. It had to be, once Abbott realized how anxious they were to find out what had happened in the jungle the night before. He could take more than that without talking. They had hanged Tomba and spared him. Why?

He looked up when the orderly offered him champagne.

"Take it, Mister," Kohler commanded across the table in his thick, accented English. "Maybe you vill need it later on."

Abbott parted his bruised lips in a smile and took the glass. If ever he had the chance—and maybe he would make it—he would square things with Kohler. He remembered the cool grimness with which Kohler had beaten him with a belt buckle until he bled from a dozen places, until Dr. Friedrich had used up his capsules of ammonia, reviving him.

Whatever it was they were after, they had succeeded, he thought. Half of them were drunk. If only he spoke German, it would be easy to understand. The table in Devoli's dining room was piled high with food and drink. Von Bruckner and eight officers sat with Abbott and that girl at one table, and across the room was another table at which sat some fifteen non-commissioned officers. All wore full uniforms for the first time. He wondered about the three naval uniforms.

And what of the woman? Where did she fit in? She had started to come into his room once when the Doctor was dressing his wounds, and the Doctor had told her he didn't need her. She was pretty in the extreme. He saw her rising now, glass in hand, as Von Bruckner cried for a toast. He understood only one word of it: Hitler.

"On your feet," Von Bruckner roared softly at him. "Get to your feet when you hear the name of the *Fuehrer*." One of the men flung a plate of food at him.

He stood up, brushing the food from his shirt. The Major repeated his toast and Abbott drank. He felt a little relieved when he saw that no one had noticed his fingers crossed, or had understood it. It was kid stuff, that finger crossing, but it made him feel better. Still, he didn't want to get shot. The way they were feeling, it seemed a distinct possibility.

After the gruel and water he had had to eat that day, the food was wonderful. He ate quickly, not caring how he looked. Now and again he glanced toward the girl, but once, when their eyes met, she looked away disdainfully. To hell with her, Abbott thought. These Nazis certainly traveled well. Von Bruckner had brought his mistress with him. Chaumont, they called her, a French woman. Well, Paris had those, too.

HE WAS still eating when Captain Mayer unsteadily rose up, his clumsy sodden fingers unfolding a sheet of paper. The other officers clamored for silence, and soon there was quiet, of a sort. Captain Mayer tried to hold the paper still and laughed at himself, but then he began reading. Abbott could make neither head nor tail of it, but whatever the paper said, it pleased the men tremendously. They applauded softly and voiced their approval, and at its conclusion another toast followed, and Abbott had to cross his fingers again.

Only this time he saw that the woman had seen him. Momentarily, her cold forehead had wrinkled, her eyes fastened on his left hand, and when they traveled up to his eyes, Abbott saw that she understood. He waited for her to say something, but she didn't. What did happen was that Von Bruckner caught the way he was looking at her.

He not only caught it, but he said something in German that made everyone laugh, and a quick, little blush spread over the girl's gay face. In a corner of the room, one of the noncommissioned officers made a gurgling, distressed sound, and as he was led out, the laughter grew louder. It was in the midst of this hilarity that Von Bruckner hammered his fist on the table for silence again.

"Herr Abbott," he said, raising his glass, and everyone drank a toast to him, throwing their glasses against the wall. And when they all sat down, the expectancy plain on their faces. Abbott knew that it was coming now, whatever it was.

"Mr. Abbott," said Von Bruckner, "I don't suppose you know you're the guest of honor here tonight?" He was leaning far back in his chair, and when he tried to nudge Prinzler, next to him, he missed, and laughing, he kicked Prinzler under the table and Prinzler howled, "Answer me, Mr. Abbott. Did you know you were the guest of honor?"

"No."

"Well, then, don't you think you ought to know why you are?"

"Yes."

"Then I'll tell you," the Major said sharply. "It is simply that you are the reason for our success. If I had not met you last night, Mr. Abbott, we might have wasted months here, trying to win the confidence of your Dr. Devoli, hoping to pry out the secret of his gorillas. But you saved us, Mr. Abbott..."

It meant nothing to Abbott. It told him, vaguely, that he had been on the right track when he thought the Major had come there for some reason connected with the Whispering Gorilla. He knew nothing else; not even where Devoli was, though Dr. Friedrich had told him not to ask and not to worry.

"You see, Mr. Abbott, I had heard about your little adventure in the Dakar yards, though I never suspected it was you when I met you. But when I found your friend Bradford in Tiola..."

Von Bruckner let his voice die away, waiting for its effect on Abbott. He was fully rewarded. Abbott felt the blood rushing to his head, felt his tongue grow thick. "You...found...Bradford?" he said.

"Yes," Von Bruckner replied, gleefully hammering his fist down. "Or rather," he amended, with a polite nod to the girl, "Miss Chaumont found him for us. Miss Chaumont, this lovely young lady on my right, is an old friend of the Third Reich. She followed your trail to Tiola, on the orders of the Dakar police, but in Tiola she found not you, but your friend Bradford. Last night when I returned to Tiola, Miss Chaumont led us to Bradford. Once we had him, realizing who he was, it was not too difficult to decide who you were, especially with your limp..."

He reached out and patted the girl's hand in an affectionate manner. "That fortunate discovery convinced me that it was hopeless to proceed cautiously with a man who sheltered the Reich's enemies. It was a desperate move, Mr. Abbott, but it turned out to be a masterstroke. For when you returned from the jungle last night with the Doctor, we quickly discovered the secret of his gorillas."

His voice had risen to a somewhat triumphant pitch, his face completely aglow with pleasure and champagne. "You understand?" he said, leaning forward. "We know the secret of their obedience…"

Abbott shook his head. It meant nothing to him. "Bradford," he breathed. "Where is he?"

A frown came over Von Bruckner's face. "Mr. Bradford is dead," he said, waving a hand impatiently. He kept regarding Abbott, and there was a tiny note of disappointment in his voice when he asked, "So you see why you are the guest of honor tonight?"

SLOWLY, Abbott had gotten to his feet. He stood there, brokenly, their faces swimming before him. The minute gleam of hope that had lived all day was snuffed out. It was over now. He picked up his glass and filled it, then raised the brimming glass.

"You're wrong, Major," he said. "The real guest of honor is Miss Chaumont," Then, slowly—because he had all the time in the world, because they could not anticipate him—Abbott whipped his hand across the table. The champagne flew out of it and splashed violently into the girl's face.

Over the instantaneous pandemonium, Von Bruckner's outraged voice bellowed, "Beidermann—*halt!* Mayer! Kohler! *Nein!*" He strode among them, tearing their hands from Abbott, letting him stand there, breathless and alone. His features were red with anger. "No," he said, jerking a hand for the officers to put away their guns. "Not so easy. The final triumph belongs to Miss Chaumont. She must have a prisoner to bring to Dakar—to be guillotined in the public square as an object lesson for the enemies of the new order." And as he spoke, he smashed Abbott across the face with an open hand, once, twice.

Abbott closed one eye and spit in Von Bruckner's face. After that, all he remembered was a hand holding a bottle, coming at him…

IT WAS very late that night when Abbott heard the noise at his window. He ignored it at first. The way his head felt, he had heard noises before. For hours he had been unable to sleep, sitting at his window, watching the moon come up and go down again. Finally, so tired that even the throbbing of his wounds could not keep him awake, he had fallen asleep in his clothes, stretched across the bed. And now, hearing the noise, he discounted it also because he knew there was no way for anyone to get to the window; it was in the upper story of a blank wall.

But that, he suddenly told himself, had been altered that day when the wing had been added. It was possible. A sloping roof came down from the new wing to his end of the house.

And there was a noise, very slight, but definite. If he had doubted it, he had now seen a hand, prying the screen loose. While he had lain there, wearily debating it, his eyes had become accustomed to the luminous darkness. The hand had pried open the screen.

Cautiously, he rolled over and slid off the bed, coming down on the floor on all fours. What the hell it was, he had no idea, unless one of Von Bruckner's gallants had decided to have another go at him. He hoped it was Kohler. He had heard Kohler howling half the night.

A second hand came in, holding a long-barreled automatic, then a foot—but at this moment, just as Abbott was about to rise up and use his forearm as a loop—he saw that the foot belonged to a woman! It was the girl coming in! He straightened himself against the wall at the instant she stood in the room. He looped his forearm around her throat, and with his other hand, twisted the gun from her. He held her firmly, expecting her to struggle, but she didn't.

He thought perhaps that he had broken her neck. He took his arm away quickly and she started to fall forward, then caught herself and spun around, holding her throat but pressing a hand over his mouth. Seeing that she was all right, he had been about to do the same thing to her, to stop her from making an outcry. Her action confused him.

She came up very close to him and whispered, "Be quiet. There's a sentry downstairs in the hall and there're more outside..."

She took her hand away and seemed to be listening intently, then she went to the door and listened there. Finally she came back to him and said, in a very soft voice, "I'm not one of the Nazis. I'm a French agent, but I'm a member of the underground, the Fighting French. You must believe me. I've no time to waste here."

Abbott felt the gun he had taken from her. He could barely make out its outlines; it was a German field pistol. "What do you want?"

"Shhhh… Quiet, we must be quiet… Not all of them are drunk." She held up a small, folded sheet of paper. "Alan Bradford…he entrusted me with this. He told me to give it to you…when he knew that he was dying." She put a hand tightly over Abbott's mouth again, as if she was afraid of what he would say or do. "I followed your trail from Dakar all the way to Tiola. Once in Tiola I found your friend. He had been brought there by a river caravan. That was three days ago, and he stayed hidden in a little inn on the furthest outskirts of the town. He was dying and he knew it—he was afraid to try making it here or sending for you…"

Abbott was silent. He kept looking at her.

"I stayed with him for three days," she went on, earnestly. "He knew who I was, what I had come for. I brought a doctor from Muerge, but there was really nothing that could be done for him at that point. When I realized he probably wasn't going to live until morning, I decided to surrender him to the Nazis. I'll tell you why later. But your friend believed in me. He told me to give you this—he said it was the answer to the puzzle and that you would understand."

Abbott took the paper. If this was some trick—but he opened the paper, peering at it in the darkness, making out the crudely drawn figure. Suddenly he felt a heavy, choking sensation. This was from Bradford—it could only have been he. He motioned the girl to stand where she was and went to a closet. There, shielding the match he lit, he examined the figure closely. It was a crossword puzzle.

1. What the *Telegram* sold.
2. (Across) Yardage equaling two first downs.
2, (Down) Last name of a famous dog.
3. Moola; Oats; Long green. (Syn.)
4. Dash the groove.
5. A hundred dollars.

HE BEGAN to fill the squares in hurriedly. It had been worked out simply, but in colloquialisms that would have been meaningless to the wrong people. Or was that what had happened? Was that why this girl had come to him this way—to hope he would solve it for them? He would deal with that later.

The first one was easy—*News*. The second...*Twenty* fitted in. The second one down—Rin-Tin-Tin, leaving *Tin*. The third, a synonym for moola, long green, composed of four letters, with *is* in the middle. *Fish*—that was it! The fourth—dash the groove. It meant nothing. Unless dash meant to be filled in. In that case—*In the groove!* And fifth, a *yard*, meaning a hundred dollars!

With the light of his last match he studied the completed puzzle. Then he read the words in the order he had written them: *News—Twenty—Tin—Fish—In—Yard.* Twenty tin fish! That meant...but it was impossible. Could the train in the Dakar railroad yard possibly have been transporting twenty submarines?

He returned to the girl. "If he trusted you, why didn't he give you the message directly, without resorting to this?"

Her voice was scarcely audible as she replied, "I wanted it that way, I didn't want to know anything that could be forced from me by torture… I still don't know what he wanted to tell you."

Abbott hesitated. The message itself was unimportant now. What did matter was this girl, and what she wanted. "But you must—" he said.

She gripped his arms tightly. "Please," she whispered fiercely. "If I must, I'll tell you everything, only let me tell you quickly. You must escape to Tiola before the Major misses me."

He could feel the tension in her hands, in the desperate urgency of her voice. "An hour after I surrendered your friend to the Nazis, he died. It was only last night that he told me you were here, and I immediately sent someone here to warn you. It was only after I had given Bradford up that I discovered Von Bruckner had been here, that his plans concerned this place. But you were not here to receive my warning, and there was nothing I could do. All I knew was that our underground had discovered Von Bruckner in Tiola, and Nazis everywhere, with great stores and equipment—and that they were up to something besides the possibility that they were hunting you. When I realized that Bradford was dying, I decided to surrender him, hoping to win their favor…"

Outside two men's voices exchanged greetings and passed on.

The girl said, quietly, "I am a beautiful woman. I would not hesitate to use any means. Fortunately, Von Bruckner sent for me this morning and brought me here. I tried to get to you during the day, but the Doctor stopped me. I did get to Dr. Devoli. He spoke to me, trying to explain something, and he gave me these."

She opened a handkerchief, which contained three pale capsules. "He wanted me to give these to Bradford. He said Bradford would understand, that they were for Carpenter—"

"Carpenter!" Abbott said, pointedly. "You're wrong…you must have misunderstood."

"I'm not certain. He spoke from fever, mentioning many things. But he did tell me that this was a drug for the gorilla, that it would clear its mind if it became hard to manage…"

"Yes," Abbott said, wonderingly, "the drug…But why—"

"He must have anticipated what Von Bruckner was doing with the gorillas. I discovered it when I went to the field near here, where the officers were engaged. I didn't understand everything then, but I saw that they had taken the gorillas and taught them to operate a little machine that was shaped like a tiny submarine—"

"A submarine! Are you certain?"

"It could have been nothing else. The gorillas were intelligent enough to manage the submarine. They were being taught to follow and ram objects, as if they were hunting at sea. Von Bruckner and the others were beside themselves with joy—"

"Why do you say gorillas? Wasn't there only one?"

"I saw only one, but I knew there were three altogether, and I heard them talking later, saying that all three had acted perfectly. This evening, before dinner, when they were already drunk, Von Bruckner sent a radio message to his superiors. That was what Captain Mayer read during dinner. It said that the task they had undertaken was already successful in all but the smallest details, and that they would be finished as soon as they had gathered up more operators. It was the word operators, in German, that made them laugh so…"

"But it's impossible," said Abbott, hopelessly confused.

She shook her head. "You must listen to me. I understand it as little as you, but there is no time to lose. Since last night, our underground has been gathering its forces in the vicinity. They must attack without delay—tomorrow night! There are a hundred men here, but they do not know the country. We are well armed. Take the pistol I brought you. I will pray for you. When you get to Tiola, go to…"

She stopped speaking, looking at him. "You do not believe me?"

OF COURSE he believed her. It was just that he hadn't yet come to understand what was happening. The facts were too many and too new for him to grasp all at once. Why had not Devoli told him the true story of the gorillas? Why had he kept it from him? And the drug…what had he expected Bradford to do with it? Why had he pinned his hope on Bradford? The story of the gorillas and the submarines was incredible, but the girl had seen it. And this message that Bradford had sent him, dying... Bradford had known how important the information was...the twenty tin fish... Von Bruckner had known too, and he had planned a fantastic blow, and if it succeeded, the twenty tin fish would be only the beginning...

"What about you?" said Abbott.

"I must stay here. I must see what they do tomorrow. After you go, I will return to his room..." She paused, touching his hand. "It is not as bad as that. He was very drunk when he took me upstairs. He fell asleep immediately. He is quite harmless, believe me."

Abbott said, "You'll come with me."

She said, softly, "I would only be in your way. You must travel fast...alone. Try to understand. Nothing matters; not our lives and desires, only victory."

"You're right," Abbott said, slowly. "But if you stay, he mustn't know you were mixed up in this." In the darkness, he looked into her eyes. He pressed the gun into her unwilling fingers. "Return this... I'll find another way to get out of here."

"There are sentries everywhere. One is downstairs, another on the veranda, a third before the house..." She held his hand tightly. "You'll jeopardize everything unless you accept my help."

After a moment, Abbott nodded. He fumbled in his pockets until he found a new book of matches. He rolled the paper with the puzzle on it to a taper. "I don't want you to carry those capsules with you," he said. "No evidence, understand?" He went back to the closet, closing it, and lit the taper.

While it was burning, the girl came to him. "I forgot to tell you about this," she said. "Perhaps it ought to be burned, too." She held out a small photograph of a dark-haired woman. "Bradford gave it to me to give to Dr. Devoli."

Abbott held the photograph in a hand he found difficult to keep steady. His eyes misted. "Poor Roselle," he murmured, and to Jeanne he said, quietly, "This is Roselle Carpenter. Once she was the wife of a friend of Alan's and Devoli...the Carpenter that Devoli mentioned..."

"Bradford loved her," she said. "The last words he spoke were of her. I thought she was his wife."

"She was Carpenter's wife. There never was another man for her. She never forgot him. Alan knew that, and he understood, but he couldn't help loving her..." He shook his head, as if to clear it. "No," he said. "I can't burn her picture. Hide it somewhere. Devoli will want it." He smiled grimly at her. "When we're out of this," he said.

He closed the closet and led her back to the window. He took the sheet from his bed and tore off a long strip. "You're in this house, aren't you? Good. We've got to have one of the staircases unguarded for a minute. When you get back to the Major's room, go out into the hall and call the sentry downstairs. Tell him to bring you a pitcher of water. That's all."

"But what will you do?"

"Don't worry about it. Now tell me what I have to do in Tiola."

A minute later, when she had finished speaking, Abbott took her hand and kissed it. "For the champagne," he whispered.

She reached up and drew his face down to hers. Her lips were soft and cool, and when Abbott pressed her to him, he felt her tremble. "For your courage," she whispered.

He lifted her to the sill. He peered out into the darkness. No sound came from below; no one was in sight. She climbed out on the roof. He gave her the pistol, and then she was gone.

HE WAITED a few minutes, then opened the door that led to the hall. He stuck his head out and looked down the open stairway and quickly ducked back. A uniformed soldier was sitting in a chair, facing the stairway. Listening carefully, he heard Jeanne's voice, faintly, then footsteps. When he looked out again, the Nazi was gone from the chair, but the next minute he saw him coming back from the other stairway, crossing the living room to the kitchen.

Swiftly, Abbott descended on tiptoe. Reaching the living room, he heard the sound of water running in the kitchen. He crouched and went to the second stairway, hiding behind a high-backed wicker chair. From a table he took the smallest of several ashtrays. He put the ashtray into the center of the strip of linen he had taken with him, and wound it securely in place, so that he had a slender, spiraled piece of cloth, weighted by the ashtray.

A moment later, the water stopped and the soldier came out of the kitchen carrying a pitcher of water. He crossed the room and started up the stairway. He was on the second stair when Abbott came out from behind the chair. With a quick, dexterous motion, he looped the linen string around the soldier's neck, so that the covered ashtray smashed squarely against the Nazi's larynx as Abbott yanked the string. The entire action took a fraction of an instant.

The Nazi's body jerked erect. The faintest gurgle came from his shattered throat, and as he brought his hands up. Abbott stuck his hand into the pitcher. The water spilled out, but the pitcher stayed on his left hand. His right hand spun the loop tighter and tighter. For a moment the two men stood thus, neither moving. Abbott half crouched over to support the soldier's weight as his body sagged more and more against Abbott, until finally the soldier's arms fell to his sides and were still.

Abbott bent down, using his body as a lever to lower the Nazi's inert form to the floor. He put the pitcher down quietly and disengaged the string from the soldier's throat. The soldier's bulging eyes were wide open, and through his parted lips a trickle of blood ran down his chin and over his uniform. He was dead, his larynx crushed and hemorrhaging; he had probably never realized what hit him.

Abbott took out the broad, triangular trench knife from the dead soldier's belt sheath. He cautiously dragged the body under a table, then put the ashtray back. He got up and sneaked along the wall to the door. From here the wall was all screen, starting four feet from the floor and going to the ceiling. If anything happened before the screen, it would be visible to anyone outside.

He lifted a chair and placed it to the left of the door, so that it was hidden from view by the closed wall. He stuck the trench knife into the floor a foot away from the chair, then he unlooped the linen string to its full length. On all fours he crept to the screened door and peered out. The sentry was standing at the far end of the veranda, leaning against one of the posts and smoking. No one else was in sight.

ABBOTT crawled back and got between the wall and the chair, and when he crouched down, the trench knife was inches from his reach. Then he called softly. "Psssst!" He waited, repeated the insistent sound. He heard the quick footsteps on the veranda.

They stopped outside the door. Evidently the soldier was looking in. "Karl!" he called, quietly. "Karl, *wobist du?*" The next moment he opened the door and started into the room.

Abbott moved the instant the door closed. He rose up and looped the string over the soldier's throat. Simultaneously he yanked the string and brought his knee up viciously into the soldier's back. The soldier's feet flew out from under him, and twisting, his hands clawing at the string, he fell backward into the waiting chair. He bounced up, and in that moment Abbott's hand flashed up from the floor. The trench knife traveled three feet through the air and sank into the soldier's ribs, piercing his heart.

Abbott had to pull hard to get the knife out. He avoided looking at the dead soldier's face. A wave of nausea seized him when he saw the red, gleaming stain on the knife, but he grinned bitterly and wiped it off on the soldier's trousers. He pulled the chair farther back and rested a moment, getting his breath.

His leg burned and ached, and there was a dull, hollow ache in his chest that made it difficult for him to breathe. He had been lucky so far. The beating had left him enough strength to accomplish the first part of his plans. He looked at the large, holstered revolver that lay quietly against the dead man's thigh. He was at home with a gun, Abbott thought. If he dared to use it, dared making a sound, he could have shot his way out. But suddenly he took the gun and stuck it into his belt. Perhaps later, when he...

Voices!

They were perhaps thirty or forty yards away, one of them loud, noisy, the other subdued. An officer talking to one of the sentries. Perhaps he was making the rounds, a tour of inspection. He had to be quick now, whatever he did.

He got up and opened the door, then walked down the length of the veranda, making no effort to hide or be quiet, and when he reached the veranda stairs he sat down on the top stair, one hand across his lap, the knife under it. He could see the dim outlines of the two men's forms silhouetted against a glow that came from one of the barns. The voices stopped and the men exchanged salutes. Undoubtedly both had heard him walking across the veranda, Abbott knew, and they had seen him—but not *him*—for they had looked, if they had looked at all, with the eyes of habit, with eyes that expected a sentry to be there. The attempt to sneak along the veranda might have been a fatal error; the slightest covert action or sound would have screamed to them.

THE sentry started walking away, his rifle over his shoulder, and the other came towards the house. Abbott tensed, sat waiting, his head slightly bowed, and well below the threshold of light. Closer and closer the steps came, and when they passed the rectangle of light that fell from the door, spilling across the veranda and the path, Abbott looked up and saw that it was indeed an officer who approached. And he saw more than that—for the officer was Lieutenant Kohler! A thrill raced through him. His hand was icy cool as it closed on the trench knife.

Kohler was five feet away when his step faltered. The area of light through which he had passed had momentarily unconditioned his eyes to the darkness. He must have seen enough to know that whoever it was that sat there, it was not the sentry, but his pace carried him another foot or two before he stopped.

"*Was tut mann—*"

He had started to speak when Abbott got up and with a single bound was on him. The words froze in his mouth. He seemed unable to move a step, but his body leaned away from Abbott, and one of his hands came up slowly, already too late to stop the thrust that had hit him and gone. The hand kept going up slowly, touching the throat that had been slashed from ear to ear, feeling the blood that spurted. Then, as the hand fell away, Kohler's body sagged. His knees bent gently and he fell face down on the path.

Abbott pulled him to the side of the house. He hid there, waiting. In the barn he heard voices. The sentry was nowhere in sight. He squatted, thinking. Then he got up and staying close to the house, he skirted the wall until he reached its end. Leaving the path, he raced across the grass to the newly built shed. Under its cover he crept to the next building. He listened, swiftly crossed an open patch and was at the back wall of the barn.

He searched the grass for a sliver of light, then, tracing it to a space between timbers, he looked through it into the barn. There were two soldiers sitting inside, stripped to the waist, sitting on oil drums and working over a small section of machinery. Two large searchlights had been trained on their makeshift table, and the barn was well lighted. To one side of them, near the stalls, were some fifteen motorcycles, several of which had attached sidecars. The soldiers spoke to each other occasionally, evidently about their work.

As he watched, Abbott saw the door swing open and the sentry come in. One of the soldiers asked a question. The sentry scowled his answer and both soldiers laughed. The sentry put his rifle down and took out a cigarette. One of the soldiers got up and knocked the match from his hand, pointing to the oil drums and berating him. The sentry said something in answer and the soldier shook his head, motioning outside.

Abbott started swinging around the walls, heading for the barn door. Time was running short. It was now almost five minutes since he had killed the first man. He had no idea of their arrangements; at any moment his victims might be discovered. He had to move fast, but above all, cautiously. And though he could kill easily, he was sick of blood.

He reached the corner just as the door opened and the sentry came out, then, without waiting, he started towards him, staying close to the wall, moving soundlessly. What had been partially true for Kohler was entirely true for the sentry—coming from the well-lit barn, his eyes would be useless for a moment in the dark. It was the assimilated knowledge of little things like this that made a successful killer, Abbott thought grimly.

HE WAS almost face to face with the motionless sentry when he took a hard hold of his gun. He fixed a finger in the trigger guard and held the hard wood-stock out. He moved suddenly, his arm coming down with the gun on the sentry's head. His other arm circled the sentry's body, catching him and the rifle. He laid them both down gently to one side of the closed door.

There was a decision to be made: Should he walk in on the two men in the barn, using the gun for authority? It would be faster. But they might decide that their lives were forfeit if they let him escape, and they might do anything. He bent down and took off the soldier's coat, putting his hand into the left sleeve. Then he took a cigarette, struck a match in cupped hands and lit it.

Holding the gun in his right hand, he stood with his back against the barn door. With his left hand he opened the door slightly, then held it past the end of the door, so that it would be visible inside. He held the lighted cigarette in that hand and he wagged his fingers in a come-here signal, being careful to keep his fingers loose, so that the motion should not appear too urgent. Otherwise, he knew, he would get both soldiers out together.

One of the soldiers called: *"Also, was ist los jezt?"*

Abbott repeated the motion.

"Zum teujel!" said the soldier, getting up. He came through the door and Abbott leaned against it, closing it behind him gently. The next moment he smashed the gun down. When he pulled the unconscious soldier away, he let the barn door swing open a trifle by itself. He waited a moment, and presently the remaining soldier called, "Paul!" No answer. "Paul!" Sharper now. Seven or eight steps. The barn door opening quickly…and again the gun smashed down.

He was feverishly anxious now to get going, but he forced himself to take the time to undress the tallest of the soldiers. Hurriedly he put the trousers over his own, buttoned the tunic, squeezed his feet into the boots. Then he strapped the sentry's rifle to his back and went into the barn. He examined the nearest motorcycle carefully, opening its fuel tank to make certain it was filled. Its mechanism, he saw, scarcely differed from British motorcycles he had used.

From one of the walls he took down a tropical pith helmet and donned it, then slung two message pouches over his shoulders. He stuck a hand into a pool of oil and lightly touched his face with it. At the last minute he remembered, and went back to the hanging tunics, rifling them and taking out some letters, which he held in his hand. He had seen too much of the German thoroughness to believe he was away yet.

He took the first motorcycle and wheeled it out of the barn. Then, still rolling it, he went for some fifty yards before, with one quick motion, he stood on the starter and got the motor going. He took the road to Tiola.

A moment after his motor had shattered the night quiet with its hammering cough, two searchlights down the road switched on, and standing in its light were three soldiers. They trained the light on him as he swept past them. They shouted at him, and he waved the papers in his hand and shouted back. *"Zum teufel!"* he yelled, wondering if it was appropriate. It sounded good.

Two hundred yards farther down, more lights caught him, and he had to swerve to avoid hitting the men. It happened once more, but each time the papers and his refusal to stop carried him through. Each time there had been rifles held in readiness; at the second post an officer had waved a pistol.

But he was through. The light of the motorcycle stabbed the road before him as he roared through darkness, going like hell.

CHAPTER SEVEN

BY NINE o'clock, Major Von Bruckner had finished his inquiry. He hardly touched his breakfast, notwithstanding the real coffee that had been brewed. Hill face was a mask of quiescent fury. Now and then he touched his head and his eyes closed in pain. He had already taken four aspirins, but there was no relief.

He had blundered that morning, badly, stupidly, perhaps irrevocably. Beidermann would not forget, he was certain; Beidermann had been Kohler's closest friend. He glanced up at the somber faces of the officers who sat with him, watching their taut, nervous movements, listening to their quiet, sparse conversation—conversation that they forced on themselves, as if all feared an otherwise inevitable silence.

He had shocked them. He had wheeled on Beidermann, furious in his refusal to attend the burial ceremonies for Kohler and the two dead soldiers. "If he were alive," Von Bruckner had cried, shaking with rage, "I would have had him shot on the spot!"

It had been a violation of the officer's code. Kohler had died doing his duty, officer in charge of the camp guard...

He remembered how he had been awakened. The dawn edging into his room, the pounding on the door. He tumbled out of bed, bleary-eyed, his head hammering with pain, and when he opened the door, Captain Mayer had started to tell him, and then, looking past him, he had seen the girl, who was still in the room. Von Bruckner had forgotten about her. He had been asleep. But Mayer say her, and he fumbled the words he spoke.

And then he had slammed the door shut, dressing quickly, saying nothing to the awakened girl. When he went downstairs he saw the two dead soldiers. Outside, still untouched, the horrible sight of Kohler's sprawled corpse, lying in mud that had been formed with his blood...

They had reconstructed what had happened, for the most part. The torn bedsheet in the American's room, the missing trench knife, later found in the barn, the stolen pistol, the uniform, motorcycle...the way he had outwitted the camp guard posts...yes, theoretically, they could trace the bloody path on which Abbott had traveled. The man was a demon, a fiend, a monster. But if Kohler had been...

And that too had been a mistake, his enraged statement that Kohler had been guilty of crass neglect of duty. He should have known better than to have said that, after what Mayer had seen— or thought he had seen. Mayer had undoubtedly told the others, and though he was wrong, there was nothing that he, Von Bruckner, could do about it.

THE best thing was to forget it. They would be here for some time yet, and there would be time enough to demonstrate, subtly, that he realized he had been wrong. Perhaps next week he would order the graves decorated, and recommend Kohler for post-humous promotion and honors. Meanwhile, there was work to be done. Things were going wonderfully well. Regarded in the proper perspective, Abbott's escape was a painful, but minor, thorn. And he might very well be caught. Two patrols were scouring the countryside for him...

"Lieutenant Faber," said Von Bruckner, "we will postpone our plans for gathering several new gorillas until this afternoon, since the cages will not be ready before then, and—"

"I must apologize, sir," said Beidermann, stiffly. "The delay—"

"Quite understandable, Captain. No apology is necessary. Still, while you are at it, it might be wise to spread your materials and make provision for thirty animals."

"That would weaken the cages, sir. We have enough steel for some ten animals, though more will be in within the week."

"I don't think they need be quite that strong, Captain. All three gorillas were very quiet last night, and while we still do not know whether they broke out the night we found the hole under their shack, it appears they have not attempted it. It seems to me that it would be better to use what we have now to train the largest number we can accommodate. Do you agree?"

"Whatever you say, sir."

"Good. And you, Faber, can spend the morning with the three we have now. Do you intend to try teaching them the torpedo mechanism?"

"I'm not sure, sir, Lieutenant Prinzler said they were behaving queerly when they were fed this morning. Perhaps—"

"I will be glad to come along if you don't think you can handle the animals yourself."

"No, sir," said Faber. "I'm sure I can handle them."

"Very well, then," said Von Bruckner, rising. "I'll see you later." He started up the stairs to his room, glancing to the veranda, where Jeanne sat. He had not spoken to her all morning; he had been a fool with her too. But sleep would settle everything. The damnable headache would be gone with a little sleep, and the rage he still felt gnawing at his vitals would be not quite so sharp...

VON Bruckner sat up in bed suddenly, hearing the shooting. He ran to the window and saw nothing. The shooting was coming from the other direction, near the sheds. Now it stopped, and everything was quiet. He glanced at his watch, dressing quickly. He had been asleep three hours; it was now past noon.

He went down the stairs and met Prinzler coming to get him.

"What happened?"

"One of the gorillas, Major-Lieutenant Diemler had to shoot it when it attacked Faber!"

The Major brushed by him and ran outside, hurrying down the path toward the house where a score of soldiers had gathered. He saw the truck used to transport the gorillas standing near the shed. Faber was leaning against it, holding one of his arms, supported by a soldier.

Von Bruckner walked into the center of the circle. At his feet lay one of the gorillas, the one that wore the brassard numbered "2" on one of its arms. It was quite dead. It had been shot at least six times and a huge pool of blood was running swiftly from underneath its body. Its jaw had been half shot off, and the bullets of the .45 automatic had penetrated its body, tearing holes in the flesh of its back.

"Lieutenant Faber, what happened here?" Von Bruckner cried.

Faber's face was ghastly white. He bit his lips, as if to hold on to himself. He looked as if he were about to fall, but he stood there, unable to speak, gulping in mouthfuls of air. At this moment, Dr. Friedrich came hurrying up, Diemler, one of the three naval officers, carrying his bag.

The Doctor took Faber's hand away. A deep, jagged wound lay open for six inches along the arm, dark and discolored, embedded with shreds of cloth from the sleeve, which had been ripped so violently that its seams had parted at the shoulder. There was hardly any bleeding. At a word from Friedrich, Prinzler and Diemler took hold of Faber under the arms and began half-carrying him to the main house.

"Not you, Diemler," said the Major. "I want you here." Out of courtesy alone, for he could hardly speak, the way he felt, the Major said to Faber, "You'll be all right, Faber. I'll be with you shortly."

A glance from Von Bruckner had sent the soldiers scurrying. Now the Major examined the locks on the house, seeing that they had been snapped shut. He walked around to the barred window and looked in. One of the gorillas, wearing the number "3" brassard, was sitting quietly in a corner, looking at the floor. The other, with number "1" on its arm, was standing crouched over in the center of the floor, as if it had been pacing until this very moment and had stopped when it heard the Major at the window. A moment later it bounded across the floor and stuck a hand through the bars, narrowly missing its grab at Von Bruckner, who had jumped back.

THERE was a sound from inside, and the gorilla withdrew its arm. It gripped the bars and shook them until the timbers of the house shivered, its mouth open and fangs exposed, then abruptly it was gone.

Von Bruckner shook his head. He started back to the house.

"Lieutenant Diemler, tell me what happened here. Everything."

"We came back here, Faber and I, to bring back the first gorilla and get another. The first had been completely useless—"

"Useless? How do you mean?"

"Entirely, sir. That was the number "3" one. When we opened the door, it came out of its own accord and went into the truck. After that it did nothing Faber ordered. It seemed to be in bad temper, though it moved very sluggishly. We took it to the field, and it was half an hour before it would get out of the truck. We brought it some raw meat, but it didn't seem to be hungry. It climbed one of the trees in the grove and stayed there until Faber sent for a saw—then, astonishingly enough, it came down, as if it understood, though of course Faber spoke German."

"Go on."

"It was useless, sir. It refused to heed a single order. It just stood or sat, as it pleased, looking at us and doing nothing. After an hour it finally got into the machine, started it, ran it aimlessly for perhaps two or three minutes, then came out. It took us almost another hour to get it back to the truck.

"We decided to try another one, thinking the first one might have been ill. When we got back, Faber kept the gorilla from shutting the door on him. He told me that yesterday, each time he brought back one of the gorillas, it closed the door behind it, as if it had to hide something. He wanted to find out what it means, so when he opened the door he slipped a board through the back space…"

"You're quite sure about this door closing business, Diemler?"

"Yes, sir. Faber will tell you, sir. He kept the door open. I was right behind him. When the number "3" gorilla went in, it tried to close the door but couldn't. Then it seemed to make some sort of sound to the other gorillas, and when Faber pointed to the number "2" gorilla and told it to come out, it came quickly.

"But the moment I closed the locks, it seemed to go berserk. The first thing I heard, turning toward the truck, was a deep, snarling sound from the gorilla. Faber backed away from it and it leaped on him, clutching at the arm he pushed into its face. But for that arm, separating him from the gorilla, I might not have dared shoot. As it was, I ran in a step and fired point-blank. Then I went for the Doctor."

They had reached the house. Von Bruckner was lost in thought, his face inscrutable, his movements slow and absent-minded. He mounted the veranda silently and looked in. Friedrich was testing a hypodermic syringe, standing close to Faber. In spite of himself, Von Bruckner's mouth stretched thin and hard. He turned to Diemler. "I want Captains Mayer and Beidermann here, immediately."

BEIDERMANN came first, wearing an open shirt and a soiled field cap, covered with sweat. "Captain Beidermann," said Von Bruckner, "one of the gorillas attacked Faber a short while ago and had to be killed. Under the circumstances, you had better return to the original plan."

"I'm half through now, sir. If I have to start again, I can't hope to have them ready before nightfall."

Von Bruckner nodded and looked away, signifying that Beidermann was free to go. When Mayer came, the Major saw that he had been told what had happened. "Mayer, I want you to radio Tripoli or Dakar and have six bloodhounds flown here at once. By tonight, if possible. And specialists to take care of them. Mention Von Zweig if you have any trouble."

"Bloodhounds, sir?"

The Major almost shouted at Mayer. But no, not Mayer. Of all the officers, Mayer had been the closest to him. He wanted...needed...someone to talk to...

"Yes, Mayer. I don't know what the American did here last night before he escaped. You remember what Benno, Devoli's houseboy, told us about the drugs Devoli gave the gorilla? Maybe the American knew of other drugs. Maybe he gave some to the gorillas—I don't know. At any rate, in the event that our American returns, and he is fiend enough to try, I don't want to lose him— and I'm not sure our guards are a match for him. So we'll use dogs to trail a dog."

"Yes, sir," said Mayer. "As a matter of fact, I was about to see you. Ten minutes ago we started receiving a radio call from Dakar. It was in the urgent 33Y code. It said 'By special order of Marshall Von Zweig and Admiral Eherhardt and stopped there. A few minutes later, Dakar said the message would be sent within the hour."

"Thank you, Mayer. Be sure to call me."

He watched Mayer walk away. Strange, he thought. Had that ass Gleichenhaus made trouble so soon? But why should Von Zweig be in it—and what, in the devil's name, was Eherhardt's name doing in the message? An answer to his own message of last night—the excellent news? Congratulations, perhaps? It could be quite awkward, such a thing, at this time. What had Diemler omitted in his story? Diemler, loyally standing by that insufferable bungler, Faber. Navy officers standing together against the army— that kind of rot.

Near the sheds, Prinzler was leading a squad of men, carrying away the dead gorilla. Blood, nothing but blood since Abbott had escaped. Like a curse on the place. The thought made his skin crawl. He was filled with a strange sense of foreboding...

He got up suddenly and went inside. Friedrich was alone, gathering up his instruments. He had sent Faber to bed, to get some rest.

"Doctor, how is Devoli?" He was surprised at the uneven pitch of his voice.

"Better, *Herr* Major. He was able to eat this morning."

"I want to talk with him."

Dr. Friedrich hesitated, his eyes on his instruments. He said, quietly, apologetically, "May I ask if what you intend to say is liable to...to excite him?"

"Perhaps."

"I cannot be responsible." The Doctor shook his head. "In a few days, perhaps, after he has regained his strength..."

Von Bruckner was about to say something, but at the last moment he turned on his heel and went out. He walked down the road for half a mile, twice passing soldiers without returning their salute. When he returned, his staff had almost finished their lunch. He excused them from waiting for him, but to naval Lieutenants Diemler and Braun, he said, laconically, "We will resume work with the gorillas in half an hour."

FOR most of the ensuing half-hour, Von Bruckner sat at the table, thinking. He was unable to eat. He sipped black coffee and smoked a long cigar. Once he looked outside, hearing Jeanne Chaumont's voice, and his eyes followed her until she was out of sight, and then, to himself, he shook his head, and his scowl deepened...

Braun and Diemler were waiting for him when Von Bruckner went outside. He noticed that both officers had their sidearms lying in holsters on a table near them, as if waiting for the Major's permission to wear them. The Major nodded towards the guns. "You may need them, gentlemen," he said. "In addition, I want six men about the house, with rifles."

He went to the shack that housed the gorillas and looked in at the window. Nothing had changed. The number "3" gorilla was still sitting, hunched over; the other was pacing, only this time, seeing the Major at the window, it stopped and stared at him, making no move. He went around to the front and put a key in the lock, listening carefully as he did so. There was no sound from within, but when he rattled the lock noisily, he heard a soft grunting that seemed to come from near the door, where the sitting gorilla was.

In a few minutes, Braun returned with a sergeant and half a squad. They formed a semi-circle around the door, standing twenty feet away. Von Bruckner, unarmed, opened the first lock, then the second. He pushed the door open with a foot.

The eyes of both animals were on him. He let his breath in and out slowly, then, raising a hand, he pointed to the number "1" gorilla. "Come out," he said, his voice strong and even. Nothing happened for a moment, and then the squatting gorilla rose from its haunches. "Not you!" Von Bruckner said distinctly. "I want the—"

Later, Von Bruckner was not sure he had heard anything. Things happened too quickly for him to be able to separate the swift movements; it might easily have been the trick of an over-wrought imagination. The number "3" gorilla, coming towards him, had stopped uncertainly, and from its half open mouth a solitary sound had come—a sound that might have been the word *if.* Whatever it was, it was never finished, for at that moment the other gorilla swung its shoulders forward and left its feet in its leap at Von Bruckner!

In the same instant the Major stepped back and out. He curled around, his back against the outside wall, then let himself fall sideways to the base of the wall. The movement had taken him beyond the reach of the gorilla and then freed the area for the riflemen, though the maneuver baffled them for a fraction of an instant. In that time, the gorilla, rushing forward, either because it had lost sight of the Major or because it ignored him, had covered half the distance to the nearest soldier, a horrible, throaty cry trailing behind it.

A fusillade of shots cracked out. The gorilla stopped in its forward motion as if it had run into a wall. Its voice stopped quite suddenly and it pitched backward on its spine. It lay there, flailing an arm, grasping the air, until Braun stepped in and emptied his pistol into its brain.

BY THEN Von Bruckner was on his feet again. He reached the open door together with Diemler. The Lieutenant had been about to slam the door shut, but the Major caught his hand. He looked in and saw the last of the three gorillas as it stood there, motionless as a tree, its head inclined, its eyes on the scene that lay behind the Major.

"Leave the door open!" Von Bruckner cried. He walked up to where the dead gorilla lay. "Take it away," he said to Braun, quietly. "We are going to try the other one."

But he couldn't disguise the unsteadiness of his hand when he took the cigarette Diemler offered him. He stood there, clotted dirt clinging to the perspiration that soaked him, smoking quickly and watching the soldiers drag off the dead gorilla. After a few moments, as if he had lost track of time, he thanked Diemler for the cigarette.

"Major Von Bruckner, perhaps...perhaps it would be advisable to wait before doing anything else."

The Major said nothing, and Diemler said, "For Dr. Devoli, I mean, sir. There must be something about these animals we do not know."

Von Bruckner shook his head slowly. Long, brittle lines furrowed his forehead. He turned the cigarette in his hand, regarding it, and when he spoke his voice had the soft, rigidly controlled note of near panic in it. "Yes, Diemler, of course," he said, as if the reasonableness of his words was a drug to soothe him. "But you see, whatever it is, we do not know—whatever it is, we must find it for ourselves. We must know exactly..."

But it was no use. His voice died away, and he knew he had made no sense. The panic was growing within him...

"Diemler, get the men ready."

The door to the little shack had been left open all this time. Now, as the soldiers assumed their positions, Von Bruckner started walking toward the open door.

"Major Von Bruckner!"

The Major stopped and turned around, and his breath escaped in a sigh, as if he had been reprieved from an obligation he feared. It was Captain Mayer who had called him. The Captain came hurrying.

"Major, this is of the utmost importance."

He handed Von Bruckner a sealed, red-striped envelope. The Major opened it and saw the heading: *Strictly Confidential: Code 33Y.*

The words swam before him, little ciphers struggling in a sea of paper. He read them a second time, a third.

"By special order of Marshal Von Zweig and Admiral Eberhardt: News magnificent. Time now of utmost importance. Assign staff to clear details, while proceeding immediately to Dakar with ten of the trained operators. Plane on the way to you, Congratulations."

Von Bruckner held his hand up to his eyes, and when he looked up they were wide and fixed. "Did you acknowledge this?" he breathed.

"Of course, sir. At once."

The Major nodded to himself. "Of course," he whispered. It was inconceivable. They wanted him to bring ten trained gorillas to Dakar. Something very important. He knew that. Ten...when he had one, and that one completely... It was imperative for him to get a grip on himself, to work out the answer, to tell Von Zweig...

"Mayer!" he cried, sharply. "The message we sent last night—what did it say?"

"I have a copy right here, sir. I'll read it: *Mission successful beyond all expectations. Operators on hand already fully capable in all but smallest details. Others expected to equal these. Will remain here long enough to establish routine, then—*"

"Stop, Mayer." He took the paper and crumpled it with a savage move. "I'll..." he began to say, when he started suddenly toward the door of the little shack.

HE TOOK no more than three or four steps, then clutched at his stomach. The blood on the ground...the blood, its horrible, nauseating odor...it was on his boots...it was everywhere...it rose from the ground, from the stained, muddy rivulets in invisible waves, choking him...

He turned around and began to retch. As the officers came toward him he waved them away. He walked back to the truck and sat down on its running board, cleaning his face with a handkerchief. "Mayer," he said. "Wire Dakar. Tell them..." But he looked into Mayer's face and he saw what he was doing.

No, there was nothing he could wire Dakar now. He had gone too far. He could not ask for time. He could not confess even temporary failure; there were no failures in the army of the Third Reich...

He heard the noise as if from a distance, the staccato bursts of the car's exhaust, the men's voices. A car came speeding through the huge, billowing clouds of its dust. It stopped before the main house and men leaped out, like gray-brown figures in a dusty dream, supporting another soldier. Lieutenant Keller, who was with them, dashed into the house. A moment afterward he came out, running towards Von Bruckner, calling the others.

"Major Von Bruckner—both our our patrols have been ambushed—"

It was the way Von Bruckner looked at him—a hard, wild look—that stopped Keller. The Major slowly rose to his feet. "What are you saying, Keller?"

"The American is in Tiola with a large force of French. Both the patrols we sent after him were annihilated! Only this man escaped."

They had brought the soldier to Von Bruckner by then. He was a disheveled, weary young boy, perhaps twenty years old. There was a long, ugly wound on one side of his head. His uniform hung on his exhausted frame in bloody, filthy tatters.

"Ambushed, sir," he practically gasped. "A hundred and fifty of them…armed with rifles…coming here tonight to attack…"

Von Bruckner, motionless, impassive, heard the story. The first patrol had gone through Tiola; the second had been contacted by a spy and told that Abbott was hiding near Tiola, gathering the Free French. But the spy had not known how far the preparations had gone…

He heard it all before he spoke—the encircling of the camp, the ambush from both sides of a deep ravine; they had shot the tires of the soldier's motorcycle and it had thrown him down an embankment. And the charge of the French, refusing to take prisoners, killing everything. And the arrival of the second patrol before it could be warned, the fierce, hopeless, out-numbered struggle.

When he was through, Von Bruckner said, quietly, "Do they know you escaped?"

"No, sir. I lay hidden for hours…they searched everywhere for survivors, killing those they found…they were afraid you might learn of their plans to attack tonight…"

The Major took a deep breath, and then he did an unusual thing for him. He shook the soldier's hand warmly and thanked him more with the slight inclination of his head than with words, and then, turning sharply to Mayer and the other officers, he motioned them to follow him a few feet away.

"Captain Mayer, wire Dakar. Inform them we are momentarily expecting an assault in force and cannot undertake to carry out the orders just sent us. Tell them we are greatly outnumbered and require assistance and heavy arms. Braun, call a staff meeting in fifteen minutes. Diemler, post every available man on guard duty and pass out full allotments of ammunition."

He took a few steps toward the house, when suddenly he stopped, returning to the shack. The door was still open; the soldiers still on guard. The Major looked in at the gorilla. It was sitting on its haunches in a corner, its eyes fixed on the square rectangle of light that was the door. For a long, still moment Von Bruckner regarded the animal, then he closed the door.

"Keller," he said, to the waiting officer, "have you seen *fraulein* Chaumont?"

"No, sir."

"Find her and confine her to her room. I hold you responsible."

LATER, at the staff meeting, Von Bruckner made his plans. He went over the gun emplacements that Beidermann had laid out, the provisions for supply, the concentration of men.

"By six o'clock," said Mayer, "three transports with parachute troops will land—"

"No, Mayer," he said, quietly. "I believe Captain Beidermann has other plans." By way of explanation, almost, he added, "Beidermann is our tactical expert, as you know; I believe it will be wisest to put the battle plan in his hands."

Beidermann, nodding, said, "The first planes, transporting the material, will be here by five, I believe? Well, then, Prinzler will go back with one of the planes to Rhamtoola, where he will meet the commanding officer of the parachutists. There, Prinzler, you will see to it that the officers and pilots are well acquainted with the terrain and our emplacements, also our signals. The planes are to leave Dakar in time to be here at nine o'clock—it will not be dark until then—but they are not to come here.

"They are to take full gasoline rations—you will so notify Dakar, Mayer? And they will hover some fifty miles from here, due south, over the jungle, about here…" He pointed to an area on the large map stretched before them. "We will be in close radio communication with them. At our command, they will proceed here, dropping their men according to pre-arranged signals. Understood?"

They went on, planning the patrol activity, arranging for scouts and spies, location of mines, deploying of emergency squads. Now that they were planning combat, their spirits were higher. None mentioned the thoughts that lay buried deep within them, the confusion and wonder at what had happened to the main plan that had brought them all here, but Von Bruckner could not keep the thoughts from his mind.

Over and over he mulled the fragmentary facts he had gathered, trying to fit them together. The battle would go well, he knew; his men were well fitted for their jobs, specialists all. But what would follow? After this momentary respite, what would he do about following the orders Von Zweig had sent? Because from the subsequent—

"What about the Chaumont girl?" Keller interrupted. "Am I to assume she is under arrest, sir?"

Keller's remark was news to the officers; none had known of Von Bruckner's order. The Major nodded. He had been thinking of her, in the back of his mind, at the moment Keller spoke.

"Yes," said Von Bruckner. "I am convinced that she had a large part in the gathering of these traitorous French..." He spoke now half to explain to his officers, half to let his words shape the direction of his thoughts, for somewhere this girl kept returning to his mind, as if she held the key to many of the new problems that confronted him.

"She must have been instrumental in arranging Abbott's escape," he went on, knowing that he was indicting himself as he spoke. "But it is certain that Abbott alone, a stranger here, could never by himself have brought this guerrilla army together. No, this Chaumont woman is a member of the underground, and her plans have been carefully arranged beforehand, for days, perhaps.

"That is why we are being so cautious in dealing with these French, for we must either kill or capture every last one of them. We must get our hands on Abbott again. It is only by getting together all the factors involved in this...this..."

HE LET his voice die away and he fingered the radio message that Mayer had brought him, the one Von Zweig had sent in answer to the Major's information about the impending attack. He tapped his fingers on the paper.

"We came originally," he said, accenting his words by a slow nodding of his head, "to spend a long time here on a plan that we considered had excellent possibilities of success. That such success was indeed possible, we have all seen. Perhaps I was premature in so informing the High Command, for they have now included us in an extremely vital tactic within the next few days."

He lifted the paper and let it fall. "Gentlemen, an American fleet is crossing the Atlantic to reinforce the British and Russians in the east. Our information is that some twenty warships are escorting almost a hundred cargo vessels of every description, with planes and tanks and munitions. Such a convoy might decide the battle for Suez, for the Caucasus...possibly the war. The Americans are expected to sail through the Mediterranean; the tactic is daring, but we expect daring from them. A few weeks ago the American carrier *Wasp* put in at Malta, you will recall.

"We must bring all our force to meet them. The Italian fleet is next to useless. Our Africa and Sicily based planes will be matched by carrier-borne planes from the fleet; our submarines cannot be expected to do much damage, especially if the British, as we expect them to, send out a large convoy of destroyers to meet them.

"But if we could put ten of our little submarines into action— into that decisive action—if we could sink the carriers and some of the cruisers—then, gentlemen, we would be safeguarding a victory that is almost ours..."

He looked around at them, knowing the effect of his words.

"Marshal Von Zweig has told us everything, you see," he nodded. "He wants us to understand how great our role is, how incalculably valuable we are to his plans. The Marshall does not know that the success we thought we had achieved yesterday is not as complete as we thought. At this moment it appears far off indeed, if not hopeless."

He lit a cigarette and waved it in a hand before him. "But it is not hopeless, believe me. The problems must be solved and they will be solved. We must now get ready to remove an obstacle, to accomplish a task with utmost caution and determination. Understanding the role of this Chaumont woman, and once we have Abbott in our hands, I believe we will find the answers that now seem so elusive to us…"

A macabre smile lit his lean features as he added, "We have not yet exhausted our resources. We have ideas, which, while they do not concern all of you immediately, may speedily end our difficulties. I leave you that thought, and I ask each of you to remember what has been asked of us. Good luck."

He watched them file out, and long after they had gone he was standing there. The smile that had been on his face had long since faded, and now, alone, he felt he could scarcely draw another breath. His mind kept exploring the myriad, meaningless tunnels of thought that had been dug in his brain, exhausting him.

He thought of the optimism with which he had spoken to his men. He had handled it well; he was certain they believed him. Now, if anything were to happen to him, they would remember that Von Bruckner had been on the verge of success. If anything were to happen to him…

It would be easy, when it was time. They would say: *"He was a man of exceptional bravery. He rushed into the enemy's point-blank fire, leading his men. His death is a great loss to the Feuhrer…"* There was no other way out for him now, and he felt almost thankful that the exit had been left him, and when he thought of the impending battle, he felt nothing…nothing but a calm, cold, numbness…

CHAPTER EIGHT

THEY were ready. In the cool of descending night, the air had a quiet, electric feel to it, a hushed expectancy. Lights flickered in several places in the camp and there was no one about, but if one listened closely, one could hear the strains of an accordion playing. That was Beidermann's idea—it sounded relaxed, normal.

Six planes had arrived during the afternoon, gliding in soundlessly. They had brought almost as much as had been hoped for, and Beidermann had toiled ceaselessly, supervising everything. Every little hillock, each declivity, was known and accounted for. The mobile force was in position, waiting the signal.

At a quarter past eleven, a courier came back with news. A French scout had been observed edging through their lines. He had been allowed to come and go. Later, other scouts felt the patrol lines, and, acting under instruction, one patrol had challenged the empty air, as it were, and allowed the scouts to go on, thinking they had eluded the patrol, deceived it into believing they were mistaken. At half-past eleven, a general movement was observed and left unhindered; a long column of the enemy was moving down in a south-easterly direction, evidently intent on attacking from the least logical sector—the south.

They were carrying several machine guns, but most of the men were armed with rifles and grenades. Approximately a hundred and fifty men were counted in the southern sector. These broke into smaller units and formed a fan. Fifty more went due east, and a small force began edging in through the north patrols.

"The attack," said Beidermann, "will begin with a surprise assault on the sentry patrols in the north. The moment we rush to their defense, the enemy will start a feint from the northeast. When we answer that, the main force will come up from the south, with the intention of taking the camp itself and whatever materiel is there. And so our plan is as follows…"

* * *

AT TEN minutes past twelve, shortly after the changing of the patrol, which was carried through normally, it began to rain. It was an unseasonal rain, warm and dirty, and coming from heavy, low-flying cloud formations that scudded before a growing wind. Far to the east there were rumbles of thunder.

Beidermann said, "The attack will begin at any moment—they cannot afford to be discovered if there should be lightning."

Five minutes later, shots were heard from the north patrol and a red rocket flare shot into the dirty sky. Pre-arranged lights began flaring everywhere in camp, and a squad of soldiers began running about with lanterns, calling loudly, simulating a camp coming to life. A few moments later, two scout cars went roaring down the road with throttles wide open. A searchlight opened up from the second north patrol and was promptly shattered. Two more patrol cars swept down the road but like the first two, they were empty, save for their drivers and a single man armed with an automatic rifle.

Von Bruckner put on a raincoat and started out the door when Beidermann stopped him. "We are fighting, Beidermann," said the Major. "Did you think I would remain here?"

"But at any moment now—"

The Major shook his head and walked past him, down the veranda, looking toward the north. Almost immediately, shooting had followed from the northeast. He knew the patrols, scattering to meet it, would fall back at first, offering little resistance. In the barns and sheds every spare motor was started running, and more searchlights began to flick on, sweeping the fields. Trucks filled with troops rode out of camp toward the northeast. After a few hundred yards they stopped and the men leaped out and started running back toward camp while the empty trucks roared ahead.

The rain was coming down in thick sheets, turning the roads to rivers of mud, putting a gray haze over everything. The northeast sector was blazing with activity. Beidermann had planted guns and mortars there long before, but the French, not knowing this, could only assume that the guns were being transported there. A small holding force, long in position, gradually began to reveal itself, firing from new, unexpected places, as if it had just arrived.

Von Bruckner started for the large barn just as a star shell went up and hung in the murky, wet sky. Far below it, tracer bullets cut the night into innumerable thin slices. Two mortars opened up, and the light of the star shell showed a dark, two-headed mountain of earth rising up suddenly, falling back silently. The French were making no attempt to gain ground, content to draw off the Germans.

In the barn, Lieutenant Keller, in charge of supply, was arranging the flow of materiel. The bulk of their forces were already moving for the south, adding to the main forces stationed there. As the Major entered, the radio speaker beside Keller spoke. It was Beidermann's voice. *"Achtung, Lieutenant Keller! Ready to move truckloads of motorcycles at once!"* There was a pause, and Beidermann spoke again, this time to the northeast sector: *"Achtung, Lieutenant Mittler! Begin counter-attack at your discretion!"* The effect of the counter-attack would lead the enemy to believe the Germans had arrived there in force.

Von Bruckner went up to Keller. "Lieutenant, you will take me in this scout car to the south sector. Assign the sergeant to your duties." He said it in a way that forbade Keller even the attempt at objection. He sat down in the car, and a moment later they left, cutting behind the barn and starting a wide circle toward where the French had concentrated their largest force.

THE sky was an angry mixture of brown and red fire, swept by rain and wind, carrying the hammer and thunder of battle in gusts. They had gone no more than a hundred yards when a searchlight, sweeping the field, caught them in its beam, and instantly, a second swung over and held them. The next instant they both swept by and the radio in the car spoke. *"Achtung, Major Von Bruckner; Lieutenant Keller! Return at once to headquarters by order of Captain Beidermann!"*

"I am going back, sir," Keller said, turning the car around.

There was nothing the Major could do. The circumstances of battle were such that even a Lieutenant might, under certain conditions, command a Field Marshal. The command of the battle was Beidermann's; it could not be countermanded without his full authority being taken away.

A star shell went up, and a second, fired in the northeast, went streaking crazily along the horizon and exploded fifteen feet from the ground, two hundred yards away. Suddenly, Von Bruckner gasped something and switched on the headlights of the car.

"The gorilla!" Keller shouted.

In that instant, as abruptly as it had started, the rain stopped. The gorilla stood there, crouching, staring into the lights of the car as if they had hypnotized it. It was breathing heavily and it was drenched, its shaggy hair clotted, glistening in the light, then slowly, it backed away and loped out of range of the lights.

"After it!" Von Bruckner cried. Swiftly, Keller started the car again, and suddenly hell opened up in the southern sector. A dozen star shells flew into the clearing sky, making it as light as day, weird with shadows and reflected light, ablaze with gunfire. The hammering of new motors mingled with the broken stutter of machine guns—that would be the mobile force, Von Bruckner realized. They would break through the enemy's fan, coming up behind it, herding the enemy toward concealed gun emplacements...

They were almost at the house when the new cry of alarm went up in camp. The searchlights had picked a mass of cavalry moving down from the silent north sector. There had been no provision for them!

Instinctively, Keller swung the wheel and started for the north, and as he did so, Captain Mayer came running out on the veranda, calling to them. But his voice was drowned out by the shouts of those who swept past him—technicians, supply men, the house guard, the radio men—all were running toward the barn, grabbing what weapons were left, jumping into cars, forging north to plug the gap.

This was Von Bruckner's chance! He climbed into the back, balancing himself as the car lurched ahead, riflemen hanging to its sides, and he fired a quick test burst from the mounted machine gun. A staccato thunder came down from the sky, and he realized that Beidermann had called in the plane and its parachutists!

Out of the night, held in crossbeams of light, the first wave of horsemen swept down toward the camp. A hundred and fifty yards, a hundred, seventy-five...sixty...and the field opened its fire on the charging cavalry! Fifty yards away, two horses reared in terror and fell back on their haunches. Another rode into them, its rider leaping off at the last moment. The moment he set foot to the ground he clutched at his belly and pitched forward. The horsemen behind him came surging through, trampling over the fallen mounts. The searchlights had made them perfect targets, but their speed had brought the bulk of them safely into such close range that the lights now revealed friend and foe alike.

VON BRUCKNER, standing erect, swung the machine gun on its pivot, guiding its hail of death. Eight or nine horsemen, having broken through the lines, wheeled and made for his car, the center of resistance. Von Bruckner swung the gun and squeezed the trigger. Two lights came full on the charging cavalry, paling the little orange flicks of fire from their pistols. The windshield was shattered and opaque; in the front seat, Keller, who had been firing a carbine, let the gun fall from his hands and slumped gently against the door. A soldier beside the Major screamed and fell over the gun.

The Major threw him out of the car with a sweep of his arm. He crouched beside his gun. He could see the men's faces, the foam on the horses' mouths. His gun spat at them, slashing them. Two horsemen went down, a third, a fourth, saber raised, fell against his mount's neck and the horse veered and headed into camp. A fifth went down as if it had run into a wall, but on they came.

Fifteen yards, ten, five—and they were at the car itself, plunging past it, wheeling, returning to attack. The world became an inferno of flame and thunder. A horseman swung up alongside of the car and slashed his saber. It cut into the side of a soldier who stood at Von Bruckner's side. The saber swung upward again and the Major fired his automatic—he could have touched the horseman. Again the Major fired and the bullet opened a black hole close to the horseman's mouth.

A group of soldiers had fought their way through the swirling melee to the car, and with bayonets they fought off the succeeding charges, thrusting the dripping weapons into horses and riders alike. Of the original group that had charged the car, none were now left. The Major's gun had accounted for more than a third of the total cavalry.

Some had broken through and continued to the house. He had heard shooting everywhere, in the barns, the sheds, the center of camp. A fire had been started in one of the sheds; it had blazed up furiously, lending a red pall to the terrible scene of death, but it had been put out. What was left of the attacking forces had gathered again for a new assault, starting closer this time.

But now the fields behind them opened with fresh, deadly bursts of fire, coming from the tommy guns of the paratroops. Von Bruckner could remember, vaguely, the sound of the plane coming and returning two or three times, and once, looking up, he had seen little puffs like small white clouds floating down close together.

The advancing paratroops broke up the new attack before it could begin. The gathered horsemen scattered to avoid forming a concentrated target, and as they each made off, the searchlights picked them up and held them until they were cut down. And now, almost for the first time, Von Bruckner became conscious of the sounds that had dinned in his ears all through the battle—men shouting, screaming, cursing, praying—horses, whinnying with terror, rearing and plunging, rifle fire and the steady clatter of machine guns. The sounds had quieted now, but he could still hear them. Somewhere near him a man was sobbing.

He saw Captain Mayer come running toward him. When Mayer was at his side, he could not hear what he was saying. He stood there, drunkenly, seeing the dead men on all sides of him, feeling the blood on his hands, seeing for the first time that his right arm had been slashed by a saber. The camp was still alive with the sounds of battle as isolated horsemen were caught, but the battle was over. The paratroops had come out of the fields and into camp.

"Major Von Bruckner—the gorilla—it's in the house!"

VON BRUCKNER, listening, could hear the occasional explosion of mortars in the south sector and once a machine gun chattered, but for the most part the only sounds there were of motors. There were still motorcycles leaving camp for the south sector—in effect, three separate battles had been fought, and now the last was ending.

Slowly, the Major turned to Mayer, hearing what he had said for the first time. "I tried to call you before," Mayer was saying, "when the gorilla first went to Devoli's room—"

"What are you saying?"

"It's in there with him—it's talking to him!"

Von Bruckner shook his head. He took hold of Mayer's arm and climbed out of the car. Then, quickly, he began walking toward the house while Mayer told him what had happened. The gorilla had escaped during the battle—it had smashed open the door to its shack and run into the fields, and then, for some reason, it had returned to Devoli's house and it had gone straight to Devoli's room. One of the men had shot at it and missed, but when the gorilla made no move, continuing on its way without molesting anyone, Beidermann had ordered the men to let the beast do what it wanted, and he had sent Mayer to call the Major.

All during the battle, the gorilla had remained in Devoli's room, talking to him. Devoli had been unconscious part of the time, and later Mayer had recorded part of their conversation. The gorilla was still with him...

Reaching the house, the Major went straight to Devoli's room. Outside the door, together with several technicians who were busy with recording machinery, was Lieutenant Faber. His eyes were shining and his face was alive with fever and excitement.

"Don't go in, sir," he whispered anxiously. "We've everything here! We've found out about the drugs—the girl has some..."

Von Bruckner nodded as Faber, listening through earphones, let his voice die away. Presently, Faber said, "Dr. Devoli wants the gorilla to leave now—to run away. It doesn't seem to understand him. He's had to say the same things over and over many times before—the gorilla is useless without the drug and—*it's coming out!*"

At a quick signal, the men backed away. Slowly, the door opened, and the gorilla came out. Its eyes were tiny and bloodshot and dull, with little understanding in them, and its manner was docile, lethargic. It started walking through the group of men, when Faber said, "Go back to your house and stay there. I'll bring you the girl and the drug."

The gorilla turned towards Faber. Its mouth opened and moved soundlessly a moment, then it spoke, and its voice was a deep, rumbling sound, throaty and uncertain. "Yes, I will...wait...but bring...the..." And then, without finishing, it ran a hand over its lips, touching them, as if bewildered by its own act of speaking, and ever so slowly, it walked away, going out.

Faber turned to two of the technicians. "Stay with it," he ordered. "See that no one harms it. Keep the men away from it."

Von Bruckner watched the great beast until it was gone. He could not understand the meaning of what he had seen, but his mind was spinning, trying to see where this fitted in with what he had thought. He felt a fire in him, a tremendous anxiety. He grasped Faber's arm—it was the bad one—and cried, "Let me hear the records, Lieutenant!"

∗   ∗   ∗

HALF an hour later, Von Bruckner said, quietly, "There are certain parts I want to hear again. I'll go through it once more," He lit a cigarette deliberately, puffed once or twice and scanned the notes he had made. One of Mayer's men was taking down the whole thing in shorthand. Beidermann, in the field, had shortly before radioed in that he had taken Abbott prisoner and was bringing him in.

"Begin," said Von Bruckner.

And so he heard it again, the incredible conversation, the soft, strained voice of Dr. Devoli speaking to the gorilla and the gorilla, seldom understanding without repetition, its mind chaotic, filled with fear of the noises that kept breaking into their conversation, starting and jumping, and Devoli trying to keep it quiet, trying to make it understand, crying out feebly…

"Get the drug," said Devoli. "There is a girl here, a friend, who has the drug you need."

"Drug…The girl is very beautiful…"

"Go to her. She has the drug I have been giving you. It will clear your mind. There are things you must understand here. The Major is my enemy. He must be destroyed. You must not do anything he—"

"Enemy? But you said…he was your friend. I want to tell you why I wore the clothes you gave me…that night in the jungle…"

"It does not matter. I understand. Listen to me! You must go to the girl. She has the drug you need. Do not do anything to these men here until you have the drug. They are my enemies."

"The girl is very beautiful. I will go to her."

"These men here are fighting against friends of mine. After you have the drug, you will understand why you must destroy them. You must save my friend Abbott and the girl, and you must not do what these men tell you to do."

"They want me to tell the others…they killed Yawwa and Moga…Yawwa and Moga were angry…they wanted to return to the jungle…and I want to return…"

"And you will return, but first you must help my friends to escape. It will be easier for you after you have gotten the drug. You must not fear it. It will clear your mind. It will quiet the emotions that trouble you. You must overcome the emotions..."

"The girl is beautiful. I want to go to her because she..."

"Listen to me. Listen to what I am saying!"

"But I want to help you. I want to take you with me. Why do you say these men are your enemies? You said the Major was a friend..."

"Listen to me. The gorillas all obey you. You must not do—"

"Pardon me, sir," interrupted Lieutenant Braun. "Captain Beidermann is arriving."

Von Bruckner got up, signifying he had heard as much as he wanted. Outside he heard the sounds of motors coming out of the south, and he went out to the veranda with Mayer. Searchlights were trained on the large central area of the camp, making everything bright. Troops stood at attention; the parachutists came out of the sheds, junior officers barked orders.

To Faber, the Major said, "Go to Chaumont's room. Search it thoroughly—tear her clothes to bits, if you have to, but bring me all her personal belongings and the drug."

THE mobile force came riding into camp, escorting trucks filled with prisoners, and at the head of the column was Beidermann, in his scout car. He had come through unscathed, a bright, calm figure in his yellow oilskin coat, blinking in the glare of the lights. He got out of the car and waited for the trucks to begin unloading. The prisoners came out of the trucks, tired, ragged, many of them wounded, soaked to the skin. They began filing into the barn quietly, like trapped animals, and then Beidermann spoke to an officer beside him, and the officer pointed to one of the prisoners, who was taken out of the line and taken off by himself, under heavy guard. It was Abbott.

Then Beidermann came up to the veranda and saluted smartly, and Von Bruckner could see how weary he was. "Sir, I have the honor to inform you that the task you assigned me has been successfully completed."

Von Bruckner took his hand and led him inside. There was little formality in the way he thanked Beidermann, and when

Beidermann started to say that he knew what the Major had done... "Without your inspired leadership against the cavalry attack, sir, all might have been lost."

Von Bruckner passed over it quickly, asking questions about the battle. Remembering how, a few hours before, he had been prepared to die, he felt an intolerable anger toward himself. He felt re-born now, confident. He spoke of the details of what had happened, asking questions about Abbott. The American had killed many men before he was captured.

"We'll deal with him later," said Von Bruckner. "We may need him, but right now we must decide as to the disposition of the others." Lieutenant Faber came down the stairs, carrying a handkerchief in one hand. He saw the two officers together and went to the other end of the room. Von Bruckner said, "I will read a general order of court martial."

"Sir, do you intend to—" Beidermann began.

"What else would you do?"

Beidermann nodded. "Technically we are correct, sir. These men have no status as prisoners of war, since their country is not at war. They are bandits, with no belligerent rights."

"Well put, Captain. You will execute them in the morning."

He went to Faber and took the handkerchief. Inside were three capsules, filled with a pale green powder. Von Bruckner's face twisted as he juggled the capsules around in his hand. "Is that all?"

"Yes, sir. She had nothing else. Some clothes, a photograph, bits of jewelry—I believe the drug was what you wanted, sir?"

"Of course. Will you tell Captain Mayer that I would like the entire staff assembled here as soon as the situation is in order? And then join me—I will be in Devoli's room."

He went down the short hall and let himself into Devoli's room. Dr. Friedrich was there.

Von Bruckner said, "What are you doing here?"

"He is very ill," said Friedrich, anxiously. "The gorilla—"

"We have dozens of our own wounded, Doctor," the Major snapped. "Join the other doctors at once."

When Friedrich had left, Von Bruckner stood beside Devoli's bed. The old man lay with his eyes open, looking up at him. Dry bits of spittle hung from his lips. His eyes were dull and lusterless, but he said softly, "I know what you're doing… You'll never win…"

Von Bruckner smiled and sat down.

He opened his hand and showed Devoli the three capsules. "I don't think you're too ill to understand this, Doctor?"

The old man's head moved from side to side. His white hair seemed yellow and brittle, and his face shone with waxy pallor. "It will do you no good," he whispered. "If you use the drug, either he will kill you…or you will have to kill him…"

"But there are other gorillas, Doctor. We can duplicate the compound of this wonderful drug of yours."

The faintest suggestion of a smile, distorted, ironic, flitted across the aged man's face. He lifted himself half out of bed on his elbows, staring at Von Bruckner. *"There is only one gorilla,"* he whispered. *"Did you know that—only one gorilla?"*

VON BRUCKNER sprang to his feet, his hands clenched, then suddenly he grabbed the old man's bedclothes and knotted them in his hands. "You old fool," he rasped. "Did you think I didn't know that?" His face was livid, his voice low and furious, but filled with triumph. "There are things about your gorilla that even you didn't know."

When he let Devoli fall back to the bed, the old man continued staring at him, and the smile remained, then little by little his eyes began to close, and his features relaxed. His breath caught in his throat once and then he was still. But even after he had died, the corners of his mouth remained fixed, as if he were still smiling.

They were still thus, the dead man and Von Bruckner, when Faber came in minutes later. Faber stood beside the bed, looking down at the old man, seeing he was dead. Slowly Von Bruckner stood up.

"We were right, Faber," he said. "There was only one gorilla— the one that spoke, the one that changed the brassards." He nodded to himself as he went on speaking, as if confirming his thoughts. "Devoli kept its understanding with this drug…"

He held out the three capsules, then one by one he opened them and spilled their contents into his palm. He looked at the powder and slowly turned his hand over, so that the little grains fell to the floor.

"But, Major, that drug—"

"No, Faber. We have no use for the drug any longer. It was a weapon in our enemy's hands—but we have a better weapon—*we know how to control the gorilla without the drug!*"

"I'm afraid I don't understand, sir."

Von Bruckner nodded. "Think, Faber, think. All this time there was one gorilla, understanding everything about us, yet doing nothing to hinder us. Why? What bond kept it here? It had not been given this drug for days—what kept it obedient? Tonight, frightened by the sounds of battle, it started to run off. Yet when it saw us, its first instinctive move was to return to Devoli. Why? And you remember how it kept saying again and again that it wanted to protect Devoli...that it thought of the girl...

"What lay behind all this? An emotion, Faber—*some kind of an emotion*... It didn't matter which emotion. It acted where the drug didn't. And now that we know this, we also know how to play on this animal's emotions..."

His eyes kindled into fire as he gripped Faber's arm, and he said, softly, "I am going to play on this animal's emotions, and the price of our victory will be the doom of our enemies! They will provide the motivating power for its emotions."

Von Bruckner left the room abruptly, moving quickly. He went through the living room where several officers had already come and went outside. There were lights in the east field, shining on the transport plane that had landed not long before. There was movement everywhere, men bringing in equipment, assisting the wounded, eating, smoking. He crossed the center of camp to the improvised hospital. It was filled with the odors of dead and wounded, with the sweet smell of ether and the sharp pungency of medicines, with the sounds, metallic and human, that followed the wake of battle.

There he took aside one of the doctors and showed him the empty capsules. "Fill these with a light green powder," he said. "It doesn't matter what—something harmless."

A FEW minutes later he left, walking toward the little shack where the gorilla had been housed, and where it had gone again. As he passed through the sentry lines, and as the soldiers saw him, the word spread quickly. He felt the tense expectancy of the soldier from whom he borrowed a flashlight. The broken door had been hastily repaired with stout timbers, but there was no lock.

Without pausing he opened the door and went in. His flashlight pierced the interior darkness with a slender white beam, like a finger searching, and the finger found the gorilla standing at the window. He struck a match and turned the wick up inside a lantern... Soft, yellow light flooded the room.

Von Bruckner stood there silently, then he held up a capsule between thumb and forefinger. "I've brought you the drug," he said, walking toward the gorilla, his hand outstretched. "Dr. Devoli and I just spoke about you. He told me the truth about you—"

"No."

The Major stopped advancing. He didn't understand the note in the gorilla's voice; the denial had been half a question. He said, "I know you were the only one of the three here that understood. I know that only you can speak. Perhaps there are things I don't know, but I am your friend, as I am Devoli's. He told me to give you this drug, that it would clear your mind..."

The great beast remained silent and immobile. The yellow light of the lantern danced in its tiny eyes, and behind it, its grotesque, enormous shadow covered the wall and hung from the low ceiling.

"You don't want the drug, do you?" said Von Bruckner. "You want the girl..."

The silence continued unbroken and oppressive. Something more strange than he could yet imagine lay in this small, hot room, Von Bruckner felt. What was it that Devoli had had in mind? He watched the gorilla, seeing its powerful neck relax, its great head sagging to its chest, and then spoke, and its voice was low and uneasy.

"Give me the drug."

The Major came up quite close to the gorilla and held the capsule out. The gorilla took it in his black, leathery hands, their surfaces dark and gleaming in the yellow light. A subdued sound, almost a groan, came from it, and when it swallowed the capsule, its hands went to its throat and it gulped in mouthfuls of air, its wet, cruel fangs exposed.

Presently the Major said, "You must be feeling better already. You know you do because it's always been that way. Your head is clear and you know I am your friend and Devoli's. If I were not his friend, would I have brought a doctor for him? If I were not your friend, would I have brought you the drug he wanted you to have?" He let his words sink in, and then he added, softly, "If I were not your friend, would I offer you the girl? Did you think Devoli and I didn't know you wanted her...?"

The gorilla looked down at the floor, then, for some reason, it brought its hands up and regarded them, the gnarled, powerful fingers half closed. It touched its face and looked at Von Bruckner.

THE Major came closer, as close as he dared. "Do you know what Devoli is going to do for you?" he whispered, his eyes wide with the wonder of his own words. *"Devoli has found a way to get you a human body! As soon as our work here is done, he is going to undertake a secret operation that will make a man of you! Do you understand that? He will do all this because he knows how much you want her..."* And now that he had said it, Von Bruckner waited. He had gambled heavily on the effect of these words; he had planned them long before, knowing what he did, conjecturing the rest, and he had gambled now when he watched the gorilla look at its hands and touch its face. It was as if he could read the great beast's mind, for as much as it wanted the girl, it realized that it was an animal. But would its fogged brain be capable of assimilating the thought Von Bruckner had planted there?

He saw the way the huge animal's head lifted suddenly, the way its eyes glistened. It forced itself back against the wall, as if to steady itself—the way a man might, hearing something that startled and shook him—and its nostrils dilated and its breathing became audible. "Devoli said that?" it breathed. "Devoli told you that?"

Slowly, the Major nodded his head. The gorilla kept looking at him, then it turned, its hands gripping the window bars, its back to him. It kept looking out of the window for a long, full minute.

"But first," said Von Bruckner, quietly, "you must return to the jungle. You must come back with many of your friends, fifteen or more of them—friends like Yawwa and Moga, and you must tell them to obey me, and you will—"

"Devoli said you were his enemy."

Von Bruckner thought swiftly. His plan was working. Everything was proceeding as he had seen it in his mind— everything but the initial distrust that Devoli had put in the gorilla's mind. Was this what Devoli had banked on? Had he felt that nothing Von Bruckner could say or do would remove the doubt Devoli had put there? It was all he had to do then...to remove that doubt—

"I cannot take you to Devoli now," he said, softly. "You saw how ill he is, and now he is asleep. But you know that there is a man here named Abbott, a good friend of Devoli's. Devoli told me after you had gone that he had asked you to save him, but Abbott is in no danger. It was only Devoli's illness that made him speak that way. If you still doubt me, I will bring Abbott here to tell you I speak the truth."

After a moment, its back still to the Major, the gorilla nodded.

Von Bruckner left quickly. Walking back to the main house he saw that men and officers paused in their duties as he re-appeared. They had suffered terrible losses in spite of the elements that favored them, for the French had fought savagely and surrendered only when resistance had become totally impossible. The battle had cast a pall over the camp, yet under it Von Bruckner could feel the pulse of excitement everywhere, like a fever running through the men.

ON THE verandah he found several of his officers waiting for the scheduled meeting to begin. He sent Lieutenant Mittler to bring Abbott to him, and sent for Beidermann. When the Captain appeared, Von Bruckner said to him, "There will be no meeting. I expect we will be in Dakar within thirty-six hours—"

"Sir, if this—" Beidermann began eagerly.

"Yes, Beidermann, matters have taken their final turn, at last. You will assume charge of the preparations for our departure. Radio Dakar and Tripoli and have planes here. We are bringing back perhaps a score of the gorillas. Your engineers will destroy everything that is left behind—not a trace of this cursed place is to remain intact…"

When they brought in Abbott, Von Bruckner was ready for him. Abbott seemed very tired. Evidently the doctors had not had time to come to him, for the bandages he still wore around his chest were torn and filthy. But in his eyes burned an implacable hatred, and his bearing was erect and deadly calm. Von Bruckner liked it better that way.

He surveyed the tall young man, saying nothing. He saw that even then, disarmed, wounded, exhausted, Abbott's eyes took in everything in the room, as if searching for something that might offer the chance to escape. How dangerous one man might be, the Major thought, when that man was determined and courageous. Scores lay dead and wounded tonight because of this man. For a moment the Major's mind flashed back to the scene of battle as it had been hours before, the smell of gunpowder, the roar of guns, the cries of men… How sweet this man's death would be; how sweet his coming anguish and torture…but quickly now—to tell him quickly, to let his resolution harden, to break him more easily…

Von Bruckner said, "You are going to perform a special favor for me, Abbott. I am going to take you to Dr. Devoli's gorilla. You will tell the gorilla that I am Devoli's friend, that Devoli trusts me, and that the gorilla is to do what I ask of it."

Abbott waited, and when he saw that the Major had finished speaking, his weary face broke the least bit and a smile started to form, but at the last moment it didn't, and he stood there. "You think so?" he said.

"Yes," said Von Bruckner, simply, and turning to Mittler he said, "Bring down the Chaumont woman."

In the moments that followed, the Major paid no further attention to Abbott. He lit a cigarette and walked about, talking to Captain Mayer who showed him the message he was sending; he met Captain Auberclauss, who had commanded the parachute troops; he studied the reports of the casualties. And when Jeanne Chaumont came down, he said nothing when she rushed toward Abbott and he took her in his arms.

He allowed them a few brief moments thus, during which neither Abbott nor the girl spoke, as if there were no words for them now, and then he quietly ordered that both be taken outside.

They were led to within a few yards of the shack that housed the gorilla, Here Von Bruckner had Abbott and the girl separated, then Von Bruckner came close to Abbott, so that his words would not be heard by the girl. "I offer you the choice that was given me," he said, his voice casual. "The gorilla will do what I want if you follow my orders...or...it will obey me if I give it the girl. You see, Devoli's almost human animal has developed a human weakness..." He could not resist a short, abrupt laugh. "...for beauty. It appears it is quite in love with her."

Having said this, the Major returned to where the girl stood and took her hand in his. For the first time since the night before, his eyes met hers. He had first dreaded this moment, then looked forward to it. There was no fear in her eyes, nothing but resignation, not even curiosity. How beautiful she was. Her full lips were partly open, her hair braided, her clothes as carefully arranged as if she were going to a dance. But he hated her, Von Bruckner knew—he hated her as much for the personal treachery she had practiced on him as for the things she represented. He could have killed her with his hands.

He gripped her wrist and took a step forward. He had been prepared for the possibility of her resistance, but there was none; she was walking with him toward the shack...

IN THAT moment, an odd, pleasurable calm came over Von Bruckner. The scene became indelibly impressed upon his consciousness. The night, cool and dark, the camp, lying around them, the stars that shone down on them, the men waiting tensely, some standing about right near them, none of them really understanding what he was doing—it was a feeling of insuperable power, and more, of revenge—and more than that, of the secure knowledge that both revenge and his plans would succeed. He was no more than a few feet away from the door now, and the timeless quality of the moment was ending, rushing swiftly now—

"I'll go," said Abbott.

He had spoken quietly, but in the hush his voice had been as loud as the report of a gun. Von Bruckner heard him, but somehow he kept on walking. He reached the door and opened it, and looked in. The gorilla was standing in the center of the room, as if it had been coming to the door and stopped when it opened.

"Don't you hear me? I said I'll go!"

Von Bruckner stood there, looking at the girl. Did she understand now what he had been about to do? He thought to himself: *What would I have done if he had not broken? Would I have taken her in?* He knew it was not what he had wanted, that he needed the girl as a constant incentive, as a motivation for the gorilla, yet the thought of what he had appeared to be doing had seized him until its hold was almost unbreakable. But now he stopped. The gorilla had seen the girl, he knew, and he drew her away from the door.

He led her back to the soldiers who had brought her, and motioned the others to let Abbott go. As Abbott started for the shack, he fell in beside him, mentally comparing Abbott and Chaumont. Of the two, when they understood what Von Bruckner was doing—and she had understood, he knew, understood it at the last moment, when Abbott had spoken—of the two, there was more emotion in Abbott. Abbott's mouth had tightened to a thin slit; his eyes were more active than ever. What had made him break? Von Bruckner wondered. He had felt that Abbott was strong enough to take anything...but not this, perhaps. Or perhaps it was because he did not realize the enormity of what he was about to do?

Joe Abbott went into the shack first, Von Bruckner a step behind him. The gorilla had backed away a few feet. Von Bruckner said, "Here is another friend of Devoli's, the man named Abbott. You know him. He will tell you that I am Devoli's friend, and that you are to do what I ask because Devoli wants it."

After a moment, Abbott said, "He is Devoli's friend. Do what he says. He is telling the truth."

"All right," said Von Bruckner.

"Leave now," He waited until Abbott had gone out, then he approached the gorilla and said, "Will you do what I ask you?"

The gorilla said, "I want the girl—I want…to take her with me…to the jungle…"

"When you return," said Von Bruckner.

"Now…before I go…"

CHAPTER NINE

HE, Olowga, had told him what he wanted. It might all be true, but it did not matter. He regarded the Major and he thought: *How long is it since I first saw this man?* It seemed a long, long time before—the night Devoli had followed him into the jungle…that had been two nights before…it was strange then, because he had taken the drug, and now when he tried to think, the thoughts remained distant and half-formed. He had tried to understand the meaning of the shooting he had heard that night; it had startled him so badly at first that he had instinctively run towards the jungle, smashing the door down, wanting only to get away, to find the quiet again—

"I promised you the girl," the Major was saying, "and you shall have her, but not until you've come back."

The thought kept drumming in his brain. Devoli had said there was a way to restore him, Olowga, to a human body. If he closed his eyes and thought about it, it was like the lights he had seen shooting into the sky. It was something that made him tremble, that made it difficult for him to speak, though he could not understand it…not entirely, not so that it was something he knew.

"I will not go…without her," he said.

He thought he would have liked to explain it to the Major, so that Devoli would not be angry. It was not that he mistrusted them…or was that it? He could not believe that they were really going to let him have the girl—but surely Devoli had meant that only after they had made him into a man again. And Devoli could do that; he had made him…an animal…

"I want the girl…to be with her…" he said. "I want her…near me…and I will come back so that Devoli can make me a man…"

It hadn't sounded like his voice then. There had been too much anger in it. But that was because of the pain he felt. Yesterday it had been almost impossible for him to think at all. It had been the shooting, the noise, that awakened his mind, and when he had gone to Devoli, seeing how ill he was, he had felt himself able to think a little, to remember to take the drug because that was what Devoli wanted.

How odd the Major looked. His face had twisted, and he nodded his head, and as he spoke his teeth showed, and he spoke very quietly and thoughtfully. "You can take the girl with you, but if you do not return with your friends, Devoli will not perform the operation that is to make you a man. Now come with me."

He wondered, at first, why the Major seemed to think that he might not return. Did he think that he, Olowga, did not want to be a man? But that could only be because he did not know that Olowga had once been a man—and so thinking, it seemed strange to him, not only the thought itself, but because he could not remember a name he had once had—and it was only then that he seemed to understand what the Major had just said to him...he could take the girl with him!

He could not understand it, but he knew he was glad. The Major had already gone out of the house, and now, slowly, he followed, and at the threshold he hesitated. In the darkness, illuminated in several places by great lights, he saw that many men were waiting outside, and he heard the Major say to one of them, "Radio instructions to all patrols that no harm is to come to the gorilla now going toward the south, nor to those that will return with him sometime within the next twenty-four hours. Make it extremely clear..."

AND then he saw the girl. She was standing among the men, and he heard the Major say to her, in an oddly strained voice, "It seems, Miss Chaumont, that you will accompany our friend on his journey."

Olowga could not mistake the expressions he saw on the men's faces, the surprise, even...horror...but the girl did not move, and her expression did not change, and she said nothing. She only turned toward him as he stood at the threshold, as erect as he could, and she looked at him.

Suddenly he came towards her swiftly. The men backed away in quick retreat. He picked her up in his arms, scarcely feeling the burden, and wheeling about, he began running with her. In an instant he was out of the lights again, secure in the darkness, feeling the night wind against his face, the grass underfoot. He went behind the house and headed straight for the jungle, and behind there had been no sound except for the Major's voice crying out, "Remember!"

The girl was not afraid. She lay in his arms without moving, and no sound came from her. He could feel her quick breathing against him, feel her skin, her flesh against him. A great, swift, burning joy was in him. He could not think, he could not do anything, but all the time he was running faster and faster, feeling the strength in him as he had never felt it before.

When he had been running for awhile—he had lost all conception of time—when he had crossed the field of spiny grass and came to the first of the streams he had to pass, he lifted the girl higher. He waded into water—right up to his chest, but he kept her dry, and then, coming out of the stream, he had heard voices near him and several little lights had shot out of the darkness, stabbing him with their rays.

The men had called to each other and he had stopped, their lights still on him, but after a moment, when they did nothing, he began running again, and the lights stayed on him until he lost them with distance as he went on.

Farther off he knew the jungle was near. He could not see it, but his knowledge was stronger than sight, stronger than the testimony of the smells that came from it, from the hundred sensory things. He knew within him, like the traveler returning home…and suddenly he became aware of the fact that the girl was crying, that she had been crying for minutes now, and he had felt her tears against his breast. He could not understand it. He had felt no fear in her, and fear was a thing he knew instinctively. But her tears and her pain were his, and he felt a strange sadness come over him, and then, still thinking so, he felt she had stopped, and she was quiet again.

He had wanted to talk to her, to tell her not to be afraid, but he could not force the words from his throat. He was afraid of what his voice would sound like, and so thinking, he saw the image of himself as he remembered it from the mirror he had secreted, and he saw himself as the girl was seeing him…and he remembered what the Major had told him about Devoli's plan. After that there was no thought, but only feeling.

WHEN he reached the jungle's edge, he took to the trees. In his eagerness he had no patience for the slow foot-travel of man-things. He held the girl with one arm around her waist and swung up into a tree, then began the swift running from branch to branch, the swinging from well-remembered vines, the occasional plunge downward to a new avenue—for the jungle here, because of the gorillas who had lived here for so many months, had become a series of avenues, of known paths and lanes.

The darkness meant little to his eyes, and nothing at all to his other senses. Long before he saw the other gorillas, he knew they were aware of his return, as he was aware of their gathering, of the word of his return being passed down through the jungle. They were coming from everywhere, heading for the clearing toward which he was going. He knew that some of them had seen the girl he carried in his arms…

By the time he reached the clearing, the sounds of the others were unmistakable. The rustling of leaves and vines, the movements of heavy bodies, their occasional grunts and calls were converging; he swung out of a tree on the edge of the clearing and dropped to the ground. Already almost a score of the gorillas were there.

He went to the center of the clearing and let the girl down on her feet. She stood beside him, swaying a moment, holding on to him, then sat down, her hands over her eyes. He had not intended building a fire, but feeling the anxiety, the trembling of the girl, and remembering her tears, he thought it would be better for her if she saw what was around her, rather than let her imagination build things in the darkness, and so he ran swiftly across the clearing and dug his hand down among the roots of an ancient, long dead tree, where, buried under moss and leaves and twigs, wrapped in cloth rags, he had long before hidden a box of matches. He gathered up an armload of dry wood and returned, and quickly built a woodpile, then struck the match to it.

All these things he thought, yet did not really think them as he once had understood the meaning of thought. His thoughts were not logical trains, dependent upon words; they were instinctive, interrelated series of desires and images. He had not thought about the girl and the fire—he had sensed her reaction and built a fire…

He watched her as the flames grew, turning the dark world of his jungle into an orange, flickering, shadowy place of huge forms and new sounds. Her face was colored by the fire, her moving eyes would catch new glints from the flames. From all sides she could see the gorillas coming out of trees, running and walking, hunched over, not like he, Olowga, toward the fire, sitting down and talking to each other quietly.

And yet, though he was not thinking, he knew certain things— and though it was highly involved for him, he knew that he knew. It was not like the drug, there was something new about this. It was the way it had been with Devoli earlier that night, when he had been able to understand little, yet had known many things of which he could not speak because he could not find the words, as if his mind was alive but unable to demonstrate it in the accepted way. Perhaps that was because the things that had once mattered to him were no longer important; what was important now was what he desired…

He had seldom come here during the night and built a fire without wearing the clothes Devoli had given him. It had been one of the many things about him that the others had never understood. But what were they thinking of this girl he had brought with him? How could they begin to understand the presence of a human here? Could they differentiate between the sexes…and if they could, as he thought, would they be able to understand that one of them, no matter how strange, no matter if it was The Strange One—would they be able to understand that one of them could feel desire for a woman, for a human female?

THEY had gathered now by the scores, those nearest the fire sitting, others standing about, moving in closer for a look at the human, moving away muttering. He watched them carefully, picking out those he knew more intimately, though he hardly knew any of them. Once one of them had called out, asking about Moga and Yawwa, though it was not really asking; the words themselves meant that Moga and Yawwa were not hunting with them any longer. Had he answered, he would have expressed the idea that neither of them could feel the urge to hunt anymore, and that the man-things had so done it, but he did not answer and none asked again. He saw they were waiting for him.

He had been standing directly beside the girl. Now he walked away, moving in a circle around the fire, his back toward it, and called out names. He, Olowga, their friend, wanted them to go with him, to give him help in a task that would bring them close to man-things, but the man-things would not harm them, nor would they harm the man-things. It was not a hunt he wanted, nor a searching for new females, but a matter that he could not explain until later.

One by one they responded. Several of those whose names he knew at once left the larger groups and came near him, others did not; but also there were some he had not called who came. Once he had to say that he asked only for males, but the words he used also meant he wanted the largest and strongest of them, and that made it sound like a hunt, but he did not explain.

He remembered there was a certain number he had been told to take back with him, but it meant nothing to him. There were many now, as many as twice the number of his fingers. They stood together, and he felt that they expected to witness a new, strange thing that would come from the mind of the Strange One. Perhaps they thought this human with him was to be part of it. Now he would tell them he was leaving her with them, that he would return later for her.

Of all those who had signified their intention to go with him, he knew one well, the one called Wotah, which meant he was quiet and even-tempered. To Wotah, he said, "You will remain here and keep watch over this man-thing. No one is to go near it, or bring hurt to it, or Olowga will be angered, and his anger is a terrible thing."

Wotah said, "It is expected that the anger of Olowga is a terrible thing, and Wotah will remain to keep watch."

Voices chorused in agreement, all eyes fixed on the girl. Olowga had never shown anger, but as Wotah had said, it was feared. Now Olowga raised a hand and pointed north, and the first of his group began moving out of the cleared area toward the trees. He turned toward the girl, and for the first time he found the courage to speak.

"Have no fear. I leave you here now...but I will return..."

"No!"

She had jumped to her feet, standing close to him, and she reached out and clutched his wrist, not letting him go. Her eyes were a mixture of wonder and fear. He realized she had never heard him speak the language of man-things before. It was as if she had been waiting for this moment.

"No!" she breathed. "You must not leave me here. You must take me back with you..." She was untying her hair now, letting the braids out, and from underneath the braids she took out a small white packet of paper. "You must take this—it is the medicine Dr. Devoli told me to give you!"

HE STOOD there, seeing her open the little packet, seeing the tiny grains of the green powder. Those who had started for the trees had stopped, and a hush had come over all, seeing Olowga and the man-thing talking to each other in a language none understood, as it had been that other night when three man-things had come.

"I have taken the medicine already," he said. "The Major gave it to me. You can see that my mind is...clear...and no harm will come to you..."

She looked at him curiously. "The Major gave it to you," she repeated, then said, slowly, "Where are you going now?"

"To bring my friends to him...to help him, as Devoli wanted..."

"No!" she cried out again. "He is Devoli's enemy! Don't you understand that? You must know that if you've taken..." She kept looking at him, shaking her head, tears running down her face suddenly. "You must listen to me..."

He, Olowga, knew she was wrong. The Major was Devoli's friend. He had proved that to Olowga. Had he not given him the medicine? Had not Devoli's friend told him so? Had the Major not told him about the operation that Devoli planned? The girl was wrong. He would leave her there, with Wotah to watch her, and he would not come back for her until the operation was over, until he had been given the body of a man-thing. Then she would not fear him, nor would she say untrue things because she feared him and wanted to return...

But, slowly, out of the dark turmoil of his brain," a new thought was forming. If he returned in the body of a...man-thing how would Wotah and the others know it was he, Olowga? Would he still be able to talk to them? Would they be able to understand a thing that he himself could not yet understand? How could he have planned such a thing? He was wrong. He could not think. Fragmentary images flashed across his mind, but he could not seize them.

One thing he knew—the girl was in pain, for she was crying, and he could not bear it. The hand she had held out to him was now at her side, tightly closed. He reached out gently and took her hand and opened it, then he took the packet out of her fingers. With a quick movement, he emptied the packet into his mouth, crumpling the paper and letting it fall at his feet.

He swept a hand out to find something to cling to and he caught the girl, then, realizing that he was dragging her down, he let her go and went reeling across the clearing. A thousand comets swept before his eyes, a thousand storms were born and died, and for an eternity it was still and silent, and the world far away. When he could breathe again, he found himself stretched out on the earth, lying on his back with the dark cloak of night overhead. He rose to his feet and felt the great throbbing pain sweeping through him.

"I must remember...I am Carpenter..."

BUT when his eyes lifted and there was the girl, standing a few feet away, he stared at her, remembering. Had she heard what he had said then? Things were returning to him, to the tiny core in him that remained always alive. He had not felt like this when the Major had given him the medicine, but it had been this way every other time—that was why Devoli had shot it at him, because otherwise the pain was too great...

He had sobbed when he spoke before; now he controlled his voice, saying to the girl, "It wasn't the medicine the Major gave me. But why did Devoli's friend tell me to believe the Major?"

"Abbott told you that?" she asked, and was about to add something, when she stopped. But he knew then, without her telling him, remembering what he had heard outside the shack, the way Abbott had shouted that he would go. Abbott had been forced into it...because the Major had said he would give the girl to him, Olowga... Strange, he thought, that he still thought of himself as Olowga, and not Carpenter. How long would the drug last this time? Its effectiveness had been constantly decreasing, and the amount the girl had given him was very small. The degeneration of the man-thing Carpenter into the gorilla Olowga was still proceeding at its terrible pace, making...

There it was again. Man-thing, he had thought, thinking the word in Olowga's language.

For a moment he could feel the fear, the...horror...that must have forced Abbott to lie. But there was hope. The new body, that Devoli had never told him about. That would change things. That was true; the Major might be Devoli's enemy and still have told the truth. He could never have imagined such a lie unless Devoli had told him the whole truth, and Devoli would never betray him. The Major had had his own reasons for telling the truth, but it was the truth. Devoli had—

Was he behaving like an animal, reacting with instinct and desire instead of thought? Was he clinging to something fantastic? It was no more fantastic than what Devoli had done to him in the first place. It was true—Devoli had found a way to restore him to the world of the man-things.

"Do you understand what I am saying?" the girl repeated.

He had not heard. His mind had been far away. He could think more clearly now, but it made little difference because he could not think anything through to the end. It was like being a man-thing, lost in an impenetrable wilderness, unable to move, and then the man-thing found a machete to help him clear a path, but then realized that he did not know the direction to take, nor would that matter, for the wilderness was too vast, too hopeless...

"You must not go back," she said.

"But if I do not go back, how can you—"

"It does not matter. The only thing that matters now is that you stay out of the Major's grasp. Don't you see that?"

Yes, he could see it. She was afraid that he would fall prey to the Major's plans again. "But the drug," he started to say, and stopped. The drug might lose its potency at any time; it was no argument.

"Devoli is still there. I cannot leave him there."

"No one matters, not I, nor Abbott, nor Devoli. Only you matter."

"Only I matter," he repeated, curiously. The words sounded so strange to him. Had she forgotten he was a gorilla? But what she said only made it more imperative that he go back for Devoli. Devoli alone knew the secret that could free him. If this girl, as she had said then, voluntarily belonged to him—he could not understand it, nor did he try to—then she would belong to him all the more when he was a man-thing again! But he could not reason with her; he was afraid to reason with her about such things. How could he tell her?

He turned to Wotah and motioned for him to come with them. He lifted the girl in his arms, and at a word from him the waiting gorillas started forward again, and he was running with them across the clearing.

FAR, far off in the east, the slightest trace of the tropical dawn was showing, a single, pale blue banner of light floating against the dark field of the sky. Overhead, though Olowga sensed rather than saw them, a few silent night birds wheeled. Not far away, a small animal ran across the plain. At the jungle's edge, the band of gorillas heard Olowga speak to them.

It was difficult, trying to tell them what he wanted them to do. He knew from their expressions, from their slight movements and grunts that the task he set before them made them wonder. It was different from what he had said before. One, Jagga, said he had spoken falsely, to trick them. He was not afraid of the man-things, but he had seen how they hunted, killing from a distance with thundersticks.

Olowga said, "You have seen how I can speak with the man-things. I have lived with them, I know their ways. I have no fear of their strength. I have lived with you, and you have seen that I fear nothing, that I have overcome everything. If you do as I have told you, we will overcome the man-things."

After that, even Jagga was silent. To Wotah he said a few words, then to the girl, he said, "If we are not back by noon, Wotah will take you wherever you direct him. You have nothing to fear now. Of all these...of all my friends, he is the most trustworthy. I would not leave you if I thought otherwise."

"Will nothing persuade you not to go?"

When he made no reply, she came closer to him and held out her hand. "Then bring back Dr. Devoli and Abbott, and God be with you..."

He felt himself trembling, and when he looked into her eyes he had to turn away quickly because there were tears there, and something more...something he had never seen there before...nor in any human eyes in so long...

Then swiftly, without touching her hand, he turned and started running, the others with him.

Across the dark fields they ran, silently, almost twenty forms in the shadowless darkness, one behind the other. Unheeding, they plunged through the streams, through the tall grass, running wet and shaggy and only the sound of their breathing to indicate them. When they reached a slight rise of land that gave to the plain itself, they stopped and here Olowga uttered a low sound. The group separated now, five remaining with Olowga, the rest under the leadership of Klaa.

Those with Klaa now crossed the ridge, moving away from the others and walking slowly toward the camp. They were obscured in the gloom in a few moments, but Olowga waited. Presently little lights went blinking across the plain in signal, and other lights answered. They had been seen by the patrols, and now their slow progress would be carefully followed, for almost immediately afterward the staccato harshness of motors echoed over the fields and motorcycles came to escort them.

OLOWGA and the five with him ran along behind the ridge and took the long circle into camp. The patrols would be withdrawn now, thinned out, at any rate, but he took no chances. They crossed the ridge half a mile east and kept running, low-crouching figures in the still night, the wind now blowing toward them. Once, near the camp, they caught the scent of man-things near them. Olowga motioned them to halt.

Alone, he crept forward. Twenty feet ahead he heard the voices of three man-things. They were sitting in a hole they had dug, and they had a long, heavy gun with them. Inch by inch Olowga came in, his heart quick with the knowledge of what he had to do. He could have circled around them and they would never have known, but later, coming back, the presence of these men where they might not be seen until it was too late, where no wind would reveal them. He could not take the risk.

He was five feet away now. He gathered himself into a ball, his great arms outstretched, poised on the balls of his feet. When he sprang there was no sound, nor was there any later. He had come down on the three men, his weight crushed them, his hands seizing two throats and smashing their heads together, and then his forearm, snapping up, had caught the third man under the chin and brought his head back with a cracking noise.

But after he had killed them, Olowga stood for a moment and looked at the dead man-things. He had never killed a man-thing before. How easy it was…how great was the power of his arms. An alien joy burned in his vitals, he breathed in deeply and smelled the sweetness of blood. For several moments everything blurred but the new sensation remained sharp, and it was only after an inner struggle that he refrained from crying out aloud.

He returned to the others quickly and motioned them on. They passed a few feet from the dead men, seeing them sitting motionless in the midst of the odor of death. He had wanted them to see that the man-things could be overcome, but now he sensed the contagion of lust and he knew he would have to watch them carefully; it had stirred them too deeply…

Then they were in the east field. Olowga listened carefully and heard the sounds of the camp awaking. He could hear the sounds of the motors from the south, and he knew that the camp had awakened early because Klaa and the others had been seen. He had to find Abbott quickly now, and then Devoli, and—

There was thunder in the sky, coming closer swiftly, and all at once it was overhead and had passed, moving out of the north. A moment later it came again from the north, like great hammers beating against the earth, then a third time. Three flights of planes—six, six, and three, flying so low that their exhausts were blue, spluttering streaks of light. The far end of the field showed lights, some blue, some white, and man-things came running from the camp.

He had not envisaged the east field being used, and already the planes were returning, and great searchlights switched on. But their noise was good. Olowga led the others on, coming to the edge of the east field and directly behind the main house. There were voices everywhere, and movement, and the clang of metal, and always more lights; it was impossible to venture out from the protection of the house.

OLOWGA thought quickly. He motioned the others to remain where they were, then edged around the corner of the newly built wing and looked into the camp. Trucks stood close together, forming a square, most of them stripped of their tires and metals and movable parts. The sheds and houses had been surrounded with wood and brush, and soldiers were pouring pungent liquids out of cans over the brush. Many of the large lights, and the guns, the mortars, were all arranged in stacks.

A soldier was approaching Olowga, spilling liquid over the brush. Olowga shrank back against the wall. The soldier stepped closer, doing his work quickly. Olowga reached out with one arm, closed his hand over the soldier's mouth and pulled him in. He held his throat for a moment or two, watching the man-thing's feet dance in mid-air when he lifted him up, and when he let him down again, the feet were still. Then Olowga took off the man's clothes and began to put them on himself. The trousers went on easily, the jacket tore in several places, but the coat held. Then Olowga picked up the deep steel helmet and put it on. He took the can and started back along the front of the house, keeping his head down and spilling the liquid.

When he reached the verandah, he quickly went up the stairs and instantly had to duck into a corner, for of the many man-things in the house, a group now came out and went down the stairs. But one of them, the last, turned back. The lights from the house, coming through the screen, had touched the sleeve of Olowga's coat. He called out, in German, "What are you doing there?"

Olowga lowered his head. The others had gone on, but this one came back up the stairs. "What is your assignment?" he barked. "Answer me at once!"

He came right up to Olowga and stuck a hand under his chin as if to lift it, but he didn't. He slowly withdrew his hand, as if he no longer controlled it, for Olowga had raised his head. Olowga took the hand that was still in mid-air and pulled the man-thing toward him with infinite gentleness. He knew the face of this young officer.

"*Wo ist Abbott?*"

But the man-thing did not answer. He stared at Olowga and tried to speak, and then he looked down at his hand, and his mouth moved again but no sound came out. Then Olowga opened his hand and let the man-thing's hand fall from his grasp, crushed and useless.

"*Wo gefindet mann Abbott?*" Olowga whispered again.

The man-thing groaned, "*In dieses haus...*"

Good. Then Abbott was in the same house with Dr. Devoli. Olowga saw how the man-thing could not move, how he had not even thought of making any outcry, and he took hold of him and broke his neck. He threw the body over the verandah railing to one side and leaped after it. He ran a few feet along the side of the house to where the new wing faced it at an angle. He gripped a railing and swung himself up. Standing poised an instant, he sprang up as high as he could, launching himself forward at the same time, and he caught the slanting top of the new verandah roof. His fingers dug in tightly and he hauled himself up.

He stood still a moment, collecting himself, getting his bearings. Perhaps three or four minutes had passed since he had left the others, and now the planes were returning, following each other in a single line and dropping ever lower, circling the field in huge, graceful arcs and coming in so that they would run along the beams of light that lay waiting for them on the ground like white paths. Their sound filled the world.

OLOWGA went along the roof to a window. It was dark and screened. He pushed his hand against it until it broke in the middle, then he let himself through and dropped into the room. Listening, he heard voices all through the house. Footsteps coming up, mounting stairs, voices calling to each other, a door opening. He went to the door and opened it, peering down the hallway. Five or six man-things stood in the hall, facing an open doorway, then others came out, and with them was Abbott. They were taking him out.

There was no time now for cunning. Olowga lowered his head and started down the hall toward the man-things. They heard him coming and turned, and already he was on them, pushing through them, and one of them screamed, "His feet! *Look at his feet!*" They had seen his bare feet beneath the overlong trousers, but now he was past them, having scattered them, and he was between them and the stairway, and they were confused and frightened, still not understanding.

He reached for one of them, grabbing him just below the knees and then raised him and hurled his body into their midst. If the hallway had been less narrow, or they better prepared, they would have brought their guns into play in the next instant. As it was, the one gun that did fire hit a man-thing, and Olowga was among them. He had gripped Abbott's clothes and sent him tumbling back into the open room, and alone with the man-things, he went for them.

They fell to all sides, smashing against the walls. He was like a hurricane of death, swift, merciless, implacable, the bloodlust in him like a fever, tearing, throwing, pounding, smashing. There was only the sound that came from his throat, a low, terrible sound. In a minute he had killed eight men, but even then he kept at them, mangling their inert bodies, unable to stop himself. Finally, when he did stop, he stood crouched over, breathing easily, covered with gore, and his hands kept moving, ever working...

He watched Abbott stoop down and take away two of the pistols from the dead men, and he had to arrange the words in his mind before he spoke, but he had only said, "I am taking you with me—" when Abbott said, "What of the girl and Dr. Devoli?"

"I have the girl, and I will go for Devoli now."

Abbott looked down the stairway. The roaring of the motors had drowned out the sounds of the short-lived struggle; those who were still down below had heard nothing. He regarded Olowga sharply, then said, "You can't go down there for Devoli now—there are too many of them. You haven't a chance—"

"I must get Devoli."

Olowga spoke softly, but with deadly sureness. He thought of the man-things below and the prospect of more killing only invited him, and when he met Abbott's eyes he saw that Abbott understood what was running through his mind.

"There are more than a hundred men prisoners here," said Abbott, speaking hurriedly. "If we don't help them, they'll be shot. We've got to do something about them first..."

"Devoli comes first."

He didn't understand, Olowga knew; Abbott didn't know why it was so important to get Devoli, more important than anything, than life itself, for without Devoli there was nothing for him, no hope and no life.

"But you'll never get out of there with him!" Abbott snapped, his eyes fixed on the stairway, his guns ready. "If we free the others, it will be easy to get him."

Olowga tried to think about it. He only knew what he wanted; he could no longer think. Downstairs he heard many voices, and someone called up to them, shouting about the delay.

At any moment the bodies might be discovered. Olowga wondered if the Major had already found out that he, Olowga, was not among the ones that had been sighted. They would not enter the camp; they would stop near it, and at Olowga's call they would scatter and return to where Jagga waited.

Olowga made no sign of acquiescence, but when he started back along the hall, Abbott was behind him. Olowga led the way through the room from which he had come and stepped out on the roof. Suddenly a random light from far off, swinging about, cut across the roof and caught both for an instant. Its arc continued a few yards, then stopped with savage abruptness and returned. Olowga had seized Abbott in his arms and leaped down. Behind them the light zigzagged crazily, searching for the strange forms it had seemingly discovered; it lingered and gave up.

MEANWHILE Olowga, landing easily, had run toward the rear of the house, still holding Abbott. Before he could remember, he had swept the corner and come into the dark grove where the other five waited. He sensed, rather than saw them, ready to spring and he retreated a step and growled softly to them. Then he let Abbott down and took off the coalscuttle helmet he still wore. But there was nothing he could do now about the clothes he wore, and the smell of man-things' blood; they were afraid, Olowga knew, as much of the sound and movement that surrounded them as of the slow advance of the tropical dawn, and Abbott's sudden appearance with him had only added to their confusion.

Abbott himself had gone stiff at the sight of them, their huge forms huddled together, outlined against distant lights in the field. He stood there, sucking in his breath, and then the slight sound was lost in the thunder of several taxiing planes as they drew closer. It wasn't until the roaring died down briefly that he said to Olowga, "Where is the girl?"

Olowga had seen Abbott trying to pierce the darkness, but the question caught him with a sudden, strange pang. Why was this man-thing concerned...but then he understood. "Safe," he said. "Across the field with...friends of mine..."

His hesitation was matched by Abbott's. He could see Abbott's eyes staring at him. Abbott said, "Wait here. I'll be right back."

He was gone so quickly that Olowga had no chance to refuse. Had he wanted to refuse? He could no longer tell; he had surrendered to the judgment of the man-thing. He thought of Devoli and of going back, but he could not move.

When Abbott returned he said softly, "Listen to me closely because I need your help. The men are locked in the barn, and there are six men and two machine guns guarding them. In front of the large shed are several trucks. The first of them contains rifles; the third has boxes of rifle ammunition. We must first overpower the guard, and immediately get the rifles and ammunition to the men in the barn. Do you understand what I am saying?"

"Yes."

"It must be done as quietly as possible because the camp is filled with men, and it must be done very quickly. First the guard, then—"

His voice broke off as motorcycles came roaring into the camp. Men went into the main house. At the same time, three trucks, their headlights on, swung out of the sheds and started lumbering across the field, ignoring the road. The trucks passed within twenty feet of the grove. When they were gone, Olowga spoke softly to the gorillas, very slowly, then he said to Abbott, "We are going."

Abbott led the way back around the house, hugging the wall, and he stopped Olowga. Men were talking excitedly on the verandah; he heard Beidermann's voice harsh and demanding. They disappeared inside and Olowga said, "The Major has come across my friends and discovered that I am not..."

He knew then, from the slow way Abbott had turned and stared at him, his face, his eyes, frozen, incredulous, that he had made a terrible mistake in speaking then, for the man-things had spoken in German, and he, Olowga, had shown that he understood! Then, suddenly, he swept by Abbott and ran across the center of camp toward the barn, the others a step behind him.

THE impulse had fallen on a bad moment for the start, for one of the six men—they were divided into two groups of three men each—was facing directly towards them. He saw the gorillas racing across the forty yards that separated them, but for a moment, perhaps because he could not be sure, in the reflected light from nearby searchlights, what they were, he gave no alarm. His hoarse shout was too late when it did come. The guns swung around frantically. The nearer one was gripped by Olowga's hand and thrown into the air, the second one said rat-tat and no more, and its bullets had plowed the earth directly in front of it.

It was over before it had begun, but the camp had had its entire attention suddenly focused on what was happening. The men who ran out of the house and those who came from the sheds saw only the end, the dead guards, the swift, blurred figures running toward the trucks, passing in and out the lights, and one recognizable figure of a man tearing down the bolts that locked the barn!

There were screams from the large shed, and the forms were running from them, from the trucks, carrying rifles and boxes, and two shots rang out from the shed. Suddenly the men from the verandah began firing at the barn doors!

Olowga had been the first to get to the trucks, and he had grabbed a great armful of rifles and loaded the others as they came. Four of them started back to the barn, and he and Puutu had gone on to boxes of ammunition. By then the men in the shed had seen them, and Olowga had run into the center of them, flinging them about. He loaded Puutu and took three boxes himself and started back when the shots came.

He hadn't heard them at once; it was only later, after an indeterminate lapse, that he remembered hearing them, for he staggered as he ran and he knew that one of the shots had hit him. Something heavy had smashed him from behind and an intolerable hotness paralyzed his left arm. He almost dropped the boxes, but Puutu, a step ahead of him, wavered as the gunfire started on the verandah, and he sprang ahead, pushing Puutu forward.

It seemed to him that the open barn door was a long way off, that he might never reach it. The brightness of the lights had trapped him and Puutu outside, and the others, who had already disappeared into the barn, could not venture out. Then he saw Abbott come out of the barn, standing beside the door, very cool and straight, the two guns in his hand spinning about as if on a slow wheel. Fire spat from his guns in tiny, continuous streaks, and over the shouting and now continuous crack of gunfire he heard the sounds of shattering glass. It was as if there were invisible cords attached to the guns in Abbott's hands, and these cords were turning off the lights one by one, until it was dark again.

In this sudden darkness, he tripped and went sprawling over some obstacle in his way, and the boxes hurtled out of his grasp. He heard Abbott's voice, and saw man-things come out of the barn and pick up the boxes. But there were more boxes on the ground than he had been carrying...and then he saw Puutu lying dead a few feet away. He had tripped over him.

ALL this time, while Olowga was getting up, while the man-things were carrying the boxes back into the barn, the gunfire kept mounting, and though there was no light to guide it, the bullets whined about them and smashed into the wooden walls behind them. He saw the open door and crawled in, and the door closed behind him. Bullets were still hammering at the heavy walls, some of them penetrating.

Some one struck a match and Olowga saw the prisoners, more than a hundred man-things. They were lying flat on the floor, passing the rifles back from the open crates. Others had opened the ammunition boxes and were passing down handfuls of bullets. In that same flare of light—Abbott was holding the match—Olowga saw several dead man-things, and the other gorillas nearby, and he heard their voices as they saw him, crying to him.

Abbott called to Olowga, "Get the others. We're getting out!"

Then it was dark again and he heard the man-things talking, their voices loud over the shooting, and when another match was struck a voice called, "Ready now, *m'sieu!*"

Abbott was beside Olowga now. "To the back of the barn!" he cried. "Tell the others to follow you!"

Lying flat on his belly, Abbott reached up and pushed the barn door open. Numerous forms were outlined against the house lights on the verandah and in front of the forms were repeated streaks of fire. The shouting increased until it was drowned out by the noise of approaching motors, and the gunfire grew heavier as more man-things arrived.

Suddenly, right beside him, Olowga heard a deafening blast as the man-things in the barn fired a volley into the verandah. Half the forms in the light fell from view. The screams and groans that followed the first volley were lost in the thunder of the second volley, and in another instant, a third.

For an instant there was complete silence in the heart of the camp and the only sounds came from its periphery. A single, low-pitched scream wailed, and in that moment Abbott was on his feet and out of the barn, followed by some ten man-things. Directly behind them was Olowga, calling to the other gorillas to follow.

Olowga ran to the back of the barn. The other man-things had broken away in different directions, but Abbott was waiting there.

He stood listening closely and the gunfire started again from other sides. There was another volley from the barn and they heard the sounds of men running out and voices shouting loudly, and all at once a machine-gun opened up, followed a few seconds later by another. A new light swung into line, but an instant after it had thrust its beam, it was shattered, and then one of the machine-guns stopped. Olowga understood—it was the other man-things who had run out with Abbott. They had scattered about the camp and were sniping.

"They can't get out!" Abbott cried. "They're trapped inside!"

OLOWGA, standing there dumbly, felt the pain in his left arm. It was hanging uselessly at his side. He had done everything the man-thing Abbott had told him and now—but at this point he heard the strange cry from the fields—the voices of gorillas! He had forgotten about them!

"What's that?" said Abbott.

Olowga lifted his head and let his voice out in a long, hollow call, and the sound silenced everything for a moment. Then Olowga said, "My friends are returning to the place where the girl wants. I am going now to get Devoli."

"Wait!" said Abbott. His face, drawn and tense, was turned to the field, and nothing of the chaos that surrounded him seemed to have any effect on him. His arms hung at his sides as if weighted by the guns in them. Then, when he turned to Olowga again, he winced as a bullet whined by, as if he had not heard the sounds before.

"We'll never get away now, any of us," Abbott said hurriedly, "unless we try something. Send one of these...of your friends here to the others. Tell them to bring the girl and to come to the far end of this east field where all the planes are. Tell them to come to the grove of trees at the far end. And when you get Devoli, bring him there—"

"It is safer in the jungle—"

"You'll never get to the jungle alive! They'll hunt you down with their patrols for sure—it's too far to the jungle and it'll be daylight in half an hour or less. But if we get to the east field, we can steal one of their planes and I'll fly us out! Do you understand?"

"Yes."

"And tell these friends of yours here to stay with me, so that you will know where to find me later. Tell the one you send now to let the others know that I will be there, that I am your friend."

"Yes," said Olowga. He turned to Weygu and grunted to him, then to the others. When he had finished he saw that Abbott had seen that his arm had been hit, that he could not move it. The pain had become a constant, numbing thing, and he scarcely felt the blood dripping down from his fingertips. The gunfire and the voices and the steady hammer of bullets had always existed; they meant nothing anymore.

"You've been hit," Abbott said.

"Go now," said Olowga. He mumbled to Weygu, and Weygu turned and ran crouching through the field. Then Olowga peered ahead and without a word he edged back around the barn.

He went back halfway to the front, then dropped down and crawled along to the next shed. From there he was able to see the place he had just come from, and Abbott and the others were no longer there. He lay very quietly and heard the voices of man-things moving surreptitiously into the shed. They were going to open fire on the barn from the side. The man-things that Abbott had been so determined to rescue were lost. The new snipers who had gotten out were still doing their work, but as the scattered forces of the Germans came back, and in daylight, it would be over soon.

Olowga crept behind the shed. He bad been thinking clearly all the time Abbott was with him, but now it was becoming difficult again. He remembered everything—that Weygu would tell Jagga and the others to bring the girl to the grove at the far end of the east field, the same grove where he had first seen the girl the day the Major showed him the strange machines. There he would bring Devoli, and then...but how was he going to get to Devoli? His task was easier now because the man-things in the house were distracted.

He would circle the camp, going from the shed to the largest shed and then to the wing of the house... A small group of man-things ran by a few yards from him, going to the back of the barn. But the sounds of the shooting had changed. It would grow intense and steady and then stop and come from a new direction, but never from the direction of the house. There were no voices now, but only the rumble of motors as new men came in. Soon the prisoners in the barn—

SUDDENLY there was shooting from the back of the barn. He looked up and saw the man-things he had seen going there. They were running into the field, and rifle fire cut down three of them. The man-things in the barn had made openings on all sides. They were surrounded, but they could not be approached closely.

He started for the largest shed, but the wind changed a trifle and he caught the odors of many man-things there. He crouched lower and circled it from the field, coming in at the end of the new wing. He went along the wall until he found a window, then he jammed an elbow into the screen and leaped up through the window.

He stood very still now. The shooting had stopped altogether. When he listened he could hear many quiet moving man-things, and subdued voices, and motors and mechanical sounds. The east end of the horizon was catching fire now. Was that why the shooting had stopped? Were the man-things in the camp going to wait for daylight?

Olowga went out of the room, into a hall, then upstairs. There was no one in the house. He went into a room, opened its screen and stood on the sill. He reached up and caught the ledge with one hand and judged the faint outlines. Then, holding tight, he raised a foot behind him and pushed against the side of the house and he sailed through ten feet of space, landing on the sloping roof below. There he found the window he had used earlier and dropped quietly into the room.

Somewhere downstairs there was movement, then voices, but nothing he could make out. A door swung open and closed, then footsteps and more voices, then the door again, very quietly. Suddenly he could understand why there had been no shooting from the house. The barn door faced the house, and if the man-things trapped in the barn opened their door, they could rake the house with fire. That meant that scarcely any of the other man-things dared to remain in this house…

He went into the hall. The dead, mangled bodies of the soldiers he had killed were still lying there. If they had been discovered, no one had had the time to remove them. They lay there grotesquely, some with their eyes open, the blood in clotted pools on the walls and floor, stiff and awkward and broken. Olowga walked through the tangle of their bodies and a queer tingle went through him.

The silence was like something alive, watching him. Again the door opened and someone came in. Standing at the head of the stairs he heard the new voice—it was the Major! Olowga heard a few words that were too faint to understand, then stepped down and lowered his head to the banister. He saw the Major's form toward the back of the room, in the darkness, two others with him, then the Major went down the hall and went into another room and the two others waited.

The desire to kill surged through him, but over it was the knowledge that he had to get Devoli. The end was in sight. Everything was in his favor now—the silent camp, the empty house, the last remaining shreds of night. He crept down the stairs. The bottom ones creaked under his weight and the men in the room turned sharply, but Olowga was lying flat on the floor.

A faint light was shining behind the two men; it came from four or five tiny, illuminated buttons on a large machine. The machine was humming now and making soft, sharp little noises—*da-da-daaa-da-daaa*—and the men were listening to it, their hands spinning dials, and one of them writing in the diffused light.

Olowga inched slowly along the floor, dragging his wounded arm. Now and again he would feel everything begin to spin around him, as if his great strength had dripped out of the wound along with his blood, but it passed if he remained still. He could see the men clearly now, their backs looming up before him. He could not get to the hall without passing them. Slowly, very slowly, he started to raise himself up, first on one knee, then up, up, until he was almost directly behind them. He stretched his right arm out and waited, and then the two man-things came closer together, close enough. Olowga reached forward quickly and brought his arm around their necks like a noose, pressing them to him, their heads close together, strangling them slowly with the strength of his forearm...

ALL through the two minutes he stood there the machine kept saying *daaa-da-da-daaa-daaa*, and the little buttons winked on and off, and the desperate, hoarse sucking sounds of the man-things grew less and less until their bodies slumped in his grasp. He let them down quietly to the floor and went down the hall to Devoli's room. He opened the door. There was no light inside. No sound came from within.

He was about to step into the room when the door directly opposite Devoli's opened and the Major came out. He took a single step into the hall and saw Olowga. He stopped in his tracks, standing with one foot before the other, then he drew the leading foot back and turned slightly, so that he faced Olowga, and he started to back against the wall but stopped himself and stood there. The light from the room from which he had just come streamed into the hall, lighting up one side of his face. It was haggard and aged and uncertain. It had been that way before he had seen Olowga.

He wet his lips and said to Olowga, "It's you."

"Yes. I've come for Devoli."

The Major turned his head toward the still chattering machine, as if he had just remembered the men there, but he saw nothing. He turned back to Olowga and said, quietly, "I've been looking for you. I wanted to tell you..." His voice cracked and dried within him. "To tell you," he said again, "that Devoli is dead. Abbott killed him..."

Olowga heard the sound of the words, but they meant nothing to him. He kept looking at the Major. "I am taking Devoli with me," he said, and the sound of his voice seemed distant to him. He saw the words he had just spoken as if they were tangible objects. They were huge letters of some solid matter, hanging in air, spelling out *I am taking Devoli with me,* but as he kept looking at them he could not read them, and they became transparent and he could see the Major's face behind them, glazed, as everything had become glazed. And then the letters began to turn and take each other's place, moving quickly, in an erratic manner, then all whirling together and turning to smoke, until there was a furious vortex before him. It stopped spinning slowly and the smoke thinned out and spread everywhere, and everything was covered with a fine, gray mist...

Olowga saw his arm reach out and grasp the Major's clothes, and he pulled the Major with him as he backed into the room. And all this time the Major had been talking.

"Abbott escaped during the night. We caught him in Devoli's room after he had killed him. He murdered him because he wanted the girl for himself. He knew Devoli was planning the operation and he was afraid you wanted the girl. He killed Devoli. There was nothing we could..."

Olowga had come to Devoli's bed. Through the covering mist he saw the still figure lying there, its face covered over with a sheet.

"Devoli," said Olowga, "I've come for you."

BUT there was no answer. He was asleep. Olowga let go of the Major and touched the still form, touched it ever so gently. Then he pulled back the sheet and looked at the relaxed face. In the darkness everything had receded. There was no longer this room. There was only Devoli and he...

He touched Devoli's face, and his black, gnarled fingers withdrew. *"Maganu,"* he whispered, to himself. *The final sleep.* Yes, that was it.

Somewhere, not far away, he heard the choking sob and felt his body racked. He fell to his knees beside the bed and the pain in him was like nothing he had ever known before, and he was beating his fist against the floor with all his strength, as if the hurt there would help take away the hurt that was in him. And then he knew that the sobbing was his, and he heard himself crying softly, uncontrollably...

"Abbott killed him. He wanted the girl. He thought that after the operation he would lose her to you because she loved you. We were too late to stop him. He murdered Devoli."

The voice had never stopped speaking. It said the same words over and over, the man-thing's voice...

And then something within Olowga snapped. Something happened to his brain, and the sorrow and pain were gone. When he stood up again there was a storm in his brain, a murderous, hysterical fury. The man-things had come and killed Devoli. Those who were his friends were not his friends. There was none he could believe. There was nothing now. It had ended for him, but before he was through—

"No!" the Major whispered, frantically. "Don't you understand what I'm saying? I was Devoli's friend—Abbott—"

Olowga brought his fist down on the Major's face. The Major was hurled across the room, falling limply against a wall. Olowga went after him, kneeling down beside the inert body. The man-thing was dead, but Olowga hammered at the face, smashing it, breaking its bones, his fist coming down again and again...

The world became filled with thunder suddenly, and fire surged through him like a thousand daggers. He spun about and leaped up only after the man-thing in the doorway had fired three shots into him, and then Olowga had caught the man-thing. He caught the hand that held the gun and pulled it and a horrible scream welled up and he was still holding the arm but the man-thing had fallen over backward and was crawling away, screaming. The shots had brought footsteps running and more voices. Olowga stepped on the crawling man-thing and kicked him, and then he was down the hall, running across the room to the stairs.

The door opened and shots echoed after him, but he could feel no pain now. He ran up the stairs, through a room to the roof, dropping to the ground and running.

THE fiery eastern sky was turning blue and white, and the fields were cold in its light. The world was cold and dismal, and far across the east field he saw the grove of trees becoming visible. He saw the great planes standing in various positions about the field, many of them near the grove, and here and there he saw man-things, not many, and all dropped from view as he ran, crouching, dodging the shots that still came from behind him, more of them now.

Thoughts flashed through his brain, even faster, bits of memories and pictures of strange faces and unfamiliar places, thoughts he could not understand. But mostly he thought of the jungle, and he kept seeing it cool and green and quiet, and knowing that he was running from it. He remembered Devoli and he heard

Devoli speaking to him and though he wanted to answer, he knew Devoli could not hear him, that he would vanish if he spoke to him.

And then the girl's face came before him, growing larger in his vision until she filled his eyes and he could see nothing. For one pierced instant there was clearness in his brain and he remembered Abbott asking first about the girl, then not letting him go for Devoli when he had first wanted to, and he remembered Abbott trying to stop the Major from letting the girl go with him. But before he could try to arrange these thoughts they were lost from him, and he saw huge, towering buildings such as he had never seen, though they were in his mind, as if the remembrance of another existence was struggling to make itself known.

He was Olowga, the creature of the jungle. He felt it in the pounding rhythm of his feet, in the burning pain of his body, in the thoughts of his brain. He wanted to kill, and when he had killed, he and the others would go back to the jungle, to live their lives as they had before the man-things had come.

Suddenly he saw them, he saw Abbott with them, and then Abbott was gone for a moment and a great roar went across the field, and he saw the air shimmering before one of the planes near the grove, and he knew that the roar came from the two whirling objects in front of the plane. He passed by one of the planes and saw the bodies of four dead men, and near another plane two men lay sprawled, facing the grove.

"*Abbott killed Devoli. Abbott wanted the girl. He was afraid he would lose her to you. Abbott murdered Devoli.*"

There was a steady hammering in his brain, a voice shouting the words over and over, and more voices joining all the time, and the Major standing beside Mogu and Yawwa and then the girl screaming the words to him, crying, wanting him to help her, and Mogu saying that Abbott had killed Devoli, and the dead man-things, all those he had killed, standing erect and adding their voices, the agony in their voices like the sounds that were coming from him, for he had been sobbing all the while as he ran across the fields.

HE WAS no more than twenty yards from the grove and the plane when he fell. He saw the earth beginning to slant and when he leaned over to right his balance, it spun around and smashed against his body. He heard the shouting in the grove and saw them come running quickly toward him, and when they were beside him he saw that they were all wearing strange white packets on their backs, that they were held in place by straps over their shoulders and chests.

However, he pushed them away, crying out loudly at them, wanting no help, and he rose slowly and staggered into the grove, the others beside him. He fell again, this time to his knees, and he was still on his knees when Abbott climbed out of the nearby plane, calling out something to him that he could not hear over the roaring of the plane and the voices in his mind. And then he saw Abbott come up close to him, and he reached out his arm and seized him, falling forward as he did so, and dragging Abbott down with him.

Slowly he pulled Abbott to him, feeling the struggling of the man-thing, hearing him shout. Abbott tossed about, his hands free, and then he had a gun in his hand, and just as Olowga caught his throat, Abbott brought a hand up and everything vanished as the world exploded, but he felt nothing except that the hand that held Abbott's throat was growing weaker.

But still he held, and Abbott's hand fell limp to the ground, and he saw Jagga and Weygu and the others standing around them, none of them moving, unable to really understand, huge, gaunt figures in the half-light and the thunder, and then through them he saw the girl come running and she fell on Olowga, tearing at his hand.

"Carpenter!" she screamed. *"Carpenter!"*

And then all the voices in his brain were quiet for an instant, and then they were crying *Carpenter* to him, but he would not release his hand…but there was something before his eyes now…a face…from the most remote regions of his mind…a face…and he looked at the picture that the girl held before his eyes and heard her voice, and the one word *Roselle*…

He closed his eyes then, but the picture remained and he knew the face—the beautiful face. His hand had unlocked its grip, covering his eyes, and when he looked up again, the girl was kneeling down beside Abbott and the picture was lying on the ground. He reached down and picked up the picture and looked at it through eyes that would not focus, but after a moment he saw the face again. He lay there, his back propped against a tree, staring at it.

He heard nothing now. He was lost in an unreal world. His mind was lucid but far removed, moving among the memories of a life that had once belonged to him. And though no sound came from him now, he was crying for everything he had lost, but slowly, peace returned to him, because he knew that death was not far away now...

FOR the first time he heard the girl's voice beside him. She was quite close to him, but when he looked at her, her face kept changing to the one in the picture he held and he was glad, hoping it would be that way when he died, that he would see Roselle last of all things on earth.

His voice was barely audible when he murmured, "Where did you get the picture?"

But when she started to tell him of Alan Bradford, he nodded his head; he had little time now, and so much to say. "Devoli is dead," he whispered. "They told me Abbott had...killed him...and I believed it..." A sudden thought had come to him, but he said nothing, seeing Abbott come toward him, stopping a few feet away.

"You know the truth now?" the girl whispered.

Olowga nodded slowly, staring steadily into the girl's eyes; and then the she waved her arm and motioned Abbott to come closer. "There are men still locked in that camp," the girl said. "Abbott found parachutes in one of the planes. He thought the only way to save them now was to drop you and the others into the camp, where you could—"

He stopped her by a feeble signal with his hand, and then he raised his voice to his friends, calling them around him. He understood everything now, and there, leaning against the tree, struggling to speak, he told them what they were to do. He told them how the man-thing would take them into the belly of the great bird, how they would fly with it, how they would not be afraid to leap out because they would float down gently. And after they were in the camp, Weygu would lead them in the destruction of the man-things. They would open the doors of the large house where so many man-things were and they would not hurt them, but only those who wore the gray clothes.

He spoke softly, sometimes repeating himself, sometimes asking Weygu if he understood. And finally he told them that many of them would enter the final sleep, but that it was good, because they were hunting for friends and because Olowga, the Strange One, told them so. When he was done, he sat quietly.

"Tell Abbott they will go with him," he said to the girl, "and stay with me for a moment longer."

He waited until the other had gone with Abbott, then he said to her, "You called me Carpenter. Swear to me that you will never tell anyone that you knew. No one must know…"

"No one will ever know."

He looked deep into her eyes then, and he saw the reflection of himself. He saw his great head and its cruel, powerful teeth, and the wide mouth across the lips of which blood kept oozing and dribbling, and he saw his own eyes, small and wondering, as if some inner self could not understand that this was he. Then he took out the picture he had hidden when Abbott came toward him and he looked at it to blot out the image he had seen in the girl's eyes…

AFTERWARD, when she had left him, he remembered that she had been crying, and some of her tears had fallen on his hand. Before the great bird had risen he had been afraid that he would be discovered in the grove by the man-things who had come into the field, shooting at the bird and Abbott and the others. But then the huge bird had roared louder than ever, scorning them, and it had swept across the field and taken to the sky, and the man-things had not come to the grove.

With what little strength remained in him then, he had risen and started south, following the course of the great bird. After it was lost from sight he still heard it, then it returned. He looked across the field toward the camp and saw a string of huge, white flowers blossom in the sky, falling swiftly into the center of the camp, and the bird had wheeled and disappeared.

He was going toward the jungle. He knew he would never reach it, but he wanted to die there, as close to it as possible, in the earth that now belonged to him. He heard the shooting that welled up in the camp, and once he saw many gray-clad figures running across a field, away from the camp, and the shooting had continued.

He was halfway across the east field when he saw Jagga and two others running toward the grove and he cried out to them. When they came to him, telling him how they had fallen like leaves from a tree, how they had killed many of the man-things and let out those in the great house, and how they had turned on those in the gray clothes and killed many of them before they escaped into the fields, Olowga felt at peace.

"Carry me back to the jungle," he told them in their own language, and in those words it meant, "Take me home."

Then, carrying him, Jagga said, pointing to the camp, "Look! The man-things have done as Olowga does!" And when Olowga looked, he saw that the camp was in flames, the fire spreading quickly and reaching for the sky.

In the stillness nothing but the roar and crackle and hush of the fire could be heard. The dawn was up and the fire was orange and red against its quiet blue, and everywhere man-things were running, tiny forms that seemed scarcely to move against the curtain of flame. He heard faint voices, and suddenly, over them, the full-throated throb of the great bird as it returned, flying low across the field. And then, as if it had seen Olowga carried by the others, its wings dipped once and it wheeled, and dipped again. Then it was gone.

But Olowga heard it long afterward, and his eyes were filled with the image of a face, and the last ebb of strength in him was still in his arm and his hand, the hand that held a picture. It fell from his grasp soon afterward, and a vagrant wisp of wind caught it and sent it tumbling across the field toward the fire.

They carried Olowga, the Strange One, home.

THE END